THE HIDDEN KING

THE HIDDEN KING

E.G. RADCLIFF

BISAC: YOUNG ADULT FICTION / Fantasy / General |
YOUNG ADULT FICTION / Fantasy / Dark Fantasy |
YOUNG ADULT FICTION / Legends, Myths, Fables / General

Mythic Prairie Books
154 W Park Avenue #141
Elmhurst, IL 60126

info@egradcliff.com
www.egradcliff.com

First edition

Library of Congress Control Number 2019901131
ISBN: 978-1-7336733-2-7 (pbk)
ISBN: 978-1-7336733-5-8 (ebook)

Edited by Kelsy Thompson
Cover design by Micaela Alcaino
Illustrated by Elena Martinez

The Cut
N
E
S
W
THE RED SEA
NO MAN'S LAND
THE WHITE CITY
BOUDICCA'S BUILDING
THE MAZE
CAVE
OLD CITADEL
FISHER'S SHORE
THE DOCKS

GLOSSARY

Ceann Beag:	Little one
A thiarcais:	My goodness
Amadán:	Fool
In ainm dé!:	Damn!
Cad é?:	What?

PRONUNCIATION GUIDE

Áed	Aid
Boudicca	Bow-di-cah
Brígh	Bree
Cadeyrn	Ca-dairn
Caoimhe	Kee-va
Cynwrig	Keyn-rik
Éamon	Ay-mun
Étain	Ay-teen
Gráinne	Grah-nya
Killough	Kill-low
Máel Máedóc	My-ell My-eh-doc
Óengus	En-gus
Seisyll	Say-sill
Suibhne	Siv-na

⌇⌇⌇

CHAPTER ONE
Ninian

MOONLIGHT CLUNG LIKE MOISTURE to the abalone walls of the cave, and the sound of lapping seawater echoed over itself in so many whispers. Ninian's feet disturbed puddles as he walked carefully, one hand outstretched to touch the age-polished wall.

He cleared his throat to announce his presence. "Evening, people."

In the back of the hollow, three shadows moved. Two stayed behind while the other stepped forward into the vague light that penetrated the cave from the rising moon. "Ninian. You're late."

No matter how many times they met, no matter where, no matter when, Ninian was always startled by her voice. Something heavy about it made it intoxicating and warm, and that violently mismatched its owner. Ninian tucked his hair behind his ear. "So?"

Brígh stepped nearer, and Ninian resisted the urge to move back. He kept his chin high while Brígh scowled with distaste. "Doran." Brígh snapped her fingers, and one of the shadows behind her placed a pouch into her hand. After weighing it in her calloused palm, she tossed it carelessly to Ninian. "There's your cut." She turned away and settled back into the shadows. "Dawn tomorrow, wait at the southern dock. Someone will give you your assignment."

Ninian traced his teeth with his tongue, letting out a disappointed breath. The southern dock lay on the *opposite* side of the city, through the Inner Maze, near the farms. Beyond the farms rose the enormous cliffs that barricaded the Maze's peninsula from the higher mainland, and from Brígh's meeting spot, Ninian would actually be able to see them: there'd be no buildings to block the view at that remote edge of the Maze. The docks were irritatingly far away—he'd have to leave in the middle of that night, a night which had already begun to slip away. "The rock between your ears is in a good mood today, Brígh," he sighed. "Meeting in such a *pretty* part of nowhere, granting me a whole *three hours'* rest." His lip twitched. "It's generous, really," he added, and watched Brígh's scarred face twist at his sarcasm. "For someone who won't even grant herself a bath."

The smack to the side of his head didn't come as a surprise, but it still sent him stumbling to catch his balance on the obsidian-smooth wall. Brígh twined a handful of his russet hair in her fist, taking advantage of its length to grip it well, and yanked his head down so that her face was level with his. "Remember your place," she growled quietly.

Ninian swore, but didn't allow his expression to show pain. "Got it, got it. Southern dock, dawn tomorrow."

Brígh released him, waved a hand languidly, and Ninian understood that he was dismissed. Careful not to slip, he made his way out of the cave and back into the night.

His feet carried him homeward without much direction from his mind. The danger of being out after dark, especially with money in his pocket, propelled him on.

"Ninian!"

Ninian almost jumped out of his skin, and he whirled around. It took him a moment to process the voice, and by the time he did, it was laughing.

"Sorry. I didn't mean to scare you."

"Like hell you didn't," Ninian gasped. "*In ainm dé.*"

Áed stepped out of the shadows where evidently he'd been waiting, and his eyes caught the moonlight. Those eyes, even after years, still ran tingles over Ninian's skin, and Ninian felt goosebumps prickle on his arms as his love's crimson irises glimmered in the dark. "Well?" Áed said, slipping an arm around Ninian's waist. "Did she pay you?"

"Uh-huh."

Áed seemed to sense Ninian's mood. "Something wrong?"

Ninian shook his head. His cheek still stung, and his scalp did, too. "Brígh got to me, that's all."

"What happened?"

Ninian sighed, and Áed released him in order to face him. "She's just *rude*."

Áed laughed softly, and Ninian lost his train of thought for a moment. He didn't think Áed fully recognized his heart-stopping effect on Ninian; frankly—and perhaps this was foolishly romantic, a concept borrowed from a book and never returned—Ninian thought he'd be happy enough if he could simply live and die with Áed beside him. "We can't all have your manners, Nin," Áed said. "Has she said who you're up against next?"

Ninian shook his head, re-focusing. "No, I'll find out tomorrow morning. Then probably fight that night."

With a sigh, Áed settled back into Ninian and put an arm around him again. "I wish there were another way."

"There's not." Ninian felt Áed stiffen slightly and knew he'd spoken more intensely than he'd meant. "I fight their fights; I get a bit of the spoils. It's fair."

He could tell without looking that Áed was pursing his lips with disapproval.

Ninian let out a breath. "It feeds us, love. What would I do instead?"

Áed was quiet for a moment. "We could leave."

"We can't leave." Ninian knew where Áed wanted to go, and the beauty of the idea only made it more painful. Even if the journey were easy, and even if Ninian were willing to risk their meager lives for something uncertain, they couldn't leave.

Well, that wasn't entirely true.

Ninian couldn't leave. His gang was not particularly forgiving of deserters—he doubted he'd even make it past the border of the city—and Áed had made it clear that he and Ninian were in it together. Gods, Ninian loved him.

"I *know* that," Áed huffed. Then he drew a deep breath and let it out slowly. "Sorry, Nin. I'll drop it."

Ninian gave his attention to the stars above them, to Áed's warmth beside him, and to the rhythm of their feet on the ground. Tomorrow was a dangerous day, just like any other, but Ninian had learned long ago that dread changed nothing for the better. The fight would go well or badly, he would win or lose, and life would go on.

Or it wouldn't.

CHAPTER TWO
Áed

IT WAS A NO-HOLDS-BARRED SORT OF FIGHT, which meant, quite simply, that Áed stayed out of it. This was frustrating, because Ninian was losing badly. Áed leaned back against the crumbling red brick of the tenement behind him and ran a crooked hand over his mouth as he took in the shouts of "*Fight! Fight!*"

"Ay, that's right," someone in the crowd yelped. "Knock his nose in, Morry, go on!"

"Shut up, you *amadán*," his buddy screeched, and Áed sighed. Morcant would wear the idiot's entrails as a scarf if he heard the poor fool call him 'Morry.' The *amadán* in question must have been completely drunk.

"Come on, Ninny," Áed called, contributing his voice to the melee for the first time. "If you don't quit, he'll kill you."

"He's already killing me!" Ninian gasped, and Áed winced in sympathy and shook his head.

One of the gigantic street torches overhead flickered and rained a shower of orange sparks over the grimy, chanting crowd. Áed looked up with a touch of worry—if that fire went out, the nighttime blackness would be nearly complete. It would probably break up the fight, which meant that Ninian's nose might be spared the trip to the cobblestones, but it also meant they would probably have to feel their way back to a lit street.

"A little help would be great!" Ninian's muffled voice came from underneath Morcant's bulk.

"What am I supposed to do?" Áed called back. He'd seen plenty of Ninian's fights; his love never needed help. Years of bitter practice had built Ninian a fearful enough reputation, but Morcant, unfortunately, occupied another realm altogether. The crowd roared as Morcant grasped Ninian by the back of his neck and held him out like a doll, and then the gigantic man tossed Ninian into the crowd, which parted and let him crumple to the ground.

"Don't kill him," Morcant demanded in his quietly forceful way. The crowd had surged forward, but it obediently retreated at the gang-leader's words. "I want him to feel it."

There were a few harsh cheers, but Morcant raised his hand, and the sound stopped. He was completely undamaged, save for a thin trickle of blood from his nose.

"I'm not done," Morcant boomed, and everyone, including Áed, jumped as he raised his voice. His eyes swept over the vagabond crowd. "Who the fuck called me Morry?"

Once Morcant's attention had moved on, Áed hurried to the valiantly fallen Ninian, who lay in a heap on the broken pavers. Ninian moaned and cracked open one blackening violet eye to glare at Áed witheringly as he approached. "Thanks for the help."

Áed rolled his eyes. "I told you to give up. It would have spared you some bruises, if you'd have listened."

"Then, when I *didn't* listen, you should have thrown yourself into the fight and wreaked some hell on that oversized bastard."

Áed held up his hands, making Ninian frown at their crooked shape. "Me, throw a punch?"

Ninian scowled. "You coulda bit him."

Áed chuckled and helped his partner to a seat. "Let's get out of here, okay, Ninny? Can you stand?"

"Yeah. Please help me."

Áed braced his feet in the pits of the road as the torch above them dimmed. "Grab my wrist."

Ninian locked his fingers around Áed's left wrist and hauled himself up, cursing his bruises as Áed leaned back to compensate for his weight. "Damn Morcant," Ninian swore. He staggered for a moment before finding a wall to slump against and shook his shoulder-length hair out of his face.

"Ninian, I can't believe they had you fight *Morcant.* I'm going to get them for that."

Ninian shook his head and dragged the backs of his fingers across his split lip. "I mouthed off at Brígh."

Áed stopped and glared at him, but Ninian was looking down, inspecting his bleeding knuckles. "Gods forbid she talk down to you," Áed said, exasperated, "Can't she tell she's addressing *nobility*?"

Ninian pointed to him, swaying a bit, and Áed held out a hand to steady him. "*Ancient* nobility," Ninian corrected with a smirk. "And anyway, guess not."

"And so she—"

"Had me fight Morcant." Ninian shrugged gingerly. "His gang's been a pain in our ass for years now, we'd have had to do something eventually. 'Course, that probably wouldn't have had much to do with me, but…" Ninian placed his palm sarcastically over his heart. "Consider me a reformed man. Hold my hand, love?"

Áed snorted and batted Ninian's hand away with his crumpled fingers. "Fuck off." Then, offering a shoulder to lean on, he supported the limping Ninian out of the alley.

Their path led them past the docks, whose black wooden fingers jutted out over the Red Sea. The torches here were more reliable, so it was possible to stop for a moment, but Ninian had to be feeling the fight. Experience said it'd be best to get him home where he could rest. Besides, the docks were not a pleasant place to stay. Torches, spitting sparks and ashes skyward, glowered over the greasy streets. The rotting docks absorbed the light into their filthy timbers, and even the thin, bottomless sea refused to reflect the torchlight with the barest sparkle. The air tasted metallic, as if the reddish water were bloody.

A few girls leaned against the railings at the edge of the water. With mouths painted apple-red and legs and midriffs exposed to interested passers-by, they pouted and eyed the two young men who hobbled past. One of the girls whistled, but Ninian shook his head apologetically. Áed could tell from the look in his eyes that he felt for her, with her tangled straw-blond hair and dark orange eyes, as she waited for someone to want her.

"Life's a bitch, sister," Ninian muttered as the girl turned away, and he spat blood onto the pavers. He had the high cheekbones and handsome face of long-defunct royalty, and Áed knew something ran in Ninian's veins that rebelled against the Maze's desperation.

In Áed's mind, hope still kept a toehold; ironically enough, it came from Ninian. Ninian, cynical Ninian, was full of stories. Ninian knew all of the histories, all of the legends, knew what was true and what was myth, and when those stories broke through the barrier of his painful realism, he shared them. It was in this way Áed knew that life was cruel, but it wasn't merciless. There had been times, and perhaps there would come times again, when the Maze had equaled even the White City, which was now isolated atop the cliffs, in glory and health.

If Áed hadn't felt powerless to help, he would try to change things. Walking through the winding pathways along the water built sorrow in his chest; it wasn't right.

"Let's pick up the pace," Ninian groaned. "I want to be home."

Áed didn't argue.

⁂

Ronan was waiting for them just inside the door, spinning a button between his fingers, and he hopped to his feet at their arrival. His bright green eyes took in the scene with the quickness of a child. "Who was it this time?" he demanded, shoving the button in his pocket with a grubby fist. "Ninian, you're all beat up."

"Your powers of observation astound me," Ninian mumbled. "Now get out of the way before you get beat up, too."

Ronan's eyes widened, and Áed nodded at him sagely. "You should see the other guy."

"Really?" Ronan followed them up the creaky stairs like an excited moth. Áed could feel the enthusiasm pouring off the boy almost tangibly, which made him smile—Ronan idolized Ninian, and Áed couldn't blame him. "Well, who's the other guy?" Ronan pressed. "Did you win, Ninian? What was it like?"

"Morcant," Ninian groaned as they reached their floor, and for a moment, Ronan looked even more awestruck. "And he's fine."

The boy frowned as Ninian eased himself into a worn-out armchair. "That's awful." Ronan huffed disappointedly, his black eyebrows crunching down. "What a roach."

"Don't let him catch you saying that. He won't care if you

only have seven years."

Ronan looked offended, but also unsure if Ninian was joking. "I've eight!"

"How do you know?" Ninian grimaced. "Áed?"

"Yeah?"

"My chest is killing me."

Áed crossed over to the chair where Ninian lay slumped. "Where?"

Ninian gestured at the spot wearily. "Here, mostly. And here. And get the little one out of here before I pass out and embarrass myself."

Ronan *hmphed*. "*Little*. Áed's younger than you, and you don't call *him* little."

Ninian rolled his eyes. "Áed has *seventeen*, mate. That's hardly a difference. You, on the other hand..."

"Come on, mate," Áed said to him, putting his left hand on Ronan's back and using it to steer him toward the door. "How was your day?"

Ronan bit his lip. "I wanted to go to Máel Máedóc's shop, but I haven't got any money, and I'm afraid he'll kill me."

"Ah, he wouldn't. But I'll go with you next time, how about that?"

Ronan nodded, satisfied, and then turned and wrapped his skinny arms around Áed's waist. "Goodnight, then."

"Goodnight, Ronan." Ronan released him and looked up with big green eyes, and Áed gestured up the rickety staircase. "Now, shoo. I've got to go fix Ninny."

Ronan laughed at the nickname and darted up the stairs; soon, Áed could hear him banging around in the flat above.

He headed back to the rooms he shared with Ninian. They'd made their home in an abandoned building, one that was too far from the docks or the Inner Maze to be of interest to Morcant or any of the lesser gangs. It left them in relative safety. The door swung with a shrill creak as Áed shouldered it closed. "Ready?"

Ninian dropped his head back and closed his eyes again. He'd managed to wrestle off his shirt, which lay in a bloody-black heap on the floor. His skin was peppered with bruises. "One of these days," he groaned, "We're going to have to do something about Ronan."

"Yeah?" Áed said offhandedly, starting to examine Ninian's chest. There was a monstrous, black-and-purple bruise blooming over his ribs, and his collarbone was crooked. Right below the left side of that collarbone, a seven-year-old brand in the shape of a crescent stood out against Ninian's skin, courtesy of his gang. "Like what?"

Ninian shrugged, then winced. "I worry, you know? We treat him like… well, like we didn't find him in a *trash pile*, and he's going to grow up soft." He opened his deep violet eyes and lingered on Áed's face. "Seriously, Áed, that boy is gonna get torn apart." He shook his head. "What are we doing?"

Áed sighed. "He's not getting raised like me." They both knew that story: Áed's mother had left him with nothing but a letter, and Áed had been raised by a stranger. Ninian could read, so he had read Áed's letter out loud for Áed to know. None of it had been good. Ninian scowled and looked away across the empty flat, and Áed gestured to the wide scar that wrapped halfway around Ninian's midriff. "Not like you, either." He prodded at a bruise on Ninian's chest, maybe a little too emphatically, because Ninian yelped. "Sorry."

"You better be." The words were right, but Ninian's voice held no steel.

"That's the problem in this place," Áed said quietly. "People *do* grow up like that. You can't tell me you regret taking him in."

Ninian groaned. "You're such a philosopher."

"Why pass up the chance to do just *one* good thing?" Ninian grunted, and Áed nodded, accepting that Ninian had seen his point. "Ronan doesn't deserve this life."

"None of us do, love," Ninian mumbled. "Except maybe Morcant."

Áed chuckled stiffly. "Right. Except him." He cocked his head, examining Ninian's collarbone from a different angle. "Now shut up and stay still."

Ninian howled loudly enough to bring down the roof as Áed used the heel of his hand to set the broken bone with one practiced, even application of pressure, and then Ninian followed up with a horrific stream of curses. Sweat beaded his brow, and his knuckles were bone-white as he gripped the arms of the chair. He squeezed his eyes shut, just not tightly enough to conceal a tear that edged from the corner. "Man," Ninian gasped. "You're *terrible*."

"You're welcome." Áed sat back on his heels and bit his lip as he gently pressed on another blooming bruise. "Love, I think you've broken a rib, too, and I can't do anything about that." He stood and crossed to a cabinet. "Sure you don't want something?"

Ninian moaned painfully. "I'd rather not."

Áed shrugged. "Your choice. But whatever you choose, you're staying put for a while. No leaving this flat, got it?"

"Got it," he mumbled, closing his eyes. He shuddered, another tear trailing behind the first, and his expression twisted. "Gods. Áed, I'm sorry, I will have that drink." He opened his eyes. "Just this once, you hear?"

Áed struggled to open the bottle; it was awkward with his hands as crumpled as they were, and his warped bones and curled-under fingers protested as he twisted the cork. He braced the sticky bottle between his ribs and elbow to pour a small amount of the liquid into an old can.

He offered the can to Ninian, who grimaced but knocked it

back in one motion. Ninian made a face. "That is *disgusting*."

"So they tell me," Áed said, clumsily replacing the cork. "That ought to help soon. Just be still." He put the bottle in the cabinet and turned back to Ninian. "You hungry?"

"Always. We have anything left over from yesterday?"

"A little."

"Does Ronan have anything?"

Áed frowned sarcastically. "I didn't realize you cared."

"Shut up, Áed. You know I care." Ninian's voice had already gotten ever so slightly slurred, like he'd just woken up.

Áed leaned out the door and called up the stairs. "Ronan?"

There were a few thumps on the ceiling, then the patter of footsteps. Ronan's dark-haired head poked around the corner, which was grimy with eons of dirty fingerprints. "Yeah?"

"Do you have anything to eat?" The boy was remarkably resourceful, and he often managed to get his hands on food that neither Áed nor Ninian had brought home. Áed suspected that he stole on occasion, but since it kept Ronan fed, neither Áed nor Ninian questioned him about it.

"Some."

"Come here and help me cut up an apple, and you can have a bit of that, too."

Ronan's face brightened, and he tripped down the stairs and pulled a little blade, fashioned from the sharpened fragment of a tin roof, from his pocket. Áed flopped to a seat in the chair across from Ninian. The old frame creaked underneath the flattened cushions and threadbare upholstery, and Ronan hummed quietly to himself as he put his knife to use. A wrinkled slice of apple crunched as Ronan popped it into his mouth, and then the boy cupped the rest in his hands and brought them to Áed. Áed's stomach growled at the pitiful meal, urging him to eat faster, but he paced himself in order to savor the sweetness of the fruit.

Ronan was offering apples to Ninian, but Ninian seemed to be having trouble picking them up. His eyes were unfocused, and his fingers missed the slices entirely, grasping only air above Ronan's hands. The boy frowned, turning to Áed. "What happened to Ninian?"

Áed had to stifle a small, out-of-place laugh. "He has a couple broken bones, so I gave him some skee."

Ronan's brow furrowed as he took in Ninian like an interesting insect. "Oh." He glanced up, all big eyes, to Áed again. "Is he alright?"

"He should be fine." That could never be a promise, but Ninian had taken worse.

Ninian finally managed to get hold of an apple slice, and he grinned at Áed before popping it into his mouth. Ronan giggled. "What a dope. Can I have some skee?"

"No."

"Why not?"

"Why do you want to act like a dope? Take another slice for yourself and go on back upstairs."

Ninian needed to eat, so Áed offered him the apple slices and watched carefully to make sure he ate them. When he was done, Áed sank back into his chair and sighed as silence settled over the flat. A few minutes later, he heard Ninian snore.

Áed pushed himself up and found his way in the dark to the window, where distant clouds churned lightning over the sea. As usual, part of Áed's mind hovered on the city beyond the fringes of the Maze, beyond the sparse, salt-soiled little farms, beyond the unscalable cliffs. Ninian, with his ancestral memory, had told stories of the White City; he described people living in tidy houses, not tipping, ramshackle towers, and streets full of food, not garbage.

Áed had wanted to travel to the top of the cliffs for as long as he could remember, and once he and Ninian had adopted Ronan, he'd wanted it even more. The first time Áed had mentioned this to Ninian, Ninian had shaken his head. "*People try to go, love, but the ones who come back say it's impossible. And the rest don't come back at all. Doesn't that tell you something?*"

"*Why would they come back?*" Áed had retorted. He would not be discouraged—the White City had become a comfort to him. After all, no amount of hoping could change the Maze, but the White City's promise reliably loomed just beyond the horizon.

Ninian had said nothing, and the argument had died. They couldn't leave, and that was just a fact: Ninian was too entrenched in his gang, and Áed would not leave him. The fact was, hardly anybody left the Maze anyway. To chase a pretty story felt like foolishness when scraping by was hard enough, and the towering cliffs jutting up from the lowland presented another deadly discouragement. People told themselves that their lives were as good as they could ever be.

It just wasn't right.

⁂

CHAPTER THREE

ÁED HAD ALREADY EATEN a little breakfast, woken Ronan, and made a halfhearted attempt to get the blood out of Ninian's shirt before Ninian even opened his eyes the next day.

Still in his armchair, Ninian moaned. "Gods, Áed, close the curtains."

"We don't have curtains, *amadán*." Still, Áed ambled over to drape his blanket over the top of the window. "How's your chest?"

Ninian groaned. "Overshadowed, in fact."

Áed blinked in alarm. "By what?"

Ninian groaned again, the sound painful and dull. "My *head*."

Áed raised an eyebrow. "Your head? I didn't think you hit your head."

"I *didn't*."

"Then—"

"I am never," Ninian said with a stone face, his voice taking on the tone of a vow, "touching that nasty skee of yours again."

Áed blinked, and then found himself laughing. "Oh, Gods," he chuckled. "You are *such* a lightweight."

Ninian grunted, but for once didn't seem to be in the mood to spar. "I haven't forgotten my orders. I'm staying put with Ronan today."

Áed rolled his eyes. "Be nice."

"I'm always nice," he groused, eyes flicking up to glare at his partner's face. The partner in question raised an eyebrow.

"There's bread for breakfast. I think you need it."

"I need a hell of a lot more than bread."

Turning from Ninian, Áed shook his head to wake himself up a bit more. His sandy blond hair was disheveled and sticking up every which way, but at least it was too short to get truly tangled, as Ninian's could. He'd never given much thought to his appearance, because that was for people who didn't live in the Maze, but he still gave it a habitual brush with his fingers.

As Áed was fetching the brickish loaf from the cupboard, Ronan poked his sleep-ruffled head through the door. "Got any food?"

Áed said, "Yes," at the same time Ninian muttered, "No, go away." Áed rolled his eyes to glare at Ninian, who just sunk more deeply into his chair.

"Why is there a blanket over the window?" Ronan asked curiously.

"Because I'm sick of looking at the Gut," Ninian snapped, crossing his arms and then grimacing and uncrossing them.

"He's hungover," Áed explained. "And cranky."

Ronan raised an eyebrow. "I'll be upstairs all day."

"At least you know what's good for you," Ninian growled.

"Don't mind him," Áed interjected.

"Mind me," Ninian countered.

"Shut up, Ninian," Áed and Ronan ordered simultaneously, and Ronan laughed his little-boy laugh and hustled over to cut up the bread.

"Gods, I hate both of you," Ninian groaned.

⁂

Áed headed out after grabbing a stale chunk of the bread. He had work to do. Ninian's fight money—which only came when Ninian won—provided income, but not enough to support three people. What's more, when Ninian was properly injured, his gang wouldn't give him another fight until he had healed enough to have a chance at winning. They all still had to eat in the meantime.

Work opportunities, however, had never presented themselves particularly willingly to Áed. With his hands ruined, Áed couldn't even join a gang; he'd tried when he was younger. Ninian had been horrified at him for even considering the possibility, and, thoroughly discouraged from that route, Áed had given up. Now, he scavenged for Máel Máedóc, bringing the man useful rubbish from the street that the shopkeeper could sell.

Áed did plan on scavenging that day, but before he began combing the alleys for abandoned coats and cracked bottles, he had something else in mind.

He turned down a side street, hands in his pockets, heading for the docks.

The sound of the sea had just barely begun to reach his ears when an arm caught him gruffly around the shoulders, pulling him into an uncomfortable sideways hold. He tensed, hands clenching in his pockets, but his assailant only laughed with delight. "You! Been wondering when you'd come back here, ye bastard!"

Áed squirmed out from under the man's arm. "Yeah." He straightened his battered jacket, casting a wary glance at the man and taking a step to the side. "Guess I couldn't stay away."

The man, undeterred by Áed's tone, clapped him on the back heartily. "You're back for more, eh?" He leaned in closer, conspiratorially. "Won't get me so easy this time."

"Surely not," Áed agreed. "Still, I'd like to try."

The man, whose name Áed could not recall, bellowed with laughter. Still guffawing, he grabbed Áed's shoulder's again and steered him roughly in the direction of the water. Against the railings, buffeted by the wind off the sea, a group of ragged people clustered around little piles of tiles and coins. "Everyone," the man announced, dropping heavily into an open space marked with a bottle of skee, "this is that fellow I was talkin' about yesternight. Remember that?"

"You weren't jokin' about the eyes," someone noted, and the man who'd introduced Áed coughed in the speaker's direction.

"I'm no liar. Red as fire, I said, and I ain't wrong. 'Bout his hands, neither. See that?" He took a swig from his bottle. "Anyhow, he's joining us." Around the circle sounded halfhearted greetings, and Áed took a seat.

Someone dealt him in, and Áed took the chance to glance around at the few assembled men and women. The woman to his right had a calculating sort of glint in her eye, but the rest of the faces were as blank as stones.

Tiles clacked on the rough pavers, but Áed didn't watch the movement of the pieces so much as he watched the faces of the players. When everyone had set their chips, peeking down at the tiles hidden in their palms, a thickset man across the circle grunted with satisfaction. "Bet time."

Licking his lips, Áed took another look around the circle. The glint had gone from the woman's eye, but her face was set to look confident; she definitely didn't have anything. The men beside her maintained perfect blankness in their faces, but Áed could feel their uncertainty rolling off of them. The man who had accosted Áed in the alley appeared relatively pleased with his lot, but Áed felt nervousness oozing from the man like sweat; Áed could practically smell it. Taking a deep breath, Áed reached into his pocket and drew out a little pouch: the last earnings from Ninian's previous fight. He set it in the center as everyone else placed their bets.

The man who'd dealt Áed his tiles spread his hands wide with an air of drama, and everyone revealed their hand. "Egh," the dealer grunted thickly. "Got a winner."

Áed let his tiles fall and collected everyone's bets. "Another round?"

He played until the good-natured atmosphere began to wane. When he caught the first frustrated, sideways glance in his direction, he stood, thanked the players respectfully, and left before anything came to blows.

The noises of the docks fell away as Áed jogged through the streets, moving briskly to bring some feeling into his legs, which had fallen asleep while he'd sat on the ground. He'd done well at the game, as usual, and, after a bit of scavenging, he hoped he'd be able to afford a decent meal. Ronan, especially, could use it. To feed Ronan, Áed would have willingly made the trip to the docks more often, but that came with certain danger. Unless he threw the games, which he couldn't much afford to do, he won, and he did *not* want to earn the kind of enemy that gambled at the docks.

Weaving expertly through the familiar streets, Áed kept his focus on the ground, in the shadows of tenements, in the gutters. The chill of the spring air felt clammy as Áed kept an eye out for any refuse with a scrap of value, and he moved with purpose, hurrying to get home.

⁂

He returned to his tenement when the sun began to set, having found a trampled glove that, with his newly-earned money, he traded with Máel Máedóc for some food. Máel Máedóc was a tall, broad man with shimmering blue eyes set deeply behind sharp, pitch-dark cheekbones, but despite his dramatic appearance, he was a gentle enough sort. His soft spot for Áed dated back years, and though Áed couldn't remember exactly how it had come to be, there remained between them a mutual respect. Though still a few coins short, Áed left with enough food to bring back home.

Áed found Ronan sitting on the tenement steps as he turned onto the dusty path toward the building. The boy looked up, his green eyes caught Áed's face, and relief washed over his expression. He jumped up and nearly knocked Áed's freshly-bought bread onto the road as he half-tackled Áed into a hug.

"Whoa!" Áed exclaimed as Ronan drew back, sniffling. "What's the matter?"

The boy opened his mouth and then closed it again, and he squeezed his eyes shut.

"Why are you outside?" Áed said more gently, and his knees touched the pavers as he knelt to be level with Ronan's tear-streaked face. "It's almost nighttime."

"I know." Ronan's voice trembled, and Áed blinked at it for a moment. He hadn't heard Ronan sound so vulnerable since he was very small.

"Hey," he said, brushing the boy's hair off of his brow. "What happened?"

A pair of crystalline tears dripped from Ronan's bright green eyes and ran around the curves of his cheeks. "I don't know what to do about Ninian."

Áed took the boy's shoulder in his own crumpled excuse for a left hand. "Why?" he said. "Did he snap at you?"

The boy shook his head and choked back a sob. Blinking,

Áed drew him closer as worry clouded his mind. Áed could feel Ronan's fear in his chest, the boy's emotions whirling and sparking alongside Áed's own.

"Shh, shh…" Áed murmured in an attempt to comfort him. He tried to silence the anxiety creeping into his voice for fear that it would upset the boy further.

Ronan coughed as a cry stuck in his throat. "Ninian said his chest hurt, and I said that was probably okay, because a bone was broken and that should hurt, right?"

"Right," Áed murmured, standing. He started moving toward the building.

Another glassy tear trembled in the corner of Ronan's eye as he hurried to follow. "But then he said it *really* hurt, and I looked, and it was red under his skin."

Áed's heartbeat was loud in his ears like his footsteps' pounding.

"And now he won't wake up," Ronan finished. His voice was pitiful, pleading. "Please, Áed, tell me he's okay." His voice crumbled as he chased Áed's long strides into the tenement.

Áed heard Ronan behind him as he threw open the door to the flat that he shared with his friend.

Best friend.

More than a friend.

Ninian lay still in his chair, the same as he had that morning. His hands, long-fingered, lay limp on the armrests as if he were a bored king holding court over an empty room.

Or rather, not empty.

Áed could sense the *bean sídhe*, the banshee, inhaling deeply as if to steal the breath from the room, preparing to wail away Ninian's life.

No. He banished the thought and forced his stiff fingers to find a pulse on Ninian's neck.

Nothing, nothing, this couldn't be happening...

There.

Ninian's heart was beating. Weakly, but beating. Áed was praying, he found, though to whom he didn't know. To the Gods whose names he invoked only in oath? To nature itself? He didn't know.

The stain was deep red under Ninian's flesh, and it radiated oddly from the spot where the rib lay broken. Áed knew what it was. He leaned over Ninian's mouth to hear faint, gaspy breathing: Ninian was suffocating as he bled out inside.

"Ronan?" Áed called, and the boy was at his side. "I need a knife. Wash it as well as you can." This wouldn't work. He knew, deep in the pit of his stomach, that it wouldn't work, it couldn't work. Blurred by impending tears in the very corners of Áed's eyes, the minute flaws in Ninian's face—the scar below his lip, the bruises blossoming on his high, handsome cheekbones—seemed to fade.

Ronan returned with a knife, his own little one.

The knife trembled in Áed's unsteady hands as he brought it to his friend's chest. "I need a candle, too." The sun was setting, and the flat was full of shadows. "Now." He heard Ronan leap into action, heard the faith in his movement. *It's okay*, Ronan seemed to be thinking. *Áed is going to make it better*. Perhaps Ninian had been right. They had raised this boy with too much naïveté.

Áed gripped the blade with both hands as Ronan returned with a packet of matches and a candle, but the boy's hands shook so hard that he burned through all of the matches before finally managing to light the bent wick. Steadier light filled the room as the fire took hold. Pressing the knife between his knuckles, Áed brought it down carefully on the red splotch, and the blade pierced Ninian's skin with a thick, strange heaviness.

The bloody reservoir bubbled from the wound in a gush as the pressure relieved. It poured like a crimson river over Ninian's pale flesh, dripping onto the floor and puddling as it flowed in a morbid waterfall to the growing puddle on the floor. Áed listened as carefully as his pounding heart would allow. As Ninian's blood poured over Áed's hands, he felt for his love's breath. It was still there, faintly, but it was growing stronger as the weight on Ninian's lungs eased. With bloody fingers, Áed felt for Ninian's pulse. It pushed against his fingers resiliently.

The discoloration faded as blood poured out, but it would be an excruciatingly temporary solution if the bone had slit a large vessel. If Ninian bled out too much onto the old floor, which was greedily quaffing his blood, he would die. If too little blood drained away, Ninian would bleed inside and suffocate.

Áed pressed his lips together, felt his eyes sting with tears, and called to Ronan. He'd relieved a lot of pressure—perhaps now, Ninian could heal on his own. His body must know that it was dying. It had to feel the urgency, had to be working beneath its deathly, blood-stained exterior to keep him alive. Áed prayed it hadn't given up.

Ronan arrived at Áed's side in an instant, bearing a cloth, and Áed took it and pressed it to Ninian's side. The blood sidled through the cloth, and Áed kept pressing as he waited for the flow to stop. He didn't know how much blood was in a body, but he knew that the parched floor was spongy with it. Too much or not enough, he could not say.

Eventually, the cloth was brilliantly red, and the bleeding stopped. The reservoir under Ninian's skin drained and the torrent thinned to a trickle, then clotted to nothing at all. Ninian had grown pale, as white as alabaster, and his cool skin was tacky with blood under Áed's touch. His slow breathing rattled in his chest. His heart, suddenly finding itself with little to pump, beat weakly and sporadically.

Ronan sat in the corner with his thin back pressed to the wall, eyes fixed helplessly on Ninian's motionless shape even after darkness fell entirely. Áed took a seat in his armchair and settled into the quiet. Against the faint rumbling of the disturbed sky, Ninian's shallow breaths were barely audible as they whispered through the heavy, lightless air. Ronan didn't sleep; Áed could hear him shifting, patient and anxious, and he realized that the mood in the room was that of a vigil. They were two people, waiting for the final ruling of deities whom they both already knew to be cruel.

Áed welcomed Ronan as, hours later, the small boy crawled from the corner and curled beside Áed in the chair. "Áed?" he murmured.

"Yes?"

There was a pause, as heavy as a stone. "I just wanted to make sure you were still there."

Áed held Ronan close and felt the child clutch his hand with his small fingers, holding on desperately to the small amount of comfort that Áed's gnarled bones could offer. "I'm here, *ceann beag*," he murmured. His own voice, like Ronan's, came unevenly. "I'm here."

CHAPTER FOUR

ÁED HAD NOT SLEPT WHEN THE SUN, edging through the hazy air, announced the new morning.

Ronan, beside him, still held Áed's hand, and the child's fingers had grown sweaty. The boy, at least, had dozed, though now his green eyes opened to blink at the brightness. "Áed?" he croaked, coughing the sleep from his voice. "How is Ninian?"

Áed extracted his hand from the child's fingers and used it to clumsily sweep Ronan's too-long bangs from his eyes. The boy's dark hair caught between Áed's fingers.

Áed had been monitoring his love's breaths all night, almost to the point of counting them, and he responded. "Living."

Ronan's replying sigh was a tiny thing, a timid expression of relief.

"Get up, Ronan," Áed said, rising from the seat himself. He extracted yesterday's packet of jerky from his pocket—Ninian's blood had marred the paper, but the meat remained clean. He handed it to Ronan, saying, "Eat. Take the bread and the apple, too."

Ronan's face showed his surprise. "All of it?"

"Yes, all of it. Go on."

Ronan needed no further prompting to tear into the meager food. Meanwhile, Áed crossed to Ninian, saying a thankful prayer to no particular God that the night was past and his love still breathed.

"Ninian," he murmured as he slipped his distorted hand into Ninian's elegant, calloused palm. The words scarcely passed his tongue. The hope that Ninian would answer was small, as fluttery as his partner's heartbeat. "Can you hear me?"

He nearly jumped as Ninian coughed and a fleck of dry blood burst from his lips.

"Ninian?" Áed was aware of Ronan watching, of bright green eyes boring into his back.

Áed dropped to his knees, and Ninian coughed again with a weak moan. His eyes opened a crack, just enough for Áed to see the sliver of breathtaking violet beneath his lids. Hope flared in his body: Ninian's state had improved from the night before, had it not? Perhaps Áed's efforts had worked, and the slim odds had prevailed. "Áed," Ninian mumbled, and Áed clasped Ninian's hand as tightly as he could. Ninian's voice didn't hold its ordinary cockiness or amusement. This voice came from a Ninian in pain.

"I'm here," Áed murmured, trying to angle himself so that Ninian could see his face without moving.

Ninian coughed again, and another clot of blood flew like shrapnel from his mouth. "Good."

Áed felt himself nodding, smiling. He couldn't help it, just the same way he couldn't help the tears that pricked at his eyes. His tongue felt thick. "Yes," he said, as a drop of salty water slipped onto his cheek. "Yeah, mate, it's good."

Ninian coughed weakly. The sound was wet. "It hurts."

"You're going to be alright," Áed said, and hoped that his voice sounded encouraging. A tendril of fear slipped into his mind and put a damper on the hope that had so recently soared.

Ninian's starry eyes blinked, and the morning light from the window lent them clear, extraordinary lucidity. "I need to tell you something."

"What?" Áed knew he sounded hoarse, but the fear in his voice showed anyway. Final words were for final moments, and that time simply could not be then.

Ninian's own breathing was quick and shallow, all raggedy. "I didn't tell you."

Áed frowned, feeling his brow crinkle, but made himself wait for Ninian to speak.

"I'm so sorry." Ninian's words were fainter. "Áed, I didn't mean to wait so long." He coughed, and this time, a glistening trail of vibrant red dribbled over his lips. Áed felt his heart plummet to a rocky bottom.

The broken rib must have pierced Ninian's lung. Just nicked it, probably, if he'd lasted this long, but… "Shh," Áed whispered softly, trying to get his love to rest. "Quiet, Ninny."

But Ninian didn't seem to hear him. "It's easy to forget," he choked, hiccupping on blood, and shook his head clumsily. "I never forgot, but I waited, and the time never seemed right, and Gods, love, I'm sorry."

"No, Ninian," Áed managed. "No, don't apologize. You don't have to apologize for anything, not to me."

"I have to," Ninian breathed, and more blood dripped down his chin. "Because…" The blood on his lower lip smeared on his upper. "Because you don't have it all, do you see… I never… never told you all of it."

"I don't understand, Ninian." This time, Áed couldn't keep the fear out of his voice, and it seeped into his tone like Ninny's blood onto the floor. "You aren't making any sense."

"Shut up… and listen then. This isn't… isn't easy." Ninian's lips were coated in blood, like he'd been drinking it. "Your letter."

Áed blinked, surprised. "My letter?"

"From your mother." Ninian took a deep, shaking breath, which rattled in his chest and made Áed's heart seize up. "I read it for you, but—" He blinked, and his expression turned confused for a moment.

"What are you saying?" It was impossible for Áed to keep down the panic in his tone.

Ninian's hand, the one Áed wasn't holding like a lifeline, dragged painfully to his head. His long fingers traced streaks of ruddy blood across his cheek and came to rest at his temple as if he was trying to hold his thoughts in place. "It's my fault." His eyes closed and Áed's heart stammered in terror, but then they opened again, slowly. Ninian's hair matched the iron-red blood that smudged under his eyes. "I was scared, love…"

Áed didn't know what to say.

"I'm a fool." Ninian laughed quietly, and blood spattered from his lips. A warm drop touched Áed's cheek and stayed there. "I'm so sorry."

"Ninian, it's alright. Just be still, just rest." He needed to convey the urgency—the absolute necessity—for Ninian to relax, to stop talking. He knew his words sounded desperate.

But then, another part of his mind murmured gently, *you already know that it's too late.*

He blinked a fresh raft of tears from his eyes, but one fell anyway. It hit the drop of Ninny's blood on his cheek and washed it down. There was no point in making Ninian rest.

"I'm sorry," Ninian breathed. "I didn't read you the whole letter. Áed, you're not… everything you think. It scared me, it did, but my love…" His chest heaved with another cough, but a faint smile spread over his lips, full of surprising, lucid happiness. "I've said it now."

Áed held Ninian's hand as tightly as he possibly could. "Ninian?"

"Not… for much… longer." Ninian's smile widened, revealing blood-coated teeth, and his eyes locked onto Áed's. "Tell Ronan it's alright."

"Nin," Áed demanded, and the panic and desperation overwhelmed him as he leaned over Ninian, frantically brushing the blood off of his love's chin as if he could undo it. "Ninian!"

But Ninian's brilliant eyes were sagging shut. His lips moved, though just a whisper came out. "Áed."

Áed shook his head helplessly. "What the hell, Ninian, you can't do this to me." Tears had earnestly begun their assault on his eyes, and they streamed down his cheeks. "Gods, no!" He shook him again, but Ninian's face had slackened, and his hand relaxed limply in Áed's grip. "Ninian!" Áed screamed, but over his own voice, he heard Ninian's breath… stop.

"Please," he heard himself begging as tears blurred his vision. "Please, Ninny, not like this. Not like this."

His hands were covered in blood from the love of his life, both old and fresh, but now blood was no longer moving in Ninian's veins. Air didn't stir in his lungs, and not a twitch of movement animated his body.

"Ninian…" Áed pressed his lips desperately to Ninian's forehead while anguish churned in his chest and stole his breath. It was a last plea—*Please, Ninian. For me. Gods, Ninny, come back for me*—but all he got was Ninian's familiar scent, warm and comforting and sullied by the smell of blood. His tears spilled onto Ninian's face and ran into his hair.

He let himself be dragged away as he felt Ronan's small hands on his shoulders, separating him from the corpse and turning him away so that he could not see. Ronan was saying something, but Áed couldn't hear what it was. He couldn't breathe, couldn't see through the tears, and he felt himself fall to his knees on the bloody floor as sobs ripped their way up from his heart.

⌇⌇⌇

CHAPTER FIVE

SURELY YEARS PASSED BEFORE HIS wracked body could breathe again. It felt like lifetimes more before he could see through the tears that veiled his eyes.

Áed rested where he'd fallen, curled up like an infant with his hands covering his face. Shaking, he moved them and found that he was facing away from the place where Ninian lay.

Dead.

Ninian was dead.

Áed used his wrists to push himself to a seat, inhaled a deep breath that tasted of rust, and forced himself to look around. How easy it would be to leave. To run down the narrow street to the Inner Maze, to find Morcant, and… what? Attack him?

Perhaps that would be best. Then Morcant would kill him, too.

He heard a faint sound to his right and turned to Ronan. Immediately, he pressed his lips together as he realized that he had fallen apart while Ronan suffered too. So much for protective instinct. He damned himself.

"Ronan," Áed murmured, and Ronan turned his head and

peeked out from under his bangs. His eyes were puffy and bloodshot, and his cheeks shone with moisture. As soon as he saw Áed sitting up, he uncurled himself, stumbled over, and collapsed once again to his knees.

Áed opened his arms, and Ronan fell into them and buried his face in Áed's shoulder. Áed held him close, and the child trembled desperately. It seemed wrong that there should still be an Áed without a Ninian. But here was Ronan; he needed Áed to stay.

Ronan sniffled. "It's my fault."

Áed shook his head. "No. Don't say that."

"I should have done something."

"There's nothing you could have done, Ronan." He pulled the boy back to look at him, and found that his tears were mirrored on Ronan's face. "Do you understand?"

Ronan nodded minutely, but he, like Áed, had nothing to say.

⁂

Neither soul moved from the flat, and neither stole anything more than brief, painful glances at the body that lay on the floor. The body whose russet hair flared out from its head like a halo and whose thin, strong arms lay motionless and stiffening by its sides. Whose eyes were open just enough to make the living uneasy.

Áed needed to do something about Ninian's body.

Áed couldn't stop his hands shaking. The haze of smoke over his vision was anger at Morcant, who had so casually struck the blow that robbed Ninian of life and robbed Áed of Ninian. The heat that sent shudders through his body was anger at himself for failing to see the extent of the damage. Was there truly nothing he could have done? His attempt to help had been useless. Crying was useless. The world had already taken everything he had, and now it had taken Ninian.

He needed to take care of the body. Respectfully, like Ninian deserved.

And here, he found himself hobbled. He fell short, like always.

He slammed his hands into the table, making Ronan jump, and felt pain course up his forearms. He drew back and did it again, and again; he felt bruises form on his left hand, and agony speared his right. With every blow, his scarred bones felt sharper against their stupid, ruined joints, and more tears brimmed in his eyes as he slammed his hands down harder, harder. He began to punctuate each blow with a word and brought them down faster and more forcefully: "I can't—even—dig—a fucking—*grave*!"

He stopped and braced his hands on the table with straight arms, trying to let the pain distract him from his grief.

Ronan was staring at him with his mouth hanging open. The boy blinked, closed his mouth, and swallowed hard.

Áed let his eyes flutter closed and drew a deep, steadying breath for the sake of Ronan, who was innocent and afraid. He extended an arm out to the side and felt Ronan tentatively nestle into it. "I'm sorry," Áed murmured, and Ronan leaned on him, trusting him.

"S'okay."

"We'll just…" He took another unsteady breath. "We'll make a pyre instead."

Ronan sounded afraid to speak, but his voice piped up anyway. Brave child. "Where will we get the wood?"

"From the building next door," Áed replied, surprised to find the answer on his lips. "We'll find a way."

⁂

After his outburst, Áed's hands would scarcely move for him. He cursed them silently as he and Ronan ripped exposed wood like scabs from the abandoned tenement beside their own and dragged them outside. It was good to have something to work at, something to think about other than Ninian's body lying on the floor of their flat.

So far, Ronan was being uncharacteristically quiet, but Áed knew the boy's mind was swirling like his own. Áed could scarcely deal with his *own* thoughts, much less those of an intelligent, vulnerable child who relied on him almost entirely. Gods, too much. It was too much.

The light was ebbing from the sky, snagging on the bottoms of the mournful clouds, by the time they set the final beam into place. "Right," Áed said quietly, knowing Ronan was listening. "It's time for Ninian to join us."

The trek up the sagging stairs seemed longer than usual, and the familiarity of the route grated against the sensation of something forever altered. Ninian's body lay where they had left it, but Áed still had to stifle surprise at the sight: *He's still here? He never stays in one place so long.* It sent a cold fist thumping into his stomach. Ninian's body looked tranquil, and Áed slowly knelt beside it. Finally, he mustered the strength to brush Ninian's eyelids down. Ninian's face was relaxed in death, something it never had been in life. Now, finally, he hadn't a care in the world. He was beautiful, with his straight nose (how had it survived so many fights intact?), his angular jaw, his high cheekbones, and full lips. He looked like a lord, like he ought to be seated on a throne someplace far away. He didn't look like he should be cold on the floor of a dirty tenement flat.

Áed had thought he was done with tears. He was wrong.

He hooked his elbows under Ninian's arms and bore the brunt of the weight as Ronan guided Ninian's feet. Áed found himself drinking in every last detail of Ninian's body, even ice-pale in death. This was the last time that he would see his love.

When they reached the pyre, Áed asked Ronan for some water and a cloth. There was one final gift Áed could give. When Ronan returned, Áed mopped the blood from Ninian's flesh and worked the rag around his stiff fingers to cleanse the dirt and blood from his skin. He gently wiped Ninian's face and brushed back his hair to remove any trace of his trauma, save for the dark bruise on his chest and the clean laceration below it. Áed worked mindlessly and regarded himself as if in a dream as he did his best to make Ninian look whole.

⸙

Áed didn't know how to light the pyre. Ronan had used all the matches the night before, back when Ninian had still been breathing, and Áed couldn't light the pyre without them. How he'd missed this fact was beyond him; he didn't think he'd forgotten, but some strange faith must have possessed him to believe that this part would resolve itself. The light faded from the sky while Ronan stood pike-straight and silent by Áed's side, and together they regarded the unlit pyre, helpless.

The last thing that Áed had wished to do, a respectable farewell, was undone.

He leaned against the pyre and bowed his head in dismal apology. *I'm sorry, Ninian, that I could not give you even this.* The wood was so dry, so ready. And there was enough fury inside of him that it seemed that the warmth of his fingers would be enough to set it alight.

He struck one of the timbers as a tear tracked down his cheek, frustrated and despairing.

The pyre remained cold.

Áed stepped back dejectedly and put his arm around a shivering Ronan. The boy's eyes shone with tears as he looked up at Áed.

A thread of smoke coiled over the ground toward their feet. Áed blinked and stepped forward, sure that he was seeing things, but then before his eyes, an ember flared to life at the base of the pyre. The miniature tongue of fire was no bigger than a candle flame, but to his astonishment it grew and licked hungrily at the wood. One tongue became two, became three, until he could feel its warmth on his skin. "What the…"

Ronan's eyes danced with the firelight, full of astonishment. "How did you do that?"

"I—" Áed stopped himself from saying 'I didn't.' Something in the statement felt wrong, as if he'd be lying. "I don't know."

"It's a miracle."

Áed agreed. The fire was gaining strength. It illuminated the brick-cobbled street and the crooked, ramshackle buildings with their sunken stoops and shattered windows, and Áed averted his eyes and stepped back as the fire spread. Flames began to curl around Ninian's body, obscuring it behind a screen of luminous orange. There rose a faint, gut-turning whiff of burning flesh.

Before long, Áed put a hand on Ronan's back and steered him back inside the tenement. There was nothing after this point that either of them should remember. Neither of them should watch. The fire would burn, burn away until the pyre was nothing but charred rubble and Ninian's bones, and Áed didn't want to see the black, sooty femurs and ribs and skull. Not of Ninian, so recently living, so recently speaking, joking, swearing and fighting, running, laughing, and caring. Áed's empty stomach heaved, and he swallowed hard.

He had a decision to make. It had been in the back of his mind, he thought, since that morning, but the time had come to face it.

Quashing quickly-rising guilt, Áed began to move around the flat to gather up their meager possessions.

"What are you doing?" Ronan's voice was small and exhausted.

Áed opened the cabinets methodically and spread the sparse contents on the table as Ronan watched. "Packing."

"Are we leaving?" The boy didn't sound like he was arguing, but he probably just lacked the energy to do so.

"Yes."

"To go where?"

"Out," Áed said. His voice felt heavy. "Out of here, that's where. The White City."

The smaller boy's silence fell as heavily as a stone.

"Go on upstairs, Ronan. Go collect your things." It pained him to do it, but the opportunity had come, and he would act. Ninian's death had taken so much that Áed didn't think the chasm in his chest would ever heal, but there was something else Ninian's death had eliminated: "If we leave now, *ceann beag*, nobody will bother us."

Ronan's nickname, meant as a comfort, had little effect. "You mean his gang?"

"Yes, that's what I mean." The gang would come looking eventually. The gang was the reason they had not left before. "Go on."

It felt almost like robbery, like stealing the child's illusion of safety, but it had to be done. Áed could not save the Maze, but he could save Ronan. Slowly, aimlessly, Ronan moved upstairs, and Áed assembled his belongings into a burlap sack. They were few. A couple of cans, a shirt, gloves that were made more of patches than original fabric. A knife so dull that Áed hadn't been able to sell it. A single coin. More importantly, he packed a comb that had been Ninian's and the letter from Áed's mother.

He paused before he placed the worn paper into the bag, staring at the rows of symbols he did not understand. Ninian's lips had once demystified the words, but now…

Ronan returned, sadly bearing his own sack, and Áed released the letter to join the rest of his worldly goods before looking up. "Are you ready?" The boy hesitated, then gave an uncertain nod. "That's my brave one," Áed murmured, and Ronan took his hand. "Let's go."

⌇⌇⌇

CHAPTER SIX

"ÁED?"

"Yes?"

"Do you know what you're doing?"

The question was so blunt that Áed blinked. He ruffled Ronan's hair the way he would have done before everything collapsed. "It's going to be alright." Alright. All right. It had never been, and never would be, all right. He shook his head to clear the haze, but he knew that his mind would stay murky nonetheless.

They'd left through the back of the tenement to avoid the still-burning pyre, and now they moved through the alleys like ghosts, untethered from the world. Grief made them weary and mindless, though Áed sensed emotion churning in himself beneath the surface. Anger and fear, both hot and bright, mounted deep inside him, but they, for the time, stayed buried beneath layers of ashy confusion.

It was properly nighttime as they neared the tightly-packed tangle of streets and glassless windows that gaped like empty eyes. This was the Inner Maze, and fear crept under grief's curtain. Ronan squeezed Áed's hand. "Áed," he whispered hoarsely. "You told me never to come here."

"I know," Áed replied. "But we have to, okay, *ceann beag*? Don't let go of me."

The boy held Áed's hand even tighter, and Áed said nothing of the ache it brought. If he thought it safer, he would have waited until morning, but he didn't know when Ninian's gang would come to check on their fighter. He'd be damned if they found Ninian dead and held the nearest parties responsible, he'd be damned if Ronan was there when that happened, and he'd be damned if they missed their only chance to get out. They approached every crossroad carefully, ears open for sounds of danger, and though the grimy route was empty, Áed held his breath. This was Morcant's territory, and the very ground felt poisoned beneath his feet.

"Can you move any faster, Ronan?" Áed murmured gently. "I know you're tired, but this is not a good place to be."

Their feet carried them deeper into the rotting metropolis, where the buildings looked wicked in the dark and their tracks were thick with filth. Fallen shingles and human refuse spackled the gutters, and Ronan shivered at the smell of decay that hung heavy in the air. "Why did we have to come this way?"

"There is no other way."

"I feel…" Ronan's voice wavered. "I feel like there's somebody watching us."

A shiver ran over Áed's skin, and he looked around. Any of the shadows could enshroud a body, and the buildings may as well be nests of hornets for the danger they could mask. "Where?"

"I don't know."

There were no torches in this unholy sector of the city, and no moon behind the clouds. There was no way to discern who lurked unseen. With a hand on Ronan's back and another glance over his shoulder, Áed urged the child onward.

"Stop."

Áed's gut clenched, and he froze.

"Turn around."

They obeyed haltingly, and from a doorway whose lintel was crooked with age appeared a figure, mirage-like. Another followed, and then one more. Together, their bulk turned the alley into a dead end.

"Do you know where you are?"

It was difficult to see, but Áed thought he recognized the silhouette in the center, the one who had not yet spoken. A spark of anger burned through the damp cloak of grief and fear. "Yes."

The left silhouette clicked his teeth, and they glinted in the darkness. "Then you know that's a problem."

The central figure held up a hand, and his underling hushed as if his breath was stolen.

At the display of authority, any doubt steamed away.

In a growl, the word escaped Áed's clenched teeth, and the world tipped as something, something hot and powerful, surged within him. "*Morcant.*"

⁂

A scratching sound clawed its way from the darkness, and a miniature, tremulous flame burst into existence. The man who held the match was practically a giant, all well-fed muscle and sinew and bone, and the weak light shone dully against muddy-colored eyes. He lifted the match, illuminating the alley, and one of his eyebrows slid up. "Well. You know whose land you're on."

The feeling in Áed's chest was furious and choking him, and he could barely speak. He'd thought, so briefly, of seeking Morcant himself—he wouldn't have done it, but now that the murderer was there before him, all of Áed's anger roiled just shy of the surface. "Do you even remember?"

Morcant stared at him for a moment. "Remember what?"

Ronan tugged on Áed's sleeve, but Áed ignored him. "Two days ago," he managed, biting the end off of each word. "The fight."

The man seemed to think for a moment, and then his mouth twitched up like his eyebrow. "I do remember you." He nodded to his men, and it seemed to Áed that the twisted smile spreading over his face was like that of the Dullahan's leering, disconnected head. "You were there for that *amadán* with the reddish hair."

Áed's teeth came together nearly hard enough to crack, and the world went briefly dark as fury poured its heat to the very tips of his curled-under fingers. "Do you know," he said in a low voice. "Do you know what you did?"

Morcant blinked. "I *won*."

Áed could no longer feel Ronan's tugging fingers on his sleeve. The alley narrowed until Morcant filled his vision.

"You *killed* him," Áed said, and his voice was louder and not quite his own.

Morcant didn't react for several beats, and in that time, anger clawed itself fully through the haze in Áed's head. He was breathing quickly, he knew that, and his wrecked hands clenched and unclenched as the silence dragged on. "I'm not surprised," Morcant said finally. "It was a good fight."

The match went dark.

Smoke twirled into the alley.

And Áed launched himself forward.

He felt it happen as he moved, as the alley dropped into darkness and the entire world closed in: a click, like lock tumblers dropping into place inside his heart.

And then *heat.*

It surged out of him, out of his chest, his bones, and his hands, red-hot and stunning and bright enough to blind as he slammed into the man who had killed his love.

Energy roared through his blood in a high, keening song. Morcant's eyes widened as he stumbled backward with a cry, and for a moment, Áed saw himself reflected in Morcant's irises.

Unrecognizable.

Burning.

One of Morcant's men reached for him, but Áed struck out and connected brutally with his head. Howling and with hair aflame, the man dropped to the ground with a sickening thud, and Áed scarcely noticed as the other crony turned and fled. His wrecked hands gripped onto Morcant's neck, clawing at his throat and searing into his flesh. Morcant was his focus. Morcant had done this, had done this, had *done* this, and Áed wanted to hear him *scream.*

The giant man was burning, but it wasn't enough. Morcant's eyes were still light, and he still writhed as fire consumed his clothes. Áed was barely conscious of himself snarling, and his voice erupted from his throat in a shrieking, inhuman grate: "*I had to burn him, you son of a bitch!*" He lunged forward, forcing Morcant onto his back against the paving-stones. "*I had to burn him! Do you understand!? Do you understand why you're going to burn?*" His hands were shining, were brilliant, were warping the air around them with heat, and Morcant tried to scramble back on his elbows. Áed was on top of him before he could move—fire billowed skyward with the force of the strike as he smashed the heel of his hand into the side of Morcant's face. The man let out a scream that made the dirty windows ring, and savage pleasure ripped through Áed's body.

Áed struck again and again, tears evaporating before they

touched his face, and kept striking as the man beneath him ceased to be a man any longer.

Sounds began to reach his ears after a time, and the demon in his chest abated enough for him to hear a broken, cracking cry. "*He's dead! He's dead!*"

Áed stopped beating and slowly rose to his feet. He turned around.

Ronan stood where Áed had left him. Tears poured down his face, dissipated in the heat, and left salt on his face. "He's dead, Áed, he's dead, you killed him, he's dead." The boy heaved, and swallowed hard. "Stop. Áed, he's dead, stop, he's dead…"

Áed frowned at Ronan, uncomprehending. "What?"

Ronan was as still as if he'd been paralyzed, save for the tears that kept coming. "He's dead, Áed, you have to see that he's dead. Please…"

Áed turned back to Morcant, who was strange in the firelight, coal-dark and caved-in.

"Áed, what are you…"

It was impossible to say if Ronan would have continued to 'what are you doing?' or left it simply at 'what are you?' because his voice trembled so much that he broke off with a gasp.

It wasn't the darkness, nor the Inner Maze, nor Morcant that frightened him now.

It was Áed.

Áed blinked and looked down at his arms, his hands. His body seemed to shine with internal light, and great tongues of fire leapt from his fingers into the air. Spellbound, he raised his hands and watched the flames surge and rage with every beat of his heart.

"Please," Ronan tried faintly. "Please, Áed. Stop."

"Ronan," Áed breathed. "What is this?"

"I—I don't know. Please."

Nodding slowly, Áed felt for the power rippling through him, and he found it as surely as his breath. With a moment of concentration, it faded, leaving bright spots on his vision, and he saw the flickering reflections ebb from Ronan's eyes. All at once, he felt cold again.

Ronan fell to his knees and covered his face, and Áed looked back to Morcant.

Bile rose in his throat. He pressed the back of his hand to his mouth and stumbled backward one, two steps. "Oh…"

He'd killed a man.

He'd killed a man, but the man had deserved it, and that wasn't the part that made him shake as he stared at what he'd done.

That fire, that force from within him that had poured forth so suddenly, warped his voice, and made his head spin with power, had felt so very, very *natural.*

"Ronan, I—" he started, but he didn't know what he wanted to say. Ronan looked up fearfully, and his wet eyes glimmered in the darkness.

"I want to go home," the boy whispered pitifully.

Very slowly, so that Ronan would not run, Áed knelt in the dust. Breathing deeply to still his shaking, he carefully reached out a hand. Ronan shrank away from him and squeezed his eyes shut, but Áed touched his shoulder, and the younger boy didn't push him away.

"What did you do, Áed? What did you do?" More tears were rising in his eyes, and Ronan quaked as he started to cry in earnest. "What did you do?"

"I don't know," Áed said honestly.

"Don't do it again," Ronan begged, and then his defenses fell completely. He buried his face in Áed's chest, where he shuddered with tears.

Áed held Ronan while the boy cried, but he was all too aware that he could provide no real comfort, not when it was he whom Ronan feared. What *had* he done? Fire had come from within him as if it had lain in wait for the moment, and he could still feel the ember of it smoldering in his core. It was familiar, and he couldn't be sure whether or not he'd always felt it. The memory of Ninian's pyre made him pause his murmuring to Ronan as it struck his mind. Had he done that, too?

What *was* he?

"*Ceann beag*," he said softly, and Ronan looked up. "We have to go, mate."

Ronan nodded and shakily began to pick himself up.

"When we're past the farms, we can rest. Alright?"

The boy didn't answer, but Áed hadn't expected him to.

He brushed the dust from his hands, and together, he and Ronan abandoned Morcant's body in the street.

⌇⌇⌇

CHAPTER SEVEN

Hours later, the sun began to warm the early sky with hints of yellow on the horizon.

They had left the Inner Maze in silence, side-by-side and lost in their own thoughts. Ronan needed to sleep; his feet dragged, and his eyes were half-closed. Every now and then he tripped and Áed automatically moved to catch him, but even if Ronan had cried onto Áed's shoulder in the heat of the moment, the boy didn't want Áed to touch him again. The pain of this didn't lose itself in the dismal swirl of Áed's mind, and Ronan always stumbled upright on his own.

There were clouds moving in, the same clouds that had churned out over the sea as Ninian's soul drifted away, and the morning light fell onto the thunderheads' bulging, gray faces. They meant a storm, Áed was sure of it, but around them, the city was thinning, and shelter would soon be scarce as they reached farmland. Still, he would rather be caught in a storm beyond the Maze than sheltered within the city, so he kept moving, and Ronan stayed with him.

The city ended and the farms began, though it was difficult to tell exactly where. The buildings became smaller and fewer, and the ground abandoned dust and cobbles for earth. Áed and Ronan's feet didn't land on paving-stones or brick, but instead shifted through sandy, starving soil as they followed a narrow path that, according to the prints in the dry ground, a farmer and his ox had beaten through the fields. The leaves of the taller plants—oats, perhaps—brushed at Áed's elbows as he led the way, and the stems crackled, *shush*ing with a sound like wind. The land was hilly, as if the undulating waves of the sea had frozen in place. Ahead of them by some miles were trees, and rising behind the trees were the cliffs, and neither of them could see anything after.

The storm clouds took their time rolling in over the Maze, but having them at his back gave Áed the feeling of being chased. Eventually, Ronan caved to exhaustion and allowed Áed to carry him, and despite hunger scraping at his stomach, Áed moved as quickly as he could.

The trees approached quickly as the farmland faded into monotony, and their shadows grew darker and all the more dramatic for the clouds were blotting out the sun.

When they reached the forest, Ronan leaned to the side and tumbled off Áed's back, where he cushioned his fall by rolling onto his back and sprawling into fallen leaves. Without the boy's weight, Áed stumbled to the nearest tree and sank down against it, gazing up into the whispering branches. "Alright, *ceann beag*," he coughed. His throat was dry, and the air was chill. "We can rest."

Ronan just stared dully at the sky.

Áed shoved his knobby fingers through his hair and rested his elbows on his knees to regard Ronan with concern. "You should sleep a bit, okay, mate? You don't even have to move, just close your eyes."

Ronan nodded, hair tangling in the leaflitter, and his eyelids fell shut. Within moments, his breathing shifted, and

Áed knew that he slept.

Áed filled his lungs with air before letting his head fall back against the bark of the tree. They'd done it. They were out of the Maze. Áed could barely process it, but they were free of the city. They were well and truly out.

Somewhere past the trees were the cliffs. They would find a way to the White City, and there they would stay, and Ronan would be well-fed and happy. Surely Áed could find work at something, he was resourceful enough for that, and they could live someplace clean and quiet. Áed reached over and freed Ronan's little bag of possessions from the child's fist, and he placed it into his own so Ronan wouldn't have to carry it. If only the crops were ripe, then they could eat! They both could do with some food.

Áed didn't let himself sleep. He wouldn't allow his eyes to close for another night, not after Ninian's death, but he sat still and watched the storm crawl in.

When lightning began its assault on the distant Maze, Áed pushed himself up and roused Ronan. The air had grown humid, and the space beneath the steadily-darkening clouds was streaky with rain. "Hey," he said, and Ronan opened his eyes blearily. "Wake up, mate."

With a yawn, Ronan pushed himself up and scrubbed at his eyes with his fists.

"*Ceann beag*, we should talk."

Ronan looked at him blankly, but there was so much turmoil behind his expression that Áed bit his lip.

"What happened back in the Maze. I know it scared the hell out of you." Áed could feel that clearly.

Tentatively, Ronan bobbed his chin.

"I know you're angry with me."

Again, Ronan nodded.

"Talk to me, mate."

Ronan looked to the ground and started crumbling the

dry dirt in his hands. He chewed his lip ferociously, but couldn't seem to find the words. Áed gave him a moment, and eventually, Ronan spoke. "I never knew you could do that." The boy swallowed hard. "You killed him."

Yes. Yes, that was true: Áed had taken a man's life. Violently. Right in front of Ronan. He felt sick to his stomach. "I am so sorry, *ceann beag*."

"You killed him with…" Ronan couldn't get the words out, but he opened his hands from fists like something was bursting from them. "You weren't *you*. I thought…"

Áed wanted only to take Ronan into his arms and convince him that everything was alright. But Ronan was still instinctively keeping his distance, and things weren't alright anyway, so Áed pressed his hands to the ground. "Ronan," Áed said, making an effort to show the truth in his words, "I don't know what happened. I don't know how I did that. It startled me, too." Gently, slowly, he reached out and lifted Ronan's chin so that the boy made eye contact. "I would *never* hurt you. Do you believe me?"

Hesitantly, Ronan opened his mouth, then closed it again. Then, in a small voice, he said, "Yes."

"Good," Áed replied with a small sigh of relief. He moved his hand from Ronan's chin, and Ronan didn't look away. "I'm sorry we had to leave, but it's going to be better now. I promise." Ronan would understand later. When the wound of Ninian's death healed a little, then he would see. Áed stood and held out his hand, and after a moment of pause, Ronan took it. "Come on, *ceann beag*. There's a long way to go."

The forest wasn't terribly thick, and this was fortunate. Brambles and thorny twigs snatched at their ankles, but they couldn't do much to damage Áed or Ronan's already-tattered trousers. Saplings stretched toward the sun, and the older trees grew crookedly. Moss that was green and rich affixed itself to flaky bark, and most of the plants looked rather sickly. Áed and Ronan picked their way over fallen trunks where fungi sprouted like spongy balconies, stepping through patches of diluted sunlight that filtered through the leaves overhead. They didn't talk, and the quiet that hung between the scrawny trees pressed both Áed and Ronan more deeply into his own thoughts.

The woods spanned fewer miles than the farmland. Before long, the trees became sparser, and the screen of branches ahead of them thinned. "We must be getting close to the cliff," Ronan said tiredly, breaking the silence for the first time in hours. He glanced at the sky, at the clouds that had nearly reached them. "Hopefully."

For a while, they walked uphill, weaving between saplings whose leaves danced at their passage, and at the top of the rise, they emerged from the trees.

And there it was, rising from the land ahead of them. A rough wall of stone, terminal and stoic, as impassable as the unforgiving sea.

Ronan's mouth fell open at the sight of it, and even Áed let out a little stunned breath.

"Áed," Ronan said quietly. "We can't climb that."

Áed nodded. "I know, mate. Don't worry, we aren't going to." Scaling the cliffs had never been part of Áed's plan, and he'd been dreaming about this journey for enough years to have considered the possibilities. "Remember Ninian's stories?"

Ronan pressed his lips together and looked away, but he replied with a quick nod.

The mention of Ninian scraped knives across Áed's heart, but he made himself continue. "The White City and the Maze used to be one city." He took a few steps toward the cliff. "So what does that tell you?"

"I don't know."

"It means that once upon a time, people had to be able get from one part to another." He began walking along the bottom of the cliff. "There's a way, mate. We just need to find it."

⌇⌇⌇

The clouds at their backs seemed to have paused over the Maze, but the air had gotten heavy and still in anticipation of the storm's arrival. Áed and Ronan stumbled along the base of the cliffs, unsure what they were looking for but determined to find it.

Wind picked up as time ground on, and leaves began blowing from the trees to dance skyward as the air met the cliff. The sky, hazy above them, was turning a faint silver-green as the impending storm filtered away the sunlight's last warmth. Áed's feet met the earth with increasing weariness, but he had his goal in mind and would not be deterred from it; he paused only when Ronan stopped breathlessly, and then he encouraged the boy onward.

The face of the cliff was changing as they moved, becoming rougher and pocked with minerals, and in places, lichens affixed themselves to the rock. Ivies and creepers trailed down the stone, sometimes obscuring the cliff entirely, and Áed gave one of the vines an experimental tug. The plant released its hold and came falling down; they wouldn't be of any use for climbing if it did come to that.

Suddenly, Áed had an idea, and immediately, he kicked himself for not having had it sooner. "Ronan," he instructed, "Brush away the ivy." As Ronan obeyed, Áed began clearing aside the swaying creepers. Behind the green leaves was nothing but rock, but Áed broke into a jog along the cliff with one hand pulling the ivy away as he went. Fine tendrils snatched at his fingers, but he kept moving.

He skidded to a stop, took a few steps backward, and yanked away the ivy. Ronan caught up behind him, and when he saw what Áed had found, he gasped.

Áed licked his lips and squinted into the cave. It smelled damp, like forest things and wet stone, and a breeze whispered through the air. The mouth of the cave was tall enough to accommodate them, but the inside was dark as a tomb.

"Áed, look." Ronan pushed away more trailing ivy and pointed at the edge of the rock. Around the straight edges of the opening, carvings settled into the rock. Pointed, spiraling knots, endless and deliberate, crept upward, framing the doorway. The strange light of the storm filled them with shadows, and they seemed to move in the corner of Áed's eyes.

"This has to be it, *ceann beag*," Áed said. He'd expected to feel jubilant, or at least grimly triumphant, but he didn't. He couldn't. "Wait here a moment."

Carefully, with hands outstretched, he felt his way forward. The light from the doorway scarcely carried beyond the entrance, but he could tell from the echoes of his breathing that the chamber was large. His foot hit something on the ground and he tripped, but his hands met stone before he fell.

"Áed?" Ronan's voice came uncertainly from the entrance.

"I'm fine," Áed called back, feeling around him. "I found stairs."

He heard Ronan's footsteps tentatively enter the cave.

"That's it, mate," Áed said. "Follow my voice. Over here—ah, there you are." He found Ronan's shoulder and gave it a squeeze. "I'm going to go first, okay? Stay close."

Ronan shivered under his touch. "It's so dark."

"I know." Áed didn't think Ronan would want him to try to break the darkness, and Áed definitely didn't want to either. The ember in his chest was very awake, and it scared him.

They moved up the damp stairs cautiously, careful of where they trusted their weight. Moss made the stone, untended for who knew how many hundreds of years, as slippery as oil, and if the hewn steps had ever had railings, they'd long since rotted away. As the two moved higher, Áed kept a hand on Ronan, all too aware of the invisible distance below them.

As they climbed higher, faint light began to permeate from somewhere above. It grew stronger as they approached it, and they moved faster once they could see. "Almost there," Áed murmured. "We're so close, mate."

Wind began to twirl through the chamber, wind that smelled fresh and stormy, and when Áed and Ronan crossed the last step, their feet fell on scruffy grass poking up between cracked paving stones.

The stairs, obscured by the grass, disappeared into the ground behind them. The edge of the cliff, which overlooked the farms, the Maze, and the vast Sea that spread to the horizon, plunged downward not twenty paces from where they emerged, and Áed stood for a moment, catching his breath. It appeared as if they were eye-level with the storm's rolling thunderheads, and beneath it all, their old city looked almost beautiful in the deadly light. "Look, Ronan," Áed said softly. "You can see the docks."

Ronan's eyes caught the storm and appeared earth-gray as he squinted across the expanse. "I can't find home."

Áed bit his lip and searched as well, but the crumbling flat was indistinguishable from anything around it. "Me neither," he murmured, and turned away. It didn't matter anymore. "Come on. We're going to get caught in the storm."

The landscape atop the cliffs was hilly and speckled with white-trunked trees, but it didn't take the two long to crest a rise and slow their steps. They stopped at the peak of a gentle knoll, cracked pavers barely intact between silvery birches, and looked toward their grail.

The White City sparkled under the storm-filtered sun, the color of bleached bones. Straight-backed buildings crowned the hills in both directions, boundless and magnificent.

"*A thiarcais*," Ronan said softly, and had Áed been able to form a thought, he would have said the same. There were the rising turrets, as if plucked from a story, there were the glittering windows. There were the sturdy, sloping roofs and the clean streets, and as Áed stared, he was sure that he saw security, warmth, and a future embedded like chips of mica in the walls.

Ronan needed no urging to start forward again, and Áed hurried after him.

⌇⌇⌇

CHAPTER EIGHT

THE VERY BRICKS UPON WHICH they walked shone white.

Agape, Áed and Ronan drank in the sights they passed. Even in the outskirts of the city, the buildings seemed to glow with health, and each was adorned with decorative brickwork or boxes of trailing flowers, terraces, and tidy shutters. Warm light spilled from windows, and smoke rose merrily from the chimneys; the few people who had not yet taken shelter from the impending tempest wore clothes of fur and fabric in a thousand colors.

The surroundings grew only richer as Áed and Ronan moved further into the heart of the city, for the buildings became taller, more ornate, and here and there a walkway arced gracefully above their heads. Ahead of them loomed a soaring citadel of white stones that dwarfed the buildings around it as it stretched its spires heavenward, and it took Áed's breath away as he craned his neck to see flags snapping at the very pinnacles of the towers. He shook his head firmly to ensure he wasn't dreaming, and the vision stayed.

But there *was* something wrong. He glanced over his shoulder, half-expecting to catch a glimpse of motion there, but all he saw was the misty, pre-storm rain. He nudged Ronan. "Keep your eyes out, *ceann beag.*"

"Alright," Ronan said. "Can we go inside?"

Áed nodded. Surely someplace had open doors. The storm was building, and Áed's uneasy feeling was only mounting as the rain stole away more visibility, as if he'd unconsciously noted something that set him on edge. "We'll find somewhere. But remember what I said, and stay alert."

As it turned out, Ronan spotted them first.

Two men behind them, taking advantage of the hazy air to follow at a short distance, ducked behind parked carriages or into doorways whenever Áed or Ronan looked back. Ronan elbowed Áed, who peeked back in time to see one of them slip out of sight. "Right," he muttered. "I see."

"Should we run?"

"Not yet."

"Please don't do the… you know." Ronan made a gesture with his hands that suggested fire spitting from them. "Don't do it."

Áed wasn't entirely sure whether it was his to decide, but he nodded. "I won't. I promise."

They wove through the streets, avoiding obvious glances at their stalkers. The White City, it seemed, wasn't free of criminals, and it was tempting to shout that for the Gods' sake, they had nothing left to steal. Instead, they hurried through the fog, hoping to lose the men in the winding streets. Ronan elbowed him again. "Áed? They're doing something."

Áed squinted through the mist to see a couple quick movements before the shadows slunk out of sight again. His skin chilled. Their gestures were of men coordinating a hunt.

"Do we run now?" Ronan asked.

Another glance confirmed that the men were no longer

trying to hide. "Yeah. Run."

The man in front gave a shout, a quick whip of a noise that cut through the sound of Áed and Ronan's footsteps. Their feet pounded unevenly and found purchase on the milky-white brick, and scattered pebbles clattered away. The men behind them sounded like beasts, all weighty footfalls and grunts, and their voices died eerily fast in the clammy air. Beside Áed, Ronan's pallid face flushed with splotchy blushes that rode high on his cheekbones. The men behind were stronger, Áed knew, and they were gaining ground. He could hear their footsteps drawing nearer.

"Here!" Áed cried, pushing Ronan in front of him as he darted into a recessed doorway. The locked door handle gave way to a kick, and Áed shouldered it open. They darted inside, he pressed the door shut and, without stopping to think, slammed his palm to the handle. Upon impact, the weak metal glowed with heat and fused the door to the frame with a slither of smoke. Áed motioned to Ronan, who had stopped running, nose wrinkled. "Come on," Áed said. "Come on, this way."

"How do you know?"

"I don't. Now, move."

They'd burst into a shop of some sort, lined with shelves of bottles and herbs, and to the right rose a narrow staircase. Áed tore up the staircase, urging Ronan on ahead of him. The place smelled warm, like spices and cleanliness, but Áed couldn't pause to enjoy it—at the base of the stairs, shouting and pounding sounded at the door. "*In ainm dé*, are they still coming?" Áed swore. What in the world could they want so badly?

The stairs led to two doors, and Ronan quickly leapt to try the handles. Neither knob would turn. Áed cast about rapidly, and, acting on a flash of insight, kicked aside the neat doormats: There beneath the mat of the second door lay a silver slice of saving grace. Ronan scooped up the key, shoved it into the doorknob, and pushed the door open, and Áed elbowed it closed and locked it behind them.

They stood for a moment and caught their breath, panting from the exertion. Áed dropped to a squat, bracing his elbows on his knees, and Ronan collapsed next to him. In the sudden quiet, the world felt safe for a moment, just one fragile, water-drop moment, cocooned in warmth and the smell of chamomile.

Áed collected himself and looked around the apartment they'd invaded, and he gave a low whistle. "*A thiarcais.*"

Ronan stood and, still breathing heavily, gaped around.

Never had either of them seen such luxury, from the cheerfully-painted walls to a beautiful table of inlaid wood farther inside. No sound came from deeper within; it was empty, and Áed took a step forward and glanced about. "Who *lives* here?"

"A queen," Ronan suggested. The rain, which now beat heavily on the window, had left shining droplets on his hair. Now that they were in relative safety, Áed noticed the lavender circles under the younger boy's eyes. Ronan's head drooped, and his little shoulders were rounded.

Áed put a hand on Ronan's back with an encouraging smile. "I'll bet there's food in here."

Suddenly, beneath his hand, he felt Ronan tense. The boy froze, and Áed instinctively froze as well.

From the hallway outside the door: footsteps. Not the heavy, loud movement of the men who pursued them, but someone with a light tread nearing the door in quick, even steps. Áed nudged Ronan around the corner, and the boy kept quiet.

A scrape sounded at the door, and the footsteps stopped. Áed sighed sharply. "Of course."

There came a jingle from outside, then a click as keys bit

into the lock and turned, and Ronan pressed himself flat against the wall. "How do we hide? If whoever's out there lives here, they can't *not* notice us."

The door squeaked as it opened, and another presence joined the room. A rustle of fabric on fabric brushed through the air, and then timid footsteps crossed the floor. "Hello?" a woman's voice called out cautiously. "I know someone's here."

Both Áed and Ronan held their breath.

"Cynwrig, you'd best not scare me."

Áed elbowed Ronan until he had the boy's attention and mouthed, 'You talk.'

Ronan's eyes bugged, and he pointed to himself as if there were someone else Áed could have meant. *'Me?'*

Áed nodded, and Ronan balked. "Trust me," Áed whispered.

Ronan pursed his lips and drew a deep breath. His eyes were fixed on Áed, who nodded, knowing that Ronan's voice was still high and unthreatening. "Um… hello."

Áed heard the woman jump, her footsteps skittering backward on the floor. "You're not Cynwrig."

"No. I don't know who that is." Ronan poked his scruffy head around the corner, but not before Áed caught a glimpse of his frightened face. "I'm sorry we're in here."

She made a squeaky sound. "We? Who else?" Shakily, the lady peeked around the corner. Her skin, whose smoothness placed her in her mid-twenties, held as little color as a phantom. Her eyes, a pale pink, lent the only hint of blush in her terrified expression, though her entire person seemed to glow with the warmth of her yellow dress.

"Hello," Áed said, keeping his voice low. "I swear we won't hurt you, please don't panic."

"What… who… why are you…?" The lady tripped over her words, unable to articulate a thought. She looked like she might either faint or scream.

"Seriously, we aren't going to do anything, please don't scream. Please, *please* don't scream."

"I—I won't." She gulped, her throat bobbing. "What are you doing here?" From her inflection, Áed could tell clearly that she was doing her best to reassert control. Her intentions, from what Áed could read of them, were shifting reactively: Run. Fight. Stay calm. He tried to keep his tone measured.

"Hiding, at the moment," he replied honestly.

"From whom?"

"Not sure. Thieves, maybe. But I think they're outside. So please don't scream, or they might hear."

She shook her head, and a touch of color returned to her face and spread ever so slightly across her high, round cheekbones. "I just came from outside. There's nobody there."

Ronan sagged against the wall in relief, leaving a streak of dust on the wallpaper. "Oh, thank the Gods."

There must be another door, Áed thought, if the lady had gotten in. He wondered how long it would be until somebody noticed what he'd done to the doorknob.

"Um," she said, turning a trifle pinker. It was a good sign, and made her appear far less likely to faint. "Who are you?"

"Áed," Áed supplied, and gestured with his chin at his companion. "And this is Ronan."

She blinked, still standing in the exact same position as when she'd first come around the corner. She looked ready to run or grab the nearest hard object to wield. "He's your brother?"

Ronan glanced at Áed. "Áed takes care of me."

"Oh." She swallowed again, trying to regain composure. "I see." She took a deep breath through her nose, eyes still flitting around as if searching for a weapon. There was a candlestick on a nearby table, and she edged toward it.

"What's your name?" Ronan asked shakily. Then he shrank back, unsure if that was an acceptable thing to say.

She blinked, not expecting that question, and replied automatically. "Boudicca." As soon as she'd answered, she narrowed her eyes warily at Áed. "What's in your pockets?"

He'd slipped his hands there, he realized, out of habit. "Nothing. My hands." To prove it, he slid them out and held them up.

Boudicca drew a sharp breath, but she actually leaned forward so her yellow-clad shoulders parted from the wallpaper. "Oh, my."

"I know." His fingers were gnarled, and the knuckles were too large for the bony digits that curled crookedly around each other as they crushed inward. The backs of his hand warped where his fingers torqued sideways into the curve of his palm. He spread those fingers as much as he could, letting Boudicca's eyes scrutinize the tortured appendages.

"How do you, ah," she began uncertainly, and cleared her throat. "How do you do anything?"

"He doesn't, mostly," Ronan interjected. "I do it for him."

"You don't have to *talk* for me too, mate."

Boudicca's lip gave an infinitesimal twitch, and the tiny smile seemed to put a crack in her wariness.

The tension seemed to be broken, at least temporarily. Boudicca stood up away from the wall, although she maintained her distance and her movements were as tightly coiled as a spring, ready to lunge for the candlestick. "So." She pressed her lips together. "Where did you come from? You look a little…"

"Dirty?" Ronan offered.

"Well. Yes."

"We're from the Maze," Áed replied. When it was clear she didn't understand, he elaborated. "The city at the bottom of the cliffs. By the sea."

Boudicca didn't seem to believe him. "You're from Smudge?"

"Smudge?"

"The city on the Red Sea." She shook her head. "But they say it's deadly. And people live like cockroaches."

Áed nodded. "Then I suppose we're from Smudge."

Her mouth fell open. "You aren't supposed to be here."

Ronan frowned. "What do you mean?"

"The king's forbidden it."

"You have a king?"

She only seemed more lost. "The *Gut* has a king. King Seisyll." Her eyes flitted back and forth between them, searching for hints of recognition. "You don't know of the king?"

"No."

It didn't particularly shock Áed that someone had claimed authority over the Maze. It was a wild place, and its inhabitants paid little attention to proclamations of power unless they were in a gang whose turf was threatened. "Why has the king banned us?"

Her hand twitched toward the candlestick again, but she seemed to decide against it. "It's for our safety. Smudge is dangerous."

"That's true, but I wouldn't worry. Trying not to starve keeps people too busy to mount an invasion." Although he couldn't deny that they probably would, given the chance.

She blinked again, her pink irises shining as she latched onto a word. "People are starving?"

Áed nodded wordlessly, silenced by her ignorance.

She swallowed hard, and her right forefinger picked at the cuticle of her thumb. "I never thought of that." Suddenly she seemed to see them fully, and her eyes scanned them up and down as she took in the grime and tattered clothing.

Under her unsullied gaze, Áed felt an unfamiliar self-consciousness. "Well, I don't suppose..." She swallowed, like she was trying to decide what to do. Áed could tell when she made up her mind, because she set her jaw with a feathering of muscle. "Do you two want to clean up?"

⌇⌇⌇

CHAPTER NINE

SHE LED THEM DOWN THE HONEY-colored hall, casting vigilant glances behind her as she motioned to two paneled doors. "Bathrooms," she said quietly, opening the doors for them. "Go ahead and bathe, use as much soap as you need." Áed noticed her unconsciously wrinkle her nose, and he flushed with embarrassment. It was a very odd feeling. From the bathroom on the right, Ronan's voice piped up.

"How do you get water up here?"

Áed eavesdropped as she explained how to use the faucet, and with a twist of her hand, a stream of hot water poured out of the spigot and splashed merrily into a white basin. She dropped in a fat bar of soap, and bubbles rolled to the surface of the filling tub. She closed the door for Ronan, and Áed moved into the bathroom across the hall. He clumsily mimicked Boudicca's motions to turn on the stream of water, and he let it run until steam rose from the basin.

The sumptuous surroundings made him dizzy. Was it truly possible that people lived this way? As the bathtub filled, he couldn't help but compare his reflection in the mirror to the people he had seen on the streets. His cheeks, hollow with hunger, sharpened his cheekbones and deep red eyes, and his sandy hair lay lank and filthy. His chest and arms were far too skeletal, their muscles taut and corded over his ribs and prominent collarbone. He blinked at himself, and felt that he saw himself clearly for the first time in his life. It wasn't pleasant.

Shivering at the lingering chill from the rain and the trek from the Maze, he stepped into the bath. Immediately, a moan of pleasure escaped his lips, and he sank up to his chin to be engulfed in the warm water. For a moment, he just floated and let the heat penetrate his muscles, unknotting the lifetime of tension held in them. He had never known it was possible for something to feel so glorious.

Taking a deep breath, he pulled his head underwater and rubbed his hands vigorously through his hair to loosen the tangles and grime. The chilly air of the bathroom refreshed him as he came back up and located the soap, and he put it to use attacking every mote of dirt.

When the bathwater turned gray, he emptied the tub and sat, shivering, as it refilled with fresh water. He rubbed the soap into a soft lather in his hair and behind his ears, losing himself in the novel experience of becoming entirely clean. A third time, he emptied the bath and filled it up again, and this time he simply floated, ears under the water so he could hear his heartbeat.

There came a rap at the door. He started, instantly alert, but then Boudicca's voice came from beyond. "Áed? Are you done?"

He took a deep breath, relaxing. "Nearly."

"Well, there are towels on the counter, and I've found some clothes for you. They're my brother's. They'll probably be too big, but I'll just leave them out here."

He blinked in surprise at her generosity. "Thanks."

Her footsteps tapped off down the hall, and, taking a

towel to hold tightly around his waist, he opened the door a crack. Dry air spilled into the steamy bathroom as he took the pile of clothing and clicked the door closed again.

Boudicca's brother was larger than Áed was. The sweater fit somewhat better than the pants that were too long and a bit too wide, but Boudicca had anticipated this and included a belt in the bundle. With a roll of the cuffs, everything fit admirably.

He folded his old garments into a tidy pile in the corner of the bathroom along with the now-damp cloth he used to dry himself before he opened the door. Followed by a swirl of lingering steam, he padded down the hall and back to the front room. Boudicca looked up from the table where she had been reading and stood. "That's better, isn't it?"

Áed nodded sincerely. "It's unbelievable. Thank you."

She nodded, still appraising him. "You look like a different person."

"I feel that way, too."

Boudicca took a deep breath, straightened her skirt, and nodded. She didn't seem to know what to say next, and the silence felt awkward. "So…" she murmured, trailing off.

Áed filled the gap. "Who is Cynwrig?"

A cautious smile played over her face. "He's the brother whose clothes you're wearing."

"Oh." Áed cocked his head. "Does he live with you?"

"No, I'm alone." She swallowed, pressing her lips together. When she opened them to speak, color ran into them again, even fuller than before. "Speaking of which." She sank back down into her chair and traced absentminded patterns on the table with the tip of her fingernail. "I'm sheltering outlaws, aren't I?"

Áed slipped his hands into his pockets. "You said the king's banned us. So I suppose."

"You look a lot different now that you're clean, and, you

know, not dressed in holes." She coughed uncomfortably. "But you are easy to recognize, aren't you?"

Áed frowned. That was likely true, but he didn't know why it would matter.

"What did you do? To have the Guard after you?"

"What?"

She regarded him intensely. "While you were in the bath, two men from the August Guard came to my door and asked if I'd seen a blond man with red eyes, or a black-haired, green-eyed boy. They said they'd followed you here."

Fear rose in Áed's throat and soured on his tongue. The men who had pursued him and Ronan had not been looking to rob them. They had been of this *August Guard*, and now were searching for them. He knew he was staring at Boudicca with alarm. "What did you tell them?"

She looked down, her face flushing pink as she traced even more quickly over the tabletop. "I told them I hadn't."

Áed swallowed hard and released the breath he was holding. "Thank you. Gods, thank you."

Boudicca cleared her throat almost daintily. "Since I'm breaking the law for you, I'd like to know a bit more about who you are."

It seemed like a reasonable request, so he sat, took a moment to organize his scattered thoughts, and started from the beginning of the story.

⌇⌇⌇

When Áed heard Ronan emerge from the bathroom, he paused, and Boudicca looked up to Ronan and smiled.

"What are you talking about?" Ronan asked.

"Everything," Áed replied. "Add what you will."

The story continued through the winding alleys of the Gut, from the Maze to the pyre, from the pyre through the farms and the cliffs. He didn't mention Morcant, or how the man had met his end, and even when Ronan added to the story, the boy kept quiet about that as well. Amazement rolled off of Boudicca in waves as she listened to their descriptions of the Maze's grungy streets, and tears actually collected in the corner of her eye when Áed tried to talk about Ninian. He couldn't do it, and stopped mid-sentence. Boudicca didn't ask for any more.

The story concluded in her apartment, and she leaned back thoughtfully. "That's incredible." She bit at the end of her nail. "It's almost unbelievable, actually. I *wouldn't* believe it if I hadn't seen the way you looked. I've never heard anything like it before."

Ronan had more pressing issues, however, and he looked up to Boudicca. "Miss Boudicca? Do you have any food?"

⁂

Boudicca clattered around in the kitchen while Ronan sat at the table with his legs tucked under him. Áed stood in front of Boudicca's bookcase, admiring the different colors of the bindings, the varying thicknesses of the pages, and the stamped images on the covers. In some books, pictures took up space on the pages, and he examined these with great interest in an attempt to glean the story.

Boudicca poked her head around the corner, stepping out of the room where delicious cooking smells gathered. She saw the book he was holding and smiled. "Found the most boring book in my collection, I see."

"Boring?" He looked down at the pictures again. "You could have fooled me."

She laughed. "*A Compendium of Herbal Remedies?*" She leaned on the doorway. "I use it for reference. It's like a healer's encyclopedia."

"Really?"

"What did you think it was?"

"I was trying to figure that out."

She cocked her head in puzzlement. "You didn't read the cover?"

Áed laughed, closing the book and sliding it back into place. "I can't read."

Color rose immediately in her cheeks. "Oh, I'm sorry!"

He smiled, waving her off. "Don't worry about it." When she continued to look down, her face pink, he chuckled. "I'm not offended. I only ever knew one person who could read, and that was Ninian."

Still flushed with embarrassment and biting her lip hard, she cleared her throat and wiped her hands on her apron. "Well. I just came out to say that dinner's ready."

Dinner.

A thiarcais.

It was *nothing* like he'd expected.

Rather than a few bites of dry bread and a couple apple slices, maybe supplemented by a strip of salty jerky eaten out of their hands, Boudicca put plates on the table and laid out silverware that glinted in the fading daylight. She made them sit, refusing help, and the most extraordinary smell that Áed had ever experienced anticipated the main dish. As Boudicca entered, Ronan kicked Áed excitedly under the table, but Áed was too distracted to reprimand him.

Curls of steam rose from the surface of the dish Boudicca brought, accompanied by an aroma that convinced Áed that he might eat the entire thing in one bite. Ronan could not be stopped when Boudicca served him: he scooped up a massive forkful of scalding food and shoveled it into his mouth, and his face flushed with either delight or pain.

"Mmph!" he declared. He swallowed with some difficulty, and a wisp of steam escaped from his mouth. "Hot! But good! Gods, that's good!" And he loaded another bite.

Áed couldn't hold back anymore either. He tried to take it more slowly than Ronan, getting a reasonable amount onto his fork, but as soon as it passed his lips, the manners Ninian had taught him vanished like the steam in the air.

It was the best thing he had ever tasted.

He barely breathed as he polished off his entire plate, swallowing just as the next bite reached his mouth and ignoring the scalding heat. In the time it took Boudicca to take four tidy bites, both Áed and Ronan polished their plates.

Áed leaned back, the food in his stomach radiating warmth like he'd swallowed a coal, and contentment spread through him. Ronan was starting on his second helping, and Áed, who'd stopped himself from licking the plate, eyed the rest of the dish before serving himself some more. Boudicca looked amazed. "I'll have you over often," she said softly, and Áed wasn't sure he was meant to hear. "Nobody has ever been so appreciative of my cooking."

Áed swallowed a bite and came up for air. "Why *not*?"

She laughed, a light sound. "It's just shepherd's pie. And it's over-salted and a touch burnt."

"Really?" Áed took another bite, trying to taste what she was talking about, but it was impossible to discern anything negative about the warm flavor and bliss that accompanied it. "I can't tell."

"Perhaps you ought to slow down." She glanced to Ronan, who was still shoveling. "I'm afraid you'll vomit."

True enough, now he paused, Áed did already feel extremely full. The feeling was completely foreign, and somewhat unpleasant. He set his fork down next to the rest of his unfinished meal.

Unfinished.

There was enough food in the White City that he left his

meal *unfinished.*

Ronan looked a bit sick as well, and he dropped his fork onto his plate with a clatter. "Whew!"

"Full?" Boudicca asked with a hint of smile behind her words. She'd set the dish down not more than five minutes before.

"Yes," Áed replied. The word evidenced his amazement.

"The sun's setting." Boudicca considered Áed thoughtfully. "Do you have anywhere to go?" When Áed shook his head, she nodded, chewing on her bottom lip. "I feel like I ought to let you stay." She tilted her head slightly, regarding them both with eyes that were lilac in the evening light. "Would I regret it?"

Ronan looked interested by her statement. "Why would you regret it?"

"She's asking if we would rob her, or assault her, or do some other horrible thing," Áed explained.

"Oh."

Áed shook his head. "Of course not."

To his surprise, she seemed satisfied. "I've only one extra room."

"That's fine." He laughed, a touch bitterly. "Honestly, Boudicca, I don't understand our luck, that we came to this flat out of every other place we could have hidden. Thank you. For everything." He smiled sheepishly. "And I am really sorry about breaking in."

She smiled at his gratitude. "I can forgive you, I think. But I'm not going to leave the key under the mat anymore."

⌇⌇⌇

CHAPTER TEN

BOUDICCA SHOWED THEM their quarters. "This is where Cynwrig stays when he visits," she explained, pushing open a door at the end of the hall. "Which is almost never. There are plenty of his things still in there."

"We won't bother anything."

She shook her head. "Bother it all you like. He has more than enough, as he makes obvious by leaving so much with me."

At the sight of the bed, its colorful quilt and thick mattress nestled between dark wood posts, Ronan slumped involuntarily. "Could I sleep *now*?"

Boudicca laughed. "Whenever you want." The air in the room was fresh with the smell of linen, and a curtained window looked out over the empty street and the *thrush*ing rain. It did look remarkably appealing. Boudicca shot a glance at Áed. "Aren't you tired?"

"Exhausted. But not ready to sleep yet."

She cocked her head in confusion.

"I'm still..." he sighed through his nose, looking at the bed with longing. "We started Ninian's fire only a day and a night ago."

Ronan understood and looked at the bed guiltily. "You still have a night left."

Áed nodded, glum not only at the reminder of Ninian, which felt like an open wound, but at the fact that he wouldn't be able to sleep in the fine bed.

"Wait," Boudicca interjected, polite but confused. "What?"

After some surprised blinking at Boudicca's lack of knowledge, Ronan explained. "You can't sleep for two nights after the burial, or burning, I guess, of a love." He glanced up at Áed reluctantly. "Should I stay up too?"

It touched his heart that Ronan was prepared to do that, but he shook his head. "You're too young for it to count for you."

Boudicca frowned. "I've never heard of that tradition."

"Really?" Áed yawned, frustrated already at his heavy eyelids. "I thought everyone had." He began ticking them off on his crumpled fingers. "One night for an acquaintance, if you went to the funeral; two for a friend or a partner; three for a parent; four for a son or a daughter."

Ronan elbowed Áed, smiling in the way he did when he wanted a serious answer but didn't want to show he cared. "Hey, Áed."

"Yeah?"

"How many nights would you stay up for me?"

"Oh, Gods," Áed muttered, taking Ronan by the shoulders and pulling him into a backward hug. "Don't die anytime in the next fifty years, okay?"

"I won't."

"Good."

"But if I did…"

Áed sighed, rocking side to side and feeling Ronan move with him. "For you, *ceann beag*?" He took a deep breath and exhaled it slowly, tightening his grip on Ronan until the boy squeaked. "I don't think I'd ever sleep again."

⁂

Once Ronan was comfortably in bed, and Áed had bid him goodnight and closed the door, Áed trudged back to the table and sat down with a sigh. Boudicca rustled around lighting candles before waving out the match and joining him. "So."

"So." He rested his elbows on the table, propping his chin on them and looking up at where she stood.

She pressed her lips together, taking a deep breath in through her nose. "So you have to stay up all night?"

He nodded.

After a moment's consideration, she sat down at the table as well. "You're going to have trouble with that, aren't you?"

"Probably."

She nodded decisively. "I'll stay up with you."

Áed smiled wearily, lifting his chin off his arms. "How much of that decision was made from fear that I'll rob you while you sleep?"

"None." She spoke too quickly, and he chuckled.

"Boudicca, you are the closest thing to a friend we have in this place." He leaned back, stretching as the chair creaked softly. "Trust me. I won't risk turning you against us."

She snorted, and then realized she had snorted and laughed a pert, sparkling laugh that made Áed smile despite himself. "I hope you wouldn't steal from me anyhow."

He cracked a wan grin. "Being honest, it'd depend on the situation."

Boudicca sighed and leaned back, regarding him with guarded interest. "Suibhne must seem so strange to you."

Áed frowned. "Suibhne?" He pronounced it *siv-na*, as she had. It sounded like a name meant for a person. "Is that what you call this place?"

She nodded. "What do you call it?"

"The White City."

"That does make sense." Boudicca thought for a moment. "I've never met anyone from Smudge, you know. You're a bit strange to me, too."

"You expected something different." He knew it was true, and didn't bother to make it a question.

She smirked. "King Seisyll says you're all barbarians."

"Why *does* he hate us?"

"He says it's because of the danger Smudge poses." Her shoulders rose and fell. "Seisyll has always been… different. People say that he's not entirely stable." At Áed's look of interest, she propped her elbow on the table and went on. "He was married when he was young, but it was tumultuous. He couldn't keep his hands off of other women, if you understand my meaning. But then his wife died in childbirth, and his infant son shortly after, and the king became erratic."

Áed mirrored her with his elbows on the table, intrigued, and Boudicca seemed fueled by his curiosity.

"He declared laws and repealed them days later, raged at his advisors, didn't sleep. He became obsessed with control. Eventually, one of his advisors—" her face twitched in faint disdain, though Áed didn't know why—"convinced him to put the Council of the King, which is Seisyll's cabinet, in charge of the city's mundanities, but that only gave Seisyll more room to fall apart. He actually—" She swallowed and looked a little uncomfortable. "He started taking outings to Smudge and coming back with stories of… well, stories of women he'd… overpowered."

Áed's brow crinkled with disgust. "*Why?*"

"Some say he's gone quite mad."

"He sounds terrible."

"Mm. Dangerous to say that. But you understand that he hates Smudge. He channeled his grief into Smudge."

"Let me get this straight." Áed brushed his hair off his forehead. "Are you saying he went to the Maze and did those things because he was *sad*?"

"I suspect that it was also an excuse to satisfy his, ah, carnal tendencies, but yes. Some people react very destructively to tragedy, and the king has never possessed the strongest of minds. He wanted a way to reassert his dominance when he felt he had no control." She shook her head sadly. "So, yes. I'm fairly confident of this."

Áed appraised her, impressed. "You're clever."

She smiled. "Thank you. Although, it is my job." She covered a yawn behind her hand. "I'm quite talented with healing, so I've seen a lot of warped minds."

Perhaps the fact that she was a healer influenced her willingness to shelter Áed and Ronan. "You're just naturally helpful, then."

She shrugged with a little smirk. "Well. I do *like* getting paid for it." She pointed toward the door with her thumb. "My neighbor, Gráinne, owns the apothecary downstairs, and I run the practice. I do it all: injuries, illness, childbirth." The smirk widened. "I'm even quick with a bit of magic, if the situation calls for it. Mostly for young folks in love."

"Magic?" There were a few people in the Maze, recluses, mostly, who claimed to be able to call on the power of the fae to speak with the dead or divine the future, but Áed had always stayed well away. "You don't say."

"Sure," Boudicca replied. "Sometimes, the herbs aren't enough." She inclined her chin towards his hands. "Just out of a healer's curiosity, what happened?"

"I'm not sure. I think they must've broken a long time ago, but I can't remember the event."

Boudicca sighed. "Terrible. I'm afraid something like that

is beyond even my little witchery."

Áed leaned back again and cast around for something else to talk about. He'd never been wholly comfortable with anything pertaining to the fae. "You have a brother, right? What's the rest of your family like?"

She easily accepted the change of subject. "Yes, Cynwrig's my brother. I have a stepbrother, too, whose father married my mother. I like my stepbrother well enough, but I don't like Elisedd—that's my stepfather—particularly well. My mother and real father both died."

"Oh. I'm sorry."

"It was a long time ago." Her gaze unfocused in thought for a minute. "Speaking of family, I'd rather if Cynwrig didn't meet you. I don't think that anything would come of it, but let's keep your presence hidden for the time." Áed agreed, and Boudicca's eyes brightened. "So. The Festival of Fire starts the day after tomorrow."

"That's right, isn't it?" He had entirely forgotten about the yearly celebration of spring. "What do you do to celebrate?"

"What do *you* do?"

He shrugged. "Set things on fire. Then people get drunk and dance, and it's good fun." A snippet of memory fluttered over his mind: Ninian, who didn't drink, chatting with a ring of four girls at once as Ronan watched wistfully from the window. Áed had teased Ninian endlessly afterward—what the hell was he going to do with a girl?—and they'd eaten bannocks cooked over the fire.

"Then it's not so different," Boudicca said with a glinting smile. "Here, we light a massive fire, and then everyone uses a bit of it to light their home hearths. Then we eat, drink a lot, and dance." She glanced to the window and wrinkled her nose. "Assuming this rain lets up." Brushing her hair over her shoulder, she stood. "Would you like a drink?"

"Oh." He wasn't sure. He was exhausted enough to be

numb without one, and that numbness, the out-of-the-world-for-a-while feeling, was the only reason he ever drank. It seemed rude to refuse, though, so he shrugged. "Sure. Thanks."

She stepped into the kitchen, and he heard glassware clinking. Her footsteps tapped out of the kitchen, and once she entered the candlelight, he could see she carried a dark bottle and two glasses.

Áed awkwardly accepted a glass with both hands and held it as Boudicca poured a stream of liquid into it, and then she sat and poured a glass for herself. "You can handle a drink, can't you?

He chuckled, smelling the cup out of habit to check for the bitter tang of poison. Instead, it smelled sweet, almost fruity. "Yes."

"Good." She took a sip and lifted her glass, and the orange candlelight caught the smooth curve of the cup.

Áed took a sip and raised his eyebrows. "What is it?"

"Elderberry wine." She raised an eyebrow at him. "You've never had wine, have you?"

"No."

"I can tell." She smirked at him. "You're going to get it up your nose." Settling back, she ran her pinkie around the edge of the glass until it sang, and then she sucked the resulting droplet of wine off her finger. The storm outside made the window frames creak with wind. "So. Might be a long night."

"Thank you for staying up with me."

She nodded and lifted her glass. "To Ninian."

Áed's throat tightened, and he raised his cup. "To Ninian."

⁂

Conversation lagged and then flowed, coming in short,

sleepy bursts throughout the night, and Boudicca's chin bobbed and then steadied as she battled sleep. For Áed, it became one long, quiet vigil as Boudicca dozed. The rumbling of thunder made the perfect accompaniment to his bleak thoughts: Tonight was about Ninian. Tonight, he relived the moments he had shared with his love, and tomorrow, he would put them away.

It became almost a dream as he moved through recollections like bright shadows, pausing to linger over some, brushing past others. Ninian screaming as Áed set a broken wrist, cursing at Áed, his sorry luck, and whichever person he'd beaten that time. He recalled a fourteen-year-old Ninian steering the four-year-old Ronan toward the rusty washbasin, talking over the younger boy's protests at the chill of the water, promising that it wasn't that bad, and that he could have an apple afterward. And there was Ninian at Máel Máedóc's with Ronan, chafing under the huge shopkeeper's stony blue gaze as he showed Ronan one of the few books in the Maze. Ninian and Áed, alone at night in their flat with nothing to hear but each other's breathing and the sound of the sky.

Boudicca poked him and he jerked up, realizing he had been dangerously close to drifting off. Shoving his fingers through his hair, he blinked around. "I wasn't sleeping."

"It's alright," she said, clearly disbelieving.

"Ungh." He stretched, arching his back to a chorus of pops. "When did it start being morning?"

Boudicca yawned. "The sun only just came up."

Her yawn was contagious, and at the appearance of the light, his vision swam. "Hey, Boudicca…"

She nodded, covering her mouth again. Her nose scrunched up when she yawned, stacking wrinkles on her forehead. "Yes. Go to bed."

He couldn't even summon the energy to express his

gratitude as he stumbled to the bedroom, ignored Ronan's sleepy protests, and crawled under the covers.

⌇⌇⌇

CHAPTER ELEVEN

HE WAS AWOKEN BY A SCRAPING SOUND, followed by a beam of light hitting him squarely in the face. Groaning, he rolled over and squeezed his eyes shut. "It's been ages, you know," a woman's voice said, and he cracked his eyes open a sliver.

He lay in a truly wonderful bed. No wonder he felt so well-rested. Anyone would be, after sleeping in a thing of beauty such as this. Blinking, the past few days caught up with him, and, as his pleasant mood deflated, his surroundings began to make sense. "Ugh," he muttered, propping himself up on an elbow and looking over his shoulder. "Boudicca?"

"He lives!"

"Guess so." He sat up fully, rubbing his eyes with the backs of his wrists and squinting in the brightness.

She crossed to the door. "You've been sleeping for a day and a night."

That got his attention. "What?"

Her hair, plaited into a bun on the top of her head, bobbed as she nodded with a chuckle. "I took Ronan down to the market and bought him some clothes that fit better, and then we went to the bakery and got him a sticky bun."

Áed was still blinking at the sun's glare through the window, but now he blinked in surprise as well. "*Cad é?*"

"What?"

"You went out?" he demanded, unaware of her confusion, and rubbed his eyes again to clear the film of sleep. He couldn't tell why it shocked him so much, not when Ronan went around the Maze, a far more dangerous territory, alone. Boudicca nodded, raising her eyebrows.

"Yes," she said, sounding a touch miffed. "He liked the bakery, especially."

That was good, wasn't it? Áed shook his head, trying to banish his inexplicable defensiveness. "How does he seem to be holding up?"

"Well, as far as I can tell. He's in the kitchen right now, I have him kneading dough for bread." She twirled her finger at him. "Also, nobody here speaks that other language of yours, so you'd best forget it quickly if you don't want to stick out."

"What? You don't?"

"Nobody does."

"Huh." Áed rolled over and tumbled gracelessly out of the bed. "Boudicca, I can't believe you let us stay this long." As soon as they could leave, he resolved to do so. Maybe, if he promised to find a way to pay her back, they could borrow clothes. That way, Áed could look for a job so that they could find a place of their own to stay. If they were careful, nobody would have to know where they came from, and they could start their new life.

"Well," she said, narrowing her eyes thoughtfully as she regarded him. "Maybe I've decided that I like the company."

Áed snorted. "I thought you could get in trouble for sheltering anyone from the Maze."

"Make sure you say 'Smudge,'" she corrected, raising an

eyebrow. "You really are going to have to blend in if you don't want to get arrested."

"Sorry. Smudge." Saying 'I'm from Smudge' almost felt like a betrayal of his home. It couldn't be right to take its enormous complexity, its despair and its hope, and refer to it all as a pathetic smear of dirt, but Boudicca had a point. And, he reminded himself, he hated the Maze.

"And yes," Boudicca went on, turning to breeze out the doorway. Her tone was a bit rebellious, and pleased with itself for being so. "I am fully aware of the risks."

When Áed went into the kitchen, Ronan greeted him cheerfully enough, although Áed could still see darkness lurking in his big green eyes. It would be a long time, he knew, before that darkness faded, but he could take comfort in their safety. It seemed that things might be stabilizing. "Good morning!"

"Good morning." Áed yawned again, eyeing the dough all over Ronan's hands. "How much of that is staying on your fingers instead of going into the loaf?"

Ronan shrugged. "I've never done this before."

"It's all supposed to go in that ball, mate. Unless you feel like sticking your hands in the oven."

"That what you did?" Ronan quipped, and buried both hands in the dough again with a smirk.

"Low, mate." Áed tousled Ronan's hair good-naturedly. "Is that going to be breakfast?"

Ronan looked at his work critically. "I hope not."

Boudicca peered over his shoulder. "It looks good. Here." She took his hands in hers and began scraping off the dough that clung to them, patting it onto the loaf. "Now we're going to wait for it to rise." She crossed to the sink and rinsed off her hands while Ronan massaged soap into the crevices between his fingers. "And in the meanwhile, we can eat."

Ronan joined Áed outside the kitchen door while Boudicca bustled around the kitchen.

The boy leaned on Áed. “I like it here.”

Áed put an arm around him. “Yeah?”

The younger boy nodded. “Yeah. I do.”

Áed opened his mouth to respond, but then Boudicca stepped out of the kitchen carrying a tray, and, distracted, Ronan hurried over to the table.

⁂

“So,” Boudicca said. She began many sentences with “so,” Áed noticed, and suspected that, once observed, that kind of trait would become irritating in a different person. “The Festival of Fire.”

Áed blinked. He’d forgotten again. It occurred to him that in the whole time he had stayed in Boudicca’s flat, he had not gone outside. In truth, he had not even given the view from the window more than a cursory glance, and he knew that if someone were to ask him what lay beyond the glass, he’d have no idea.

Boudicca was still speaking, oblivious to his musings. “I think we ought to go and celebrate. It’ll be so crowded that nobody will notice you.”

“Are you sure?”

“There will be so many people, nobody will pay you any mind. Besides, you’re clean, and you’re dressed properly. Wear some mittens, and you won’t stick out at all.”

Ronan tugged Áed’s sleeve. “I’d like to go the festival.” His eyes held glimmers of excitement.

The hope in his expression worked like a weevil into any reluctance Áed harbored. Ronan had grown up too fast, but it could be different now. He could feel free, enjoy himself, grow up happier. Still, he looked to Boudicca. “Surely you’re going with someone already."

She shook her head. "No, I go alone, and then I mingle. I never have plans on festival nights." She smiled at Ronan. "Maybe this year, I could change things up."

Ronan's sparkling eyes fixed hopefully on Áed's face. "Please, Áed, I want to go…"

Áed ruffled his hair, smiling at him and then gratefully at Boudicca. "Of course, *ceann beag*. I do, too."

⁂

The weather was still damp, and so Áed scrounged around in the guest room closet for a coat. When he had found one, he headed down the hall to find Boudicca fastening a stylish, asymmetrical hat with pins to her thick locks. Áed frowned. The brim flattened near the front, hiding part of her face. "I think that hat's broken," he said.

She looked up and made surprised eye contact through the mirror on the back of the door. "What? Oh." She caught what he meant, glanced back at the mirror, and narrowed her eyes alluringly. "It's meant to be like that. A little… mysterious." She winked at Áed's reflection in the glass. "Who's the girl under the hat? Makes it a game."

He blinked, feeling entirely lost. "I had no idea my ignorance of hats could have such complicated social implications."

Tossing her head back, Boudicca let out a peal of laughter. "You're funny!" She turned to face him so she no longer addressed his reflection. "You know, for someone who can't read, you have an impressive vocabulary."

"Thanks," he responded self-consciously. "It's from living with Ninian." Ninian had eaten up words when there had been nothing else to fill him, and it occurred to Áed that not all of Ninian's legacy had been lost. "You're going to the festival with the intent to flirt?"

"Of course." She took her coat from the rack, a long black duster that flowed all the way to the ground. She left it unbuttoned so the fiery carmine of her skirt showed through. "What, don't you?"

"Flirting..." He pretended to consider for a moment, cocking his head. "Hmm. Nope."

"You ought to try it. Not now, I mean, I'm not trying to be insensitive, but you're handsome enough. There's always fun to be had in that." Her words were entirely frank, and he knew that she was stating what she saw as a fact. It surprised him.

"Ronan!" Boudicca called, and Ronan raced into the room excitedly. Boudicca handed him a coat, and the boy began, with excitedly clumsy movements, to find the armholes in the black fabric.

"Say," Áed asked, curiosity shifting onto a different subject. "Where did you find clothes that fit Ronan? Before you bought some, I mean."

"I borrowed them from Gráinne, the apothecary owner, who has a grandson about Ronan's size. Which reminds me." She clasped her hands in front of her. "If we meet anyone I know, you two are visiting cousins."

"Understood."

"Are we going?" Ronan chirped, bouncing up and down on the balls of his feet.

Boudicca opened the door, and Ronan hopped out into the hallway, eyes shining. "Yes, we're going! Come, come!"

The top of the stairs was just as it had been two days ago, smelling of spices with an air of quiet between the doors. This time, however, the hall wasn't empty, and Áed stiffened, bracing for a conflict as an old woman emerged from her apartment. A smile crowned her creased cheeks, and her reddish hair was streaked with silver-gray beneath a festive yellow hat. Ronan stared.

"Hello, dear!" the old woman sang, and Boudicca, who had turned to lock the door, looked up. Immediately, she broke into a warm smile.

"Good morning, Gráinne! How are you?"

The old lady grinned. "Oh, I'm never better! But how about you, Boudicca? Looks like you have guests?"

"Oh, yes! My cousins."

The woman's grin only widened. "You know, I won't even bother to ask which part of the family they're from." She smiled kindly at Ronan, who returned the expression timidly, stepping closer to Áed. "Well? Are you going to introduce us?"

"Of course." Boudicca slipped the keys into a pocket of her long coat and gestured to Áed. "This is Áed, and his little brother Ronan." Gráinne beamed at them. "Áed and Ronan, this is Gráinne."

Gráinne extended a hand, and Áed shook it apprehensively, hoping the mitten was thick enough to disguise the wrongness of his hand beneath it. The old lady didn't seem to notice anything out of the ordinary as she smiled at him maternally and moved on to Ronan. Áed closed his eyes for a moment, offering up a prayer of gratitude to whomever listened, and opened them again to find Gráinne beaming. "Are you all excited for the festival?"

That got Ronan nodding. "Boudicca is going to teach me how to dance!"

"Well, you couldn't find a better teacher." Gráinne winked at Boudicca, who smiled back easily as Gráinne adjusted her hat. "I must be off, dears. Boudicca, lovely to see you, and it was a treat to meet you both."

"Likewise, Gráinne," Áed replied politely, and she grinned at him.

"Enjoy the festival!" With that, she moved past them

down the hall.

Boudicca smiled after her. "She treats me like a daughter."

"How many years does she have?"

"Fifty-two."

Ronan's eyebrows popped up. "Seriously?"

"Yes. Why?"

Ronan glanced at Áed. "The oldest person I know is Máel Máedóc, and he has… what?"

"He's in his forties, I think."

Boudicca frowned, her rosy eyes blinking. "The oldest person you know is in his forties?"

"Yeah."

She shook her head, looking baffled. "The oldest person *I* know has seventy-nine."

"Seventy-nine!" That was unheard of. Unimaginable. What did someone even *look* like when they had seventy-nine? "*A thiarcais.*"

"Ah," Boudicca reminded him. "None of that, remember? You're from here."

They reached the bottom of the stairs, and, passing the side door that was still fused closed, Boudicca led the way through the shop. When they emerged from the teetering wooden shelves, she pushed open the door to the outside.

Immediately, sensation engulfed them.

Yellow and white flowers hung over the doorway, creating a curtain through which to pass, and in the white-brick street, even the carriages held white-thorn branches and sprigs of frizzy blooms. A magnificent bonfire, roped off with garlands of flowers, roared at the end of the street, and people sat on a few barrels nearby while others maneuvered around them, hoping to fill their cups with whatever the kegs were serving. Along the side of the road, bands of musicians had set up, and they strummed on lyres and blew into flutes, creating a cacophony of competing melodies that echoed through the crisp air. A group of children tore down the road, each carrying a doll made of grass and tiny blossoms.

Áed stepped off the stoop. "Goodness."

Ronan was bouncing again, tugging them toward the celebration. "Come on, come *on*!"

The fire beckoned to Áed, but Ronan wanted to see the musicians, so Áed allowed himself to be led. He watched with amusement as Boudicca took hold of Ronan's hands and started teaching the boy where to put his feet for a dance. Ronan concentrated as hard as Áed had ever seen, and Áed didn't stifle the smile that spread over his face at the sight. The musicians grinned too, and they cheered when Ronan tripped his way out of step and covered it with a proud bow.

Ronan, beaming, looked to Áed, who took his hand and nodded toward the road, which burst with color and motion and things to see. "Want to explore?"

Ronan responded with an enthusiastic nod, and the trio set off down the street.

⌇⌇⌇

CHAPTER TWELVE

IT SEEMED LIKE THEY DID IT ALL that day. They went to the bakery, where they got sticky buns with tops decorated in yellow flowers. Ronan wanted to ride in a carriage, and so they took a bouncing ride around the city to watch the revelry. Boudicca showed Áed and Ronan how to twist hawthorn flowers into a crown, and she cheerfully looped a spray of blossoms around the brim of her hat to match her companions. There were so many little fires around, so many flowers and fluttering ribbons, that Áed felt almost dizzy.

When finally they returned to Boudicca's street, the sun had fallen low in the now-cloudless sky. The bonfire then appeared exceptionally bright, and it gleamed like a beacon through the deepening chill. The crowd around it grew and made merry in the warmth. The mood was jolly, and people had begun dancing around the fire, clapping to the rhythm of drums that echoed from the bands along the streets. Boudicca pushed off through the crowd for a moment, leaving Áed frowning and looking around after her, but eventually his eyes caught on her flame-colored dress as she pushed her way back toward them. She carried two mugs, one of which she handed to Áed. "Here. Cheers."

Ronan looked on with interest as Áed took a drink. The wine warmed him from the inside out, though it tasted different from what Boudicca had shared with him at her flat. Boudicca finished a drink, caught his curious expression, and answered his unspoken question.

"Rhubarb."

He nodded, taking another drink. "I like it."

She took another long draw, and Áed raised an eyebrow. Even at the Festival of Fire back in the Maze, he only ever let himself get a little tipsy. Perhaps here it was safe to be drunk in public, though Áed personally didn't intend to test that.

"Can I try?" Ronan whined, tugging on Áed's sleeve. "Please?"

He raised his eyebrows at Ronan's begging face. "You won't like it."

"How do you know if I don't try it?"

Áed rolled his eyes and handed Ronan the mug. It was the Festival of Fire, and a tiny bit wouldn't do much more than make him feel grown-up. "One sip."

Thrilled, Ronan accepted the cup with both hands and brought it to his lips, eyes crinkled with anticipation. Instantly, though, his nose wrinkled, and he handed the mug back with a scowl. "Blech!"

Laughing, Áed took the mug back. "Told you so."

"How do you drink that? I need to clean my tongue!"

"I like it."

"And as for your tongue," Boudicca chimed in, "People are starting to bring out food to share. You'll be able to chase away the taste soon."

"Food?" Ronan perked up, looking around. Sure enough, people were traveling back into the buildings, returning with tables and delicacies to go upon them. Someone moved the garland roadblock since the street traffic was nearly gone, and the crowd spread out. Áed noticed that people were filling plates and then leaving a portion in a basket at the end of the table.

"What are they doing?" he asked, watching a woman in a flower-yellow skirt and a red blouse take an entire loaf of bread and toss it in with the rest.

Boudicca followed his startled gaze. "They're offering some of their food to the fae," she explained. "Later tonight, someone will put the basket under a hawthorn tree."

Áed frowned.

Noticing this, Boudicca looked back to the basket. "Don't you do that?"

"With what food?"

"Ah. I see."

"I can't believe you give up your food to faeries." It was impossible to hide the surprise in his tone. Such abundance was foreign to him. The loaf that had just vanished into the basket could have fed Ronan for three days.

"Of course we do. But only at the festivals, when they can come through the veil for a time."

"And what if you don't?"

"Then they'll be angry. It'd be foolish to anger such a people." She seemed oblivious to his challenge. "It makes sense why they don't come after you, I guess, because you don't have much food." She hiccupped. "Then again, maybe that's the reason the oldest person you know is in his forties."

"We can't get much hungrier than we already are."

"I would just be afraid to provoke the fae." She took another drink. Áed suspected she was a little drunk as they made their way over to one of the tables and sent Ronan to squirm his small frame between the crowding people to bring back plates of food. He brought back two for

Boudicca and Áed, each laden with meat, gravy, and greens. They found a couple of kegs to sit on and put their plates on their laps as they watched the crowd swirl around them, eating, drinking, and dancing in groups to the beat of the drums. The firelight shone on their faces, casting bright orange light that fell abruptly into shadow.

Áed gripped his knife as best he could with his mittened left hand, too nervous to take off the gloves and too hungry to ignore the chance to eat. Ronan rejoined them shortly, his own plate burdened with more dessert than meat, which prompted Áed to raise an eyebrow. "What?" Ronan griped. "I got the food."

The illumination from the bonfire, as well as the constant distractions, had prevented Áed from noticing when darkness had come, but he noticed it then, noticed the billows of sparks pluming from the top of the fire and edging out gracefully into the twilight. The women in the crowd wore dresses in the hues of the fire, crimsons and golds, yellows and deep pinks. He caught a glimpse of a woman, her hair pinned under a blood-red hat, who wore a dress of violet-blue in the shade of the flames at the heart of the inferno. The air itself felt shimmery.

Áed frowned. Something strange had just caught his attention, and he didn't know what it was.

He nudged Boudicca. "What was that?"

She pouted—evidently he'd interrupted some story he hadn't noticed she'd been telling. "What was what?"

He wasn't sure. It was the impression of another person in a room, that sensation of another beating heart occupying the same space, but with people all around, that didn't make sense.

Ronan burped and then laughed, startling Áed from his thoughts, and Boudicca joined in the laughter and leaned over the side of the keg to refill her drink. Her laughter made Ronan giggle even more, and he hugged himself, hiccupping. The cheer of it all made Áed smile despite himself, though he couldn't shake the feeling.

Boudicca, setting her empty plate down on the keg, turned to Áed and extended her hands. He raised an eyebrow, noting her clumsy movements and her slightly unsteady stops. She was a little drunk. "Come on," she said, and her pink eyes glimmered deeply in the glow of the flames. "Dance with me."

Áed shot Ronan a glance, but the boy nodded, grinning. "I'll be fine."

"It's safe," Boudicca assured him, taking his hands and pulling him up. "Look, there are children everywhere."

She was right. Everywhere around them, boys and girls, some younger than Ronan, scampered through the crowd. He supposed that he wasn't too worried. Ronan blended right into the crowd, and he knew how to handle himself. Boudicca tugged on Áed's hands, and he let her draw him into the throng. When they stopped, Áed realized that the drums had quickened their rhythm, and the dancing had picked up into a flurry of beating boots. Boudicca held up her hands, and Áed put his against hers as he caught the beat in his head.

Boudicca laughed with delight, stepping back and then in as he mirrored her on the opposite side. Her skirt flared like a windflower in bloom and brushed the tops of his shoes when she twirled. She finished the turn with her back to his chest; her arms crossed over her waist, and Áed held each of her hands. Then he chuckled as he realized he was enjoying himself. "What?" she demanded, looking up at him with eyes that held the firelight.

He shrugged, still keeping step, and twirled her out again as everyone around them did the same. The effect was like an eddy in flowing water. "I've never danced with a woman."

"But you *have* danced."

"I danced with Ninian."

She didn't press. Instead she spun to the side, throwing out her arm, before she once again stepped in and put her palms to his. "Did Ninian teach you to dance?"

He nodded, holding her back to him again. "Yeah."

They rotated through the motions again, and their feet beat a rhythm on the ground that complemented that of the drums. The fire flickered over faces, disappeared into black coats, and glinted off teeth and eyes as it washed the paving stones in red light. Boudicca's voice was almost drowned in the sea of dancers, but it still carried to him as she spun away. "So how did he learn?"

Áed caught her as she twirled in to him and leaned over so she fell backward against his arms. She raised an arm above her head and let her knuckles touch the ground before he swept her up again. "Oh, that's a long story."

He felt her shrug in his arms. "We have all night."

That was true. The fire was still raging, pulsing energy through his bones, the merrymakers showed no signs of slowing, and food and wine remained plentiful on the tables. He suspected that, like in the Maze, the party would last until the sun came up. "Ages ago," he explained, "After the cities split, the Maze crowned its own rulers. The kingdom crumbled, of course, so it's pretty lawless now, but Ninian had noble blood from the Maze's royalty." He stepped aside as another pair of dancers swung close, and Boudicca matched the movement as part of the dance. "His mother felt that everyone who came from such a bloodline should know certain things." Boudicca ducked under his arm, keeping time, and he let her spin back in. "There's not a lot of room for royalty in the Ma—Smudge, I mean, but he could read, write, dance. He had manners, a hell of a vocabulary, that kind of thing. He knew all of the histories."

"What happened when he learned it all?"

"He never did." Áed shook his head sadly. "He came close, but his mother died when Ninian had nine years. His father, too, from the illness of his mum."

Boudicca's sympathetic sigh crystallized in the cold air, a puff like smoke floating away into the fiery sky.

The feeling of another presence struck Áed again like a slap, and he nearly gasped. None of the dancers were watching him, a nervous look around him verified that, but the sense fired hot sparks down his spine. He turned around, positive he was being watched, and his heart leapt painfully to his throat. There, in the darkness beneath a blossom-covered awning, red eyes blinked at him. The owner of the eyes leaned against the wall, graceful as a ghost, and, meeting Áed's stare, pushed away from the building and loped to the fire *just* too smoothly to seem human.

"Áed," Boudicca asked. "Are you quite alright?"

He closed his eyes hard, and when he opened them, the vision had vanished into the flames.

He shook his head firmly. Perhaps that rhubarb wine had been stronger than he'd realized.

"I thought I saw something."

"Ooh," Boudicca replied. "The veil's thin tonight. Perhaps it was one of the fae."

Áed sighed. "I've never really believed that."

Boudicca's eyebrow popped skyward. "What?"

"It's never made sense to me," Áed said. "Why would they actually come here? To play mischief and eat our food?"

"No!" Boudicca rolled her eyes. "Well, *yes*, but not like that. The fae are a cunning race, yes, but they aren't *mischievous*." Evidently her point was important to her, for she paused in the dance. The crowd swirled around them as if he and Boudicca were an island in the sea. "Listen," she said, "because this is important. The fae are a dangerous, frightful lot, and clever enough to know a man's intentions better than he knows them himself. Compared with fae power, you and I are *nothing*." She shivered despite the warmth of the fire. "Even when I work my little magic, I have to be careful." She nodded toward the basket at the end of the table, now full of bread and early fruit. "So we appease them with food." She gave him a look. "Maybe don't insult them."

Áed held up his hands in surrender. He didn't like talking about this.

Satisfied, Boudicca moved in toward him again and resumed the beat of the dance. As they danced, her hair worked its way loose from under her hat and fell in wispy chestnut curls around her cheeks. The fine hairs that caught the light of the bonfire shone like filaments of gold.

"I think I'd like another drink," she sighed, nodding her head to the drums.

Áed pulled his attention to her words. "Are you sure?"

"Yes, I think so."

He regarded her skeptically. "You're already drunk."

"Not enough. The Festival of Fire only happens once a year, you know."

"You're going to wake up with a headache."

"I'll be fine."

He rolled his eyes and took her hands. "It's your choice. We can find Ronan and sit down."

⌇⌇⌇

Ronan sat where they had left him, consuming a second plate laden with finger-sized cakes. He looked up and grinned before he popped another cake into his mouth and tried to speak through it. "Hello."

"Cheers," Boudicca declared, and set off purposefully

toward the food tables.

Áed sat down next to Ronan and gazed over the laughing dancers. No red eyes, no shaded figures moved among them. The feeling had gone, leaving nothing but a prickle of familiarity in Áed's chest. It had felt like the shadow had come to see him, and him specifically.

When Boudicca elbowed her way back toward them through the crowd, her lips were dark with wine and she held two mugs high. Áed moved over to make a space for her, and she sat heavily onto the barrel and nearly sloshed wine over her dress. Handing a mug to Áed, who discreetly put it aside, she tipped her chin back and took a long drink.

"Boudicca?"

Finishing, she brought the mug back down. It may have been the shifting firelight, but her eyes didn't appear to focus on him. "Yes?"

"Ah…" He trailed off as she looked into her mug with disappointment, and he realized it was already empty. It was not a small cup. "You're going to make yourself sick."

She shook her head too hard, a few stray hairs floating loose. "Naw."

He sighed as she straightened her skirts awkwardly and the material caught on the rough barrel. Sighing, Áed hopped up, took Boudicca's hand, and pulled her to her feet. Once standing, the matter of smoothing her dress was simplified, and he eased her back into a seat as she smiled at him a bit vacantly.

"Say," she said, and her words were mildly slurred. "Did you drink yours already?"

"No."

She blinked, her long eyelashes brushing against her cheek. "Can I have it?"

He considered her face, her jerky, incompetent movements, and shook his head. "Nope."

She leaned on him and dropped her cheek onto his shoulder as if it might convince him. "Why not?"

He found the brim of her hat and tugged it back gently to reveal her face. Her rosy eyes studied him while an absent smile stole over her wine-stained lips. She pouted, her elegant eyebrows coming together, and Áed had to put an arm around her shoulders as she tipped unsteadily backward. "You've had a lot."

She waved her hand dismissively and almost hit Ronan in the nose. The boy leaned back, frowning with disapproval, and Áed bit his lip to keep from laughing as Boudicca dropped her hand back onto her lap. "Pshaw. Don't be such a killjoy." Her hand flung out again, gesturing vaguely to the dancers, the dark forms of laughing people at the food tables. "It's a party. This festival only happens once a year."

He gave her hand a squeeze. "Come on. It's getting late, and at the very least, Ronan needs to get to bed. Let's go back to your apartment, okay?"

"I don't want to." Her head tipped back as she looked to him, trying to see around the flirtatious hat brim. "You take Ronan back. I'll come later."

Áed squirmed out from under her cheek and stood, but kept as tight a hold as he could on her hands to prevent her from toppling sideways. "That," he declared, pulling her up, "Is a terrible idea. Come on." Ronan hopped up as Áed let Boudicca slouch against him. "You've done a lot for us, and leaving you drunk at the mercy of the crowd would be a horrible way to repay you."

She complained inarticulately as Áed led her through the crowd, one arm around her waist and the other held as a support. Ronan trailed behind, his hands full of cakes he hadn't finished.

It was fortunate that Boudicca's apothecary was just down the street, because by the time they were free of the throng, she was dragging. Too worried about Boudicca breaking an ankle on the steps to care what anyone thought, Áed scooped her up and carried her over the threshold while Ronan held the door open.

Once inside, Áed set her down and leaned against the wall to catch his breath. The hall was dim compared to the brilliant blaze of the bonfire down the street; only a few candles glimmering in sconces along the walls provided illumination for the foyer. "Boudicca," he sighed, and she looked up at him with a dopey smile. "You are going to be so sick tomorrow."

"Probably." The word was badly slurred and accompanied by an impressive peal of too-loud laughter.

They made it to the stairs, and Boudicca gasped loudly. She broke into a drunken grin. "What?" Áed asked, glancing to Ronan to see if he knew, but he just shrugged, staring blankly at Boudicca.

"No *way*!" she laughed, tripping forward toward the steps, and Áed looked up to follow her gaze. Standing on the stairs was a shadow, a silhouette in the shape of a man. Boudicca stumbled onto the bottom step, tripped onto her knees, and looked down in confusion like she didn't know how the staircase had gotten there. Then she looked up again, beaming. "Why are *you* here?"

"Hello, Boudicca," the shadow said in a deep, even voice. It held a hint of bemusement. The stairs creaked as the figure descended, peering through the gloom. "Who've you got with you?"

"Friends." Suddenly she scowled, glaring at Áed. "'Course, he wouldn't let me get another drink."

"For good reason," Áed grumbled, and supported her by the shoulders to help her up. Addressing the stranger, he asked, "Who are you?"

The silhouette passed into a streak of candlelight, and the

yellow beam illuminated chestnut hair and a crooked nose, a mouth set in a curious half-smile. The man's features were familiar enough that Áed already knew the answer when the man said, "I'm Cynwrig, Boudicca's brother." He moved down a few more steps, and his face moved out of the light. "She's drunk?"

Áed nodded. Boudicca had mentioned that she'd rather Cynwrig and Áed not meet, but there was nothing for it now. "Very."

In a couple of self-assured steps, Cynwrig was standing next to them, hoisting his sister up and cradling her against his chest. Judging by the ease of the motion, he must have been strong. Boudicca giggled, and Cynwrig transitioned her weight to one arm, extending the other hand to Áed. "I didn't get your name."

"Áed," he replied, shaking Cynwrig's hand carefully. "And this is Ronan." He gestured down to where Ronan was standing behind his legs.

Unlike Gráinne, Áed was certain that Cynwrig noted the shape of Áed's hands beneath the thick mittens. Still, the man said nothing, only, "Pleasure meeting you," which left a swirl of nerves tingling in Áed's stomach.

Áed and Ronan followed Cynwrig up the stairs, and Ronan took hold of Áed's sleeve and clenched it in his fist.

"So," Cynwrig's voice came down the stairs, and it was impossible not to notice he shared his sister's habit. "I thought I would come by for the festival, but the key wasn't under the mat." At this, Boudicca snorted.

"I know."

"Do you have the other key?" he asked, addressing his sister, who still hung limp in his arms.

"Pocket," she slurred, jamming her hand into her pocket and frowning. "I mean, the other pocket."

Sighing, Cynwrig located the key in her pocket and

opened the door, nodding over his shoulder to Áed and Ronan. "Well, come in, then." The two followed Cynwrig as he carried his sister inside like she weighed nothing, navigated the dark room, and set Boudicca down in one of the chairs at the table. She immediately laid her head on her arms. Once she was safely seated, her brother pulled a pack of matches from his pocket and lit candles while Áed and Ronan hung up their coats. Áed removed his mittens and pushed his hands into his pockets.

Having lit the flat, Cynwrig sighed and dropped to a seat at the table. The chair creaked under him, and he flicked another match from the packet and drew a cigarette from the pocket of his coat. His eyes, a pale, clean blue, narrowed as he regarded Áed and Ronan in the light, and he held the cigarette between his lips and lit it. The end glowed like a nocturnal eye as he inhaled, and he blew out a puff of white smoke with a thoughtful frown. "Are you wearing my clothes?"

Áed bit his lip. Intuition was murmuring in his gut, and he didn't think he trusted Boudicca's brother. "It's a long story."

Cynwrig took a deep pull on the cigarette, and the smell of it reached Áed's nose. "Well," he mused, smoke encircling the same words Boudicca had used earlier. "I suppose we have all night."

⌇⌇⌇

CHAPTER THIRTEEN

IN THE SAME WAY ÁED KNEW if a gambler had a good hand, or that Boudicca was trustworthy, or that Ronan was too scared to speak, Áed knew that Cynwrig was far less sympathetic—and less impulsive—than his sister. In that moment, Cynwrig's eyes looked less like water and more like ice, their blue was deep and calculating. It would be wonderful if Boudicca were sober, but she had, unfortunately, begun to snore.

Áed could read people. It wasn't something he'd learned, but rather something that he had always instinctively relied upon, and now, he tried to discern what Cynwrig's reaction would be to the truth. Something honest and unyielding made itself known in the set of Cynwrig's face, something in the openness of his gaze and the tightness around the corners of his mouth that suggested confidence and told Áed he shouldn't attempt to lie.

"Boudicca let us stay when we were caught in the storm," he said truthfully. "She invited us to join her for the Festival of Fire, and we plan to leave tomorrow."

Cynwrig scrutinized them both and took a long drag on

his cigarette. "Interesting." He let the smoke pool in his mouth like he was tasting it before he spoke and it blew out. "So, I want to hear your long story."

Áed couldn't exactly say that they were visiting cousins, because that wouldn't fool Boudicca's brother. There was motion mounting in Cynwrig's body language, a slight tensing of his fingers and shifting of his shoulders that said he was preparing for something, and what came out of Áed's mouth was neither a lie nor a truth. Instead, he blurted, "Please don't do anything extreme."

Cynwrig raised an eyebrow. "I promise not to do anything extreme, on the condition that nothing warrants extreme behavior." He tapped ash off the end of the cigarette into an empty mug on the table. "Áed, may I see your hands?"

Áed pressed his lips together. "Why?"

"Mm. No reason." Cynwrig didn't bother trying to hide the falsehood in his tone.

As he could neither refuse nor comply without seeming strange, Áed brought his hands hesitatingly from his pockets. Cynwrig appraised them with a nod, unsurprised, and Áed's stomach clenched.

"Of all the places to take shelter," Cynwrig said with a sigh, tapping more ash off his cigarette, "this one was inopportune." He pushed himself to his feet and dropped the cigarette butt into the mug. "Did Boudicca not tell you who I am?"

Áed shook his head wordlessly. Apprehension tugged him toward the door, instinct telling him to run, but he was frozen in place by Cynwrig's ice-hard gaze.

Cynwrig had shrugged his coat onto the back of his chair, and now he reached into an inside pocket and drew out a folded piece of paper. Fingers deftly opening it, he cleared his throat and read. "Two males, one a young man, one a boy, with blond and black hair, respectively, travelled toward the Southeast Quarter and entered one of the shops there. Pursuit was impossible, as they locked the door behind them. Later, the building's residents alleged that they had seen nothing out of the ordinary. Distinctive markings: Blonde man's hands impossibly mangled. Red eyes. Young boy with green eyes. Clothes tattered, filthy. Carrying a burlap sack." He re-folded the paper and slipped it back into the pocket before raising an eyebrow at Áed. "Now, that was a report from two of my Guard. Sound familiar?"

A nerve was jangling in the back of Áed's skull and sending shards down the length of his spine. "*Your* Guard?"

Cynwrig's blue eyes bored into him. "As General of the August Guard, they are, in fact, *my* Guard."

Áed could only mouth the words. *General of the August Guard.* How had Boudicca neglected to mention that her brother was the *general* of the Guard that sought them?

Cynwrig glanced to his sister, asleep on the table. "Did she know who you were when she took you in?"

Áed shook his head quickly. He wouldn't incriminate the person who'd risked so much to be kind to them. "No."

Cynwrig looked a little relieved, but his face manifested the expression only in the slight relaxation of his brow. "Good." He had drawn himself up tall, shoulders back, in a movement so natural that it made Áed feel small, and stepped around the table. "Tell me, where are you two from?"

"Here," Ronan squeaked, but Cynwrig was unimpressed.

"Which Quarter? Which district?"

Neither Áed nor Ronan had anything to say.

"Do you deny that you have infiltrated this city from the land called Smudge?" His voice had fallen into the pattern of a script, and Áed knew with certainty that Cynwrig, General of the August Guard, planned to arrest them there and then.

"I was trying to secure a better life for Ronan," Áed said. Ronan, who deserved to be happy. Ronan, for whom Áed would stay up a thousand nights.

For the briefest of half-seconds, the ice of Cynwrig's eyes thawed, but then they frosted over again like gullies in midwinter. "Your motivation is not the current concern. Trespassers are brought to King Seisyll."

Cynwrig moved toward them again, and Áed stepped instinctively in front of Ronan. "Wait."

To his surprise, the General did.

"We didn't know your laws," Áed said quickly. "We'll go. We'll leave, and you'll never see us in your city again."

Cynwrig shook his head and reached for Áed's arm, and Áed's stomach tumbled as he quickly moved away. With the tension this high, he could almost feel the sparks on his skin. "Don't touch me," he snapped, and Cynwrig must have heard the warning in Áed's tone, for his hand hesitated.

"What would you do to us?" Ronan asked quietly. His voice was barely a whisper.

"I *will* bring you to King Seisyll, who will do as he sees fit."

At the harshness of Cynwrig's tone, tears gathered in Ronan's eyes.

Áed was still considering the odds. If they bolted, could they make it to the crowd of people in time to disappear before Cynwrig caught them? And what from there? Despite what he'd told the General, leaving the White City was not an option; there was no place to go but the woods or the churning Sea. "I'll fight," Áed said bluntly. "And Ronan will run, and you'll never find him."

Cynwrig raised an eyebrow at Áed, surely taking in the way his skinny frame swam in his too-big clothes. "You'll fight."

"Áed," Ronan choked. "You can't."

Áed did not slip his eyes from Cynwrig's handsome face, and he spoke with quiet certainty. "I can."

"You and what army?" Cynwrig said, matching his assuredness. "I don't travel without men. They're downstairs. There's nowhere to go."

The feeling of being trapped resonated behind Áed's breastbone. He didn't know what to do. He didn't know how many men Cynwrig had, or if he was bluffing, or what it would cost to take the chance. If he reached for the power smoking in his chest, would he control it, or would it burn until the building was skeletonized with the people inside it? If they ran, slammed the door, how many seconds to the stairs, to the flower drapes, to the obscurity of the night? How many hands waited ready to catch at their fleeing bodies?

Ronan's crying had roused Boudicca, who lifted her head blearily from the table. "What's happening?" she asked groggily, eliding her words. "Cynwrig?"

Cynwrig turned to his sister. His face revealed no frustration, nor anything else. "You're awake."

"Uh-huh." She scrubbed at her eyes. "What're you doing?" A frown creased her lips, and she tried to push herself up, but her eyes slipped out of focus. She staggered into Cynwrig's arms.

"Boudie," Cynwrig sighed. "Don't trouble yourself with this. Go to bed."

But Boudicca was inebriated and uncomprehending. "When did you meet Áed and Ronan?" She didn't resist as Cynwrig eased her back to a seat. "I met them yesterday or two days before..."

"They're from Smudge," Cynwrig explained with surprising gentleness, and Boudicca's forehead wrinkled. "They aren't your friends. I'm going to take care of it, okay? How about you go to bed?"

She shook her head so hard that her hair flew loose. "They're staying with me." Ronan was still sniffling, and Boudicca looked to his face with a gasp. "You made Ronan cry!" She clumsily smacked at her brother's arm. "What did you do that for?" And with that, tears began to bubble in her eyes and stream down her face.

Cynwrig ran a hand down his face as Boudicca dissolved into crying, and Ronan redoubled into even-harder tears. "For Gods' sake, Boudicca." He turned to Áed, anger finally showing on his features. "Did you let her drink this much?"

"I *stopped* her from drinking more," Áed snapped.

Boudicca, unsteadied by crying, slipped off her chair, and Cynwrig had to catch her before she became a vermilion-dressed puddle on the floor. With his sobbing sister's tears soaking his sleeve and Ronan choking on cries behind Áed, the man broke.

He deposited Boudicca rather roughly back into her chair and threw up his hands. "Fine! Fine, Boudicca, pitch a fit, you win." He whirled around to Áed and Ronan. "You can stay the night here, and I'll take care of you in the morning." He strode over to the door and leaned into the hallway. "Ahearn! Killough! At the door!" As he slammed his way back into the room, Áed heard two sets of footsteps tramp up the stairs and take up position by the entrance. Cynwrig glared at Boudicca, and then at Áed. "Congratulations." The word was frigid on his tongue. "You just borrowed some time."

⌇⌇⌇

CHAPTER FOURTEEN

DUE, NO DOUBT, TO WORRY, ÁED COULDN'T SLEEP. Beside him, washed in blackness as deep as drowning, Ronan slept peacefully. He was a curl of a person, his knees tucked nearly to his chin, and his face was as placid as a still pool while he snored softly.

Áed knew he wouldn't drift off. A twitchy restlessness was building in his fingertips and legs, and he needed to move.

He padded silently past Cynwrig's long, bulky form on the couch, past the bookshelf whose volumes' contours cast shadows like crooked teeth against the wall. A faint shine from the kitchen indicated a candle that hadn't been extinguished, and Áed squinted at the glow as he stepped into the room.

He almost jumped out of his skin when a soft sound penetrated the shadows. "Who's that?"

"Boudicca."

"Ah." His heart slowed a bit, and he sighed. "You scared me."

"I gathered that." Her voice sounded clearer than it had before, but sort of low.

"How are you feeling?"

"Sick. And still just drunk enough to be disoriented."

She sounded miserable, so Áed lowered his voice. "Headache?"

Boudicca just nodded, and he noticed that her complexion was faintly green even in the warm orange glow. "I've already thrown everything up, but I'm still horribly nauseous." A wretched moan escaped her lips, and she slid down the cabinets, dropped her forehead into her hands, and tucked her knees up to her chin. "I feel awful."

"This isn't something you do often," Áed guessed, and she shrugged.

"Sometimes. Festival nights, parties. Always starts out fun, doesn't it? Have you ever been sick like this?" She said it like the conversation was a pleasant distraction, but Áed thought that soon enough, words would feel like hammers on the inside of her head. He kept it short.

"A few times."

She rolled so her shoulder hit the wood of the cabinet, like she was trying to find a comfortable position that didn't exist. "It's horrid. Why do I never remember this part?"

"After the first drink, you don't really consider it." Áed retrieved a glass from the cabinet and, gripping it between both hands, he filled it with cool water from the sink and then brought it to her. She looked up with dull eyes, but brightened a bit at the offering and took tiny, pathetic sips as Áed returned to his spot on the counter.

"Thank you," she murmured. "That was kind."

"Of course."

Still holding the glass, she leaned forward so her elbows rested on the ground, and dissolved into a miserable heap. "I'm never drinking again." She sighed heavily, shoulders rolling in. "'Course, I say that every time."

Áed bit his lip. "Boudicca, how much do you remember from last night?

"What?"

"Do you remember your brother coming over?"

She frowned up at him. "Cynwrig came?" Then she flattened her palms into her closed eyes. "Oh, Áed, I was so drunk, that could have gone poorly. I should have told you…"

"That he's the General of the August Guard?" Áed finished grimly. "I know. We're going to need some backup tomorrow morning."

She dropped her hands and stared at him, horror-struck. "What?"

Áed leaned back on the counter. "He's still here. You cried so much when he tried to arrest us that he let us stay the night, but it isn't going to last."

"He tried to arrest you?" Boudicca moaned painfully and folded forward to press her forehead onto the floor. "He knows who you are. And I was too drunk to do anything—damn!" She let out her breath all at once. "I'm sorry, Áed, I didn't think it'd be a problem. Cynwrig hardly ever visits, and I thought I'd be able to convince him to ignore you even if he did. He listens to me, he always listens to me, but I was so drunk..."

"Shh," Áed said. "Let's get you back to bed, okay? You can't think right now. We'll figure something out in the morning." He bent down to help her up, and together, they crossed the flat to her bedroom.

When he eased her to a seat on her bed, she curled onto her side and cradled her head in her hands. "Thanks, Áed," she mumbled, her curled arms pushing the pillow into her face. It looked like she was trying to hide in it. "I'm so sorry."

He nodded despite the fact that her eyes were already closed. "We'll fix everything in the morning." When she didn't answer, Áed returned to the guest room.

The sack of his and Ronan's possessions sat on the dresser, still full, and, resigned to being awake, he took it down and looked inside. What junk, compared to Boudicca's flat. Still, all who had touched the hodgepodge of items had left their invisible mark: Ninian's lips on that tin cup, Ronan's hands on that little coil of thread.

Áed lifted out the yellowing scrap of paper that, along with his name, was all his mother had left him, and he spread it flat on the dresser. Perhaps a trace of his mother lingered on it the way Ninian or Ronan did on everything else, but he couldn't tell any more than he could tell the meaning of the writing scratched onto its surface. Lying on the dresser the way it was, the fading light of the bonfire down the street set its wrinkles into shadow and made the writing even starker against the paleness of the paper. Áed liked seeing it in the firelight. Somehow, the flickering illumination made the letter more real, so he let it lay there when he went over to sit by the window and wait out the night.

⸙

Áed almost slept in the time between the death of the bonfire and the rising of the sun, but every time he nodded off, he thought of Cynwrig beyond the door. His blood chilled, and he looked to the window (too high to jump from) and the door (too well-guarded) before pressing his lips together and trying to think of what to do.

The icy certainty that the General would arrest them with or without Boudicca's intervention spread like creeping hoarfrost in the pit of Áed's stomach and made his weary body tense. The ember in his heart flickered at the chill as if to remind Áed what was at his disposal, but Áed refused to think of it. He didn't want to hurt anyone. He didn't want

Ronan to fear him. He didn't want to be afraid of himself.

Blush had begun its spread across the sky, the color of heather, and dawn was far too close.

The best course of action, if there was such a thing, eluded him.

And the sun kept rising.

Cynwrig was already seated at the table when Áed and Ronan quit their room and ventured into the bright flat. Not knowing what else to do, Áed hesitantly placed himself at the table as well.

Cynwrig looked up at Áed, and his ice-blue eyes chilled Áed as sharply as chips of steel. Immediately, Áed was ready to fight or flee. "I feel for you," the General said, and Áed, not expecting this, blinked. "I know that Smudge is the lesser of the cities," Cynwrig continued, and his chilly stare swept over both of their faces as he spoke. "And that by coming here, you believed you were doing yourself and your ward a service." He leaned back. "But the laws of Suibhne are for Suibhne's sake, and it's to *this* city that I swore my oath."

There it was: the separation. *My* people or *your* people.

At that moment, Boudicca poked her head around the corner from her room, and, as it was her peculiar talent to captivate a room, everyone's attention turned to her.

Her hair, a frizzy, tangled disaster, emphasized the great blue bags beneath her eyes, and her fingers grasped the edge of the door for support. Wrapping her arms around her robe-cloaked middle as if she was cold, she shuffled slowly over to the table, where Cynwrig offered her his seat.

The silence draped heavily as she scrutinized the expressions on all of their faces with puffy eyes and a faintly sick expression.

Finally, she spoke in a voice that was broken and gravelly, a voice that commanded focus. "Alright. Tell me exactly what's happened."

Ronan hopped up chivalrously to get her a glass of water, though Áed suspected that he really wanted to escape the strain of the room. In his absence, Áed stayed quiet as Cynwrig explained the situation to his sister, softening everything to sickening simplicity. Indeed, Boudicca looked faintly nauseous, though it was as likely due to the last night's alcohol as her brother's honey-tongued explanations.

"I promise, Bou," Cynwrig was assuring her, leaning forward. Her smaller hand was sandwiched gently between his callused ones, and the similarities in their long, slender fingers became evident side-by-side. "You love Suibhne, don't you?"

Áed was gratified when she pulled her hand away, looking disgusted. Her eyes met her brother's with distaste, and she scowled and crossed her arms. Cynwrig looked hurt, but Boudicca's gaze did not soften, nor did her brow, which was furiously crinkled. "This is absurd."

"It's anything but."

She only crossed her arms more firmly, which completely erased her docile, sweet-looking appearance. Áed had not, in the short time he'd known her, seen her look particularly stubborn or angry, but now she donned acrimony as easily as a favorite dress.

Cynwrig stilled at her stance. "Careful, Boudie."

"Or what?" she challenged, glaring at him from under her pale eyelids. "You'll arrest me for treason?"

"I don't question orders," Cynwrig maintained, trying to take Boudicca's hand again. She leaned away and did not deign to make eye contact. "And neither should you." He glanced at Áed, who glared at him. Cynwrig sat up straighter, his brows coming together. The bottoms of his eyelids rose pensively and changed his eyes' rounded almond edges to something more angular, where harder lines belied the sentiment behind them. "That's enough." In one smooth motion, he placed his palms on the table and stood. He reached the door in two steps, and his men stood at attention. "Ahearn, the young one. Killough, the other."

⌇⌇⌇

CHAPTER FIFTEEN

ÁED AND RONAN FOUND THEMSELVES in the back of a carriage, with the man called Killough in the driver's seat snapping the reins of a glossy, char-black horse. Boudicca had hugged Áed and Ronan before her brother's men had stormed into the flat. Áed hoped that she wouldn't suffer for that, but then she was gone, pulled away as the men had shoved Áed and Ronan through the door.

Now, they sat on cracked leather, and the carriage's wheels clattered over the paving stones and bounced on the smallest of irregularities with bone-chattering jolts.

The journey, though it felt quite timeless, didn't last long before a monstrous building loomed in the window, and Áed recognized it from the first day in the White City. Flags, embossed with shimmering crests, fluttered at the parapets, and above the banners, towers rose into the sky. Killough pulled the carriage off the street and into an alley that burrowed its way between the walls, and the three were cast into gloom.

Áed could just make out the dim form of a man accepting the horse's reins and bringing it to a gentle, clip-clopping halt. Killough jumped smoothly from the driver's seat, and he beckoned Áed and the tremulous Ronan out of the carriage.

In the raw morning air, their breath rose in plumes, and Ronan huddled close to Áed. The man who had opened the door for them was shorter than Áed, though not by much, with reddish-black hair and startling golden eyes. He stood to the side with a straight back, and though his face wasn't unkind, he didn't make eye contact with either of them as he beckoned them to pass. Áed cast a glance at Killough, but the guard's face held no expression. A shiver ran down Áed's spine.

They followed the golden-eyed man deeper into the alley, where two more guards pulled open a great set of double-doors. Ribbons of chill trailed after them as they stepped inside.

The hallway into which they'd come bore an unmistakable expression of pride. Gold leaf, resplendent with the light of pure-white candles, crept up the walls to the vaulted ceiling. For half of a breath, Áed forgot why he was there and gaped.

The building was even more vast on the interior than it appeared from the street. They walked on through corridor after luscious corridor, all draped in tapestries or carved with curling, spiraled designs, before the golden-eyed man stopped short so abruptly that Áed nearly stepped on the backs of his feet. Then he realized that they'd halted before an ornate door, a door winged by two more of the August Guard with swords at their backs, and a thread of something sickening squirmed in Áed's stomach. In a clear, practiced monotone, their guide spoke. "You are about to enter the presence of King Seisyll, Monarch over Suibhne, Emperor of the Darklands of Smudge." Áed had to stop himself from letting out a sarcastic whistle, and instead bit his lip as the man continued. "When His Majesty is finished with you, I will deliver you to whatever fate the king chooses, without recourse."

When neither Áed nor Ronan responded, the man turned to the door.

The golden-eyed man stepped in first, leaving Áed and Ronan briefly between the two impassive door-guards. The gleam on their blades was as cold as Cynwrig's eyes.

From within the room, a voice echoed. It was a resonating voice, a voice that sent Ronan's hands clenching onto Áed's crumpled fingers. "Cadeyrn," the voice said, and Áed realized that Seisyll was addressing the golden-eyed guard. "What is this?"

"Two outlaws, Your Highness, from Smudge."

"Bring them in."

Bowing deeply, Cadeyrn stepped from the doorway and beckoned Áed and Ronan inside.

With Cadeyrn out of his way, Áed could see the fullness of the room. Unbidden, his jaw dropped.

Rose marble, punctuated by a florid mosaic that glittered with color, constituted the impossibly-smooth floor. Where the floor met the wall, marble gracefully transitioned into curved ribs, studded with torches, that sprouted up and soared to pointed arches and a ceiling set with a thousand shades of stained glass. The glass was not arranged into circles or arches, but instead sprawled like a breathtaking stain, scattering sunlight across the throne in a cascade of gemstone glow.

Only one other figure shared the space with Áed and Ronan, and in a testament to the size of the chamber, Áed could not discern any detail of him from the distance. It was clear only that he wore a night-blue robe, and that atop his head was a crown. Thinking of Boudicca's description of the king—half-mad—Áed's heart thrummed nervously. Ronan pressed his body close.

Their footsteps echoed as they moved toward the silent king. Details materialized: The man was tall, perhaps as tall as Cynwrig. He had sandy-blond hair, only a shade or two lighter than Áed's, and upon that hair rested a simple crown studded with brilliant white stones.

Áed and Ronan stopped, still twenty feet away, and Áed took a deep breath. He could feel the light penetrate his lungs.

The king's eyes narrowed at them, his gaze caustic. No patience lurked in the depths of his burning, bright-orange irises. "Come closer."

Tentatively, they did, and the king's eyes appeared to focus as he saw them clearly. He examined them from down his nose, hands clasped behind his back, and Áed put a protective arm around Ronan's shoulders.

"What," Seisyll said, clipping the word, "do you call yourselves?"

"I'm Áed," said Áed, doing his best not to sound intimidated by the king's height, his wealth, or the guards at the doors. "This is Ronan."

"Do you deny that you come from Smudge?"

"Would you believe me if I did?"

The king didn't answer, merely raised a regal eyebrow, and Áed's disdain for him rose a few notches.

"I came to find a better life for Ronan," Áed hurried to say, "so whatever you do with me, you can't punish him. It's not his fault. He didn't even want to come."

Seisyll let his stare fall on Ronan, who stood up straight for a moment before curling toward Áed again. Seisyll made a little hum of disapproval and focused his gaze on Áed. The king cocked his head. "You look familiar to me." He narrowed his eyes. "There's something in your face, I've seen your features before. Your eyes…" Seisyll frowned and shook his head. "It matters not." He turned away, cloak trailing behind. "You know your home as 'the Maze,' do you not?"

"We do."

Seisyll nodded, unsurprised. "I am very familiar with it. I have travelled there, seen for myself, and I know well its filth and depravity."

"M-hm," Áed said quietly. "I heard."

Seisyll faced the two again, and his gaze became only more intense. "What have you heard?" He laughed. "Boy, the inhabitants of my kingdom are my *right*."

That damned coal in Áed's chest again was growing hot again, as if Seisyll's words were blowing on it. "What do you want with us?"

"Silence," Seisyll snapped. "I do not tolerate dissent when it comes even from my most trusted of advisors, much less from the *nothing* that you are." He took a step toward them, and Áed began to see the instability that Boudicca had spoken of as Seisyll's facade, cracked by insolence, split away. "You're a fool if you think I spare you a thought. I have broken Smudge like a horse, I have killed its men and taken my fill of its women, and the worms that remain shall not crawl their wretched way into the kingdom *I* have created." With another step, he was in Áed's face, and Áed pulled Ronan behind him.

"Don't come closer," Áed said, raising his voice automatically.

But something was sparking in Seisyll's tormented head, and he would not be deterred. "I *have* seen your eyes before," he said with a curling smile. "Only then, they were full of fear and fire." The king pulled back his sleeve and raised his arm like a talisman, raised the rippled scar that crawled up to his elbow, and Áed stepped back, keeping himself between the king and Ronan. "I emerged the victor over a creature of great power. Is this the mark of a weak man?"

"Get away," Áed warned, but Seisyll was still advancing. "Stay back!"

"You don't give me orders!" Seisyll snarled. "I'll come if I will, you'll stay if I bid you. You'll throw yourself at my feet!"

Áed's skin was growing warm. Ronan felt it, he must have, because he let out a little sound and stumbled backward. Seisyll saw it as a sign of weakness and laughed, lunging forward. "Don't!" Áed shouted, but the king took him by the upper arm, yanking him away from where Ronan retreated, and Áed shoved him off.

Seisyll let out a cry as the smell of burning fabric slithered into the air, and he released Áed's arm. Áed clutched his hands to his chest, trying to contain the heat, but beyond him, it was too late: A glowing edge ate a hole in Seisyll's shirt before flames started licking up the king's body, and Seisyll roared and smacked uselessly at the growing blaze. Áed stared, shocked at the part of himself that was gleeful at the flames. The king tripped backward and fell; sunlight shone through the fire in a multitude of colors and shivered in the waves of heat that eddied in the air.

Áed snapped out of it when Seisyll stopped screaming, and he forced his appalled body forward. "Stop this," he muttered to himself, but he didn't know how. The fire wasn't his anymore, so with all the effort he could muster, he rolled the king onto his stomach. The flames, suffocated, dimmed, and then he pressed at them until only a few glowing kernels of fire remained, not burning but shifting at the seared edges of Seisyll's clothing.

The king's skin was blackened, and from his soot-darkened face, his orange eyes blazed at Áed as he knelt beside the fallen man.

"I'm sorry," Áed said, but that was all he could say. He hadn't meant to do that. He hadn't meant to hurt anyone else. "I'm sorry."

If Áed had chosen that moment to inhale, the sound would have drowned the king's next words.

"I know you," King Seisyll breathed, and a hint of a flickering smile alighted his lips so that his expression danced.

"What?"

"I know *exactly* who you are." He blinked and groaned, and his face tensed with pain. "A festival night," he murmured, and Áed didn't think that the king was speaking to him anymore. "A festival night and her eyes like fire. She said I'd be punished—tell me I'm not a foolish man..."

"You're mad," Áed said softly.

The king's hand moved as if he intended to reach for Áed, but the man's fingers stopped short as Seisyll froze with pain. "I feel that I'm dreaming," the king admitted. He let his hand fall, defeated. "I didn't realize this would happen. I didn't realize you would come of it." He closed his eyes, and his face twitched. "She *was* beautiful, you know. I liked her best. I always wanted..." He trailed off, hesitating. "Well, not like this. Not like this at all. I wanted this, but not like this at all." Seisyll's voice had fallen quiet, and the king mumbled to himself, eyes unfocused. "I always wanted you."

Áed shot to his feet as the door at the end of the chamber banged open, and Cadeyrn, followed by the guards at the door, spilled into the room. At the sight of their fallen monarch, they crossed the chamber at a sprint. "Your Highness!" Cadeyrn locked his eyes on Áed. "You! Get back!"

Obediently at the threat of the guards' swords, Áed tripped back to where Ronan sat, mute, on the rose-marble floor.

While the door-guards tended to Seisyll, Cadeyrn strode

over to Áed, fury rising like the tide, and gripped him by the collar. "What did you do?" he spat, and gave Áed a vicious shake. "*What did you do?*"

"I—I didn't mean to—"

Cadeyrn, though shorter than Áed, was much stronger, and he threw Áed to the floor so that all the wind left Áed's lungs.

Gasping, Áed pushed himself to his elbows. "I swear it was a mistake, I didn't know—"

"Get up," Cadeyrn seethed, and, without waiting for Áed to move, grabbed him by both shoulders and heaved him to his feet. Cadeyrn gestured with his chin to Ronan. "You too."

"It's not his fault, he's just a boy—"

Cadeyrn cut Áed off again, this time with an elbow to the gut. "You're through talking. Come with me."

Twisting in the guard's grasp, Áed cast desperately over his shoulder to where one of the guards was pushing Ronan away toward the opposite door. "Ronan hasn't done anything! Let him go!" He kicked out, but Cadeyrn only wrenched him backward so that he lost his balance and almost fell. "Ronan!"

"Áed!" Ronan screamed.

"Please," Áed begged. "Please, don't hurt him. He has eight years, that's all, he's never hurt anybody. It's me, all me, I swear."

"I know it's you," Cadeyrn growled. "So shut up and stop trying to kick me." He fixed Áed with his golden glare. "You attacked my king. You *will* be punished for that."

⌇⌇⌇

CHAPTER SIXTEEN

THE PATH TO THE DUNGEON TWISTED and turned. For a short while, they followed the halls of the palace, but then Cadeyrn opened a door in the gilded wall, and the men holding Áed pushed him into a passageway. The illusion of candlelit splendor fell away like a husk to reveal sweating stone walls.

They proceeded down long, narrow staircases until Áed knew they had descended stories deep beneath the earth. The earthy darkness made him panicky, especially since beside the path, bottomless chasms yawned in the gloom. Hundreds of cells passed behind them, each alike, though some revealed ghoulish faces crowned with wild hair, long beards, or bloody scratches peering through the iron bars. Surely, Áed realized, some of these people were his kin: invaders, *outlaws* from the Maze. Fear prickled at his heart as the eyes of the damned observed him pitilessly.

It occurred to him horribly that even if he managed to escape a cell, he might wander endlessly through the labyrinth of passageways, searching for the way out. The thought made him nauseous. And where was Ronan? Was he to be dragged here as well? The boy would be terrified and alone, paralyzed in the dark. Áed threw himself desperately against the guard's grip, which resulted in a blow on the back of the head from Cadeyrn that made bright spots swirl before his eyes.

After descending more stairs than Áed had ever imagined to exist, Cadeyrn stopped. An empty cell waited in the darkness, gaping like a maw, and Áed's protests fell on deaf ears as Cadeyrn pushed him forward so he fell to his hands and knees on the cold stone floor. They'd long ago passed the last torch in the wall, and Áed knew as soon as the man left, the blackness would be complete.

Cadeyrn stepped back and slammed closed the iron-barred door, and Áed heard the lock clamp into place. Cadeyrn threw his weight into it to ensure that it didn't yield.

It didn't.

"Someone will bring you water in two days' time," the guard said. Anger still simmered beneath his words. "And a meal five days after that. If you try to escape, you'll fall to your death before you even encounter a guard."

Áed did his best to square his shoulders, but the fear was overwhelming. The dungeon was freezing, and he trembled despite Cynwrig's thick gray sweater. "Where is Ronan?" he asked, wrapping his arms around himself as much for comfort as warmth and peering through the bars at Cadeyrn's stony face.

Cadeyrn blinked slowly and turned to go back the way he came, and Áed pressed himself against the cold iron of the bars to follow the receding light. Cadeyrn's voice echoed coldly down the dismal passage with the finality of a death knell. "You will never see another sunrise."

"Wait!" Áed shouted after him as the hallway plunged into darkness. "Where is Ronan?" He elbowed the bars, and they clanged with a harsh, empty echo. "Where is he?!"

He received no reply.

For the first few hours after the last footsteps had faded away, after the torch had withdrawn its last beam of light, Áed lay on the rotting cot, facing the wall and hugging himself. After a few minutes spent on tears, he'd realized he was wasting not only energy, but water.

He tried, for a time, to consider his predicament. He was stuck in a cell in the pitch-darkness, and for all he knew, Ronan was as well. Or the boy was in an orphanage, or he was being thrown to the streets, or returned to the Maze—that thought stopped Áed cold, and bile rose in his throat. What if they returned Ronan to the Maze? Alone, there were so many ways he would die. And the things that would happen before that… Áed pressed his hands to either side of his head and curled forward, breathing too quickly.

Then, harnessing the panic, he forced himself to his feet, gritted his teeth, and wrapped his mutilated fingers around the bars.

⌇⌇⌇

Ten minutes later, he collapsed onto the cot.

It hadn't worked.

He had poured everything, *everything* that he had, into fire. He had opened himself wide and let the roaring beast within him sing out like the sun. His hands had thrilled, white-hot, against the blackness of the cell, had illuminated it more powerfully than daylight, but the monstrous bars had responded only with a dull red glow. He'd kicked them. He'd screamed.

They had refused to give.

He shoved his hands, smelling of smoke, through his hair and took a deep breath, standing forcefully and stalking across the cell to brace his forearm against the opposite wall.

It hadn't worked.

Defeated and empty, he slid to the ground and pressed his forehead to the cold, damp stone.

⁂

Áed awoke to a dry throat, and swallowing provided no relief. He sat up, wondering how long it had been, and felt the dull throb of a headache developing behind his eyes and temples.

He stood up and leaned against the bars. A chill breeze swept eerily through the passageway; if he listened, he could hear it moaning as it rounded corners, like blowing over the top of a bottle. He shivered, returned to his cot, and pulled his arms deeper into his sleeves.

Helpless, he sat.

By nature, he was patient, and so it wasn't the passing hours that itched behind his dark-blinded eyes and sent his hands scrabbling over the cot like spiders, searching for something familiar. Rather, it was the way time moved as if it were freezing like his breath in the air, the way every heartbeat took longer than the last, and the way the moaning breeze drifted in and out and left naught but profound silence in its wake. There was no buzz of humanity, no thunder, no wind, and not so much as a *drip* of water to break the silence. Áed hummed tunelessly, tracing a seam in the wall and trying to keep his breathing steady.

"Ah! Do I hear music? It's been a long time."

Áed gasped and banged his shoulder on the bars with a *clang*. He stared around him, but his eyes could discern nothing. "Who's there?"

The voice was slow to reply, and when it did, it arrived with the cadence of a sigh. "Probably just a voice in my head, by now." It was a crackly voice, creased with age like a well-worn book, and it seemed to come from one of the cells nearby. "Oh, wait. You mean who am *I*?"

"Yes." Áed stood again, standing against the bars and trying to locate the source of the voice.

The voice sighed. "A fellow, if you've been interred here as well. When did you get here? I must have been sleeping."

Áed was surprised that the voice's owner could sleep through so much, what with the brilliant firelight and the shouting. "I'm not sure. Today." How many hours, he couldn't say. The conversation, even with a voice floating in the darkness, washed him with a relief so potent that he shuddered.

A wheezing sound jerked its way down the hall, and it took Áed a moment to realize that the voice was laughing. "That's terribly unfortunate."

Áed kicked an unyielding bar. "Tell me about it."

"I've been here seven years, I think," the voice said dispassionately, and a tremor ran down Áed's spine. "I once was called Judoc, but nobody calls me anything anymore," the voice continued with a lack of emotion that both impressed and scared the hell out of Áed.

"I'm… I'm sorry." He didn't have any idea what to say to that. "That's horrible."

Judoc's wheezy laugh twisted down the hall again. "It is, indeed." As if to emphasize his words, he accompanied them with a sound like he was sucking his lips to his gums, and Áed shivered again. "But you needn't feel bad for me, boy." Áed was about to feel relieved, but Judoc's voice went on. "You're in the same stew, I'm afraid."

The relief turned to a rock in the pit of his stomach. "No. I *have* to get out."

"Everybody has to get out," Judoc said matter-of-factly. "But if you're all the way down here, you aren't going to."

Áed sat and drew his knees to his chest. "So tell me, boy," Judoc rasped. "Why *are* you here?"

Áed shoved his fingers into his hair again and tried to recall what it was to be warm. "I set the king on fire."

Judoc was silent for a moment, and then he cut the darkness with a low, incredulous whistle. "You *what*?"

"It was an accident."

"My word. I'm surprised they didn't simply kill you."

Áed tried to ignore the chill that ran through him at that. "What are you here for?"

"Stealing gold, and I've made my peace with not seeing the sun again." Judoc cleared his throat. "It's good to talk, you know. I haven't heard another voice in months."

Áed winced. "If the last time you had company was months ago, and nobody ever gets out…"

He could almost feel Judoc shaking his head sadly. "Best not to think about it."

⌇⌇⌇

CHAPTER SEVENTEEN

IT DIDN'T TAKE LONG BEFORE Áed's throat was too dry to speak anymore. He tried calling out to Judoc, but he couldn't muster his voice, and the man didn't respond. Áed sincerely hoped that the old prisoner simply couldn't hear him, and that Judoc hadn't suddenly died.

It was impossible to think. Áed's headache had intensified over the course of a few hours, and the mere thought of a dewdrop made his throat clench wishfully. He didn't know how long it took for a person to die of thirst, but he knew that when he stood, the pitch-black cell whirled around him. Gingerly, he sat on the bed and vowed not to move until water arrived. He considered attacking the bars again, for his spirit was willing, but his body was weakened.

He dozed fitfully, grateful for sleep's reprieve. His dreams were fractured. He saw Ronan's face, then Boudicca and Ninian. He awoke disoriented, his head pounding.

He was hungry, too, but hunger was familiar. Of every deprivation he'd suffered, he'd never been without water, and he could think of nothing else. Thirst burrowed through his brain and taunted him with images of condensation dripping down a window, bubbling springs, and the sink in

Boudicca's kitchen.

When the sound of a tray scraping under the door finally skidded into the cell, Áed opened his eyes uncertainly, not sure what was real.

The guard's light receded down the hall, but the fading torch revealed the outline of a tin bowl. Not trusting his hands to pick it up, Áed fell onto all fours and drank straight from the dish. The water felt cool in his parched mouth and throat. He didn't come up to breathe until the bowl was empty, and then he lifted it and tipped it into his mouth so that the last few drops landed on his tongue. It was sweet, sweeter than any water he'd ever tasted, and the sweetness lingered on his tongue like the juice of an overripe apple.

Relief spread quickly, and he smiled to himself. He ran his fingers around the inside of the bowl just so they would be wet, and then he sat on the edge of his cot and waited for his headache to subside while a weight of weariness bore down on him.

Sleeping came even more easily when his head wasn't throbbing. This sleep was peaceful, not fitful; he drifted as if he were floating through soft layers of consciousness, a buoy on the waves of the sea. Even as he slept, he felt the heaviness in his limbs, as if they were pinned to the impossibly comfortable cot. Sounds filtered through his awareness, but he ignored them, succumbing to the peace of sleep.

For a moment, he dreamed that he was moving, that someone was carrying him, and that their hands were cold, but there was nothing to be done about it. The dream faded to black and didn't return.

⁂

He awoke to light and squeezed his eyes closed as pain

flashed through his dark-blind vision. Blinking, he edged open his eyelids, but the light was overwhelming and everywhere. In the time it took to orient himself, he became aware of other senses demanding his notice.

He was lying on his stomach against a smooth surface, and his head rested uncomfortably against something hard and flat. A chill wind breezed over his back, which was no longer warmed by Cynwrig's gray sweater.

He blinked, trying not to let himself panic before it was strictly necessary, and attempted to push himself up to his knees.

No luck.

His hands were bound beneath the table as if he were embracing it, and his feet were immobilized as well. A tether ran across his lower back, pinning it down.

His eyes adjusted and brought him nothing reassuring. The glare of metal: the platform to which he was tied. White walls set with silver candle brackets. A table populated with slender metal implements.

Panic won, and his breathing came quickly.

"Hello, Áed." A quiet voice came from directly to his left, but he couldn't turn his head to see who had spoken. It was an understated voice, calm and interested, but it held an oily tone that left a residue on Áed's mind like the grime on the docks of the Maze.

"What's going on?"

"Shh," the voice soothed silkily, but it did nothing to make Áed relax. "My name is Óengus." A pernicious smile laced through his words, and Áed's breath caught in his throat.

"What are you doing?"

He felt Óengus stand beside him, heard the rustling of fabric as the man moved, and he strained uselessly against the bonds. "You attacked the king, Áed. It is Áed, isn't it?" His footsteps were slow and methodical as he stepped around the front of the table, and then he paused. Áed still couldn't see him, and he suspected that this was intentional. "His Highness is suffering greatly. Now, what do you suppose we should do with his assailant?"

Áed's mouth was dry, as dry as the fields before rain.

"The punishment shall fit," Óengus said in a voice that was far, far too cheerful, and a roll of terror crept along Áed's spine.

"Wait," Áed protested, trying to shift. "I swear to you, I didn't mean to hurt him. It was a mistake, an accident." The bonds held firm as he yanked against them, and he recoiled as Óengus took another step, bringing him into Áed's sight. He was a wiry man with a ruddy face and greasy, pitch-black hair, and he had eyes to match: flat black, the color of darkness.

"Áed," he said, and a serpentine smile crawled over his thin, cracked lips. "I have to do what's right."

Áed reached for the ember in his chest and felt his body respond, but his hands were under the cold metal table, immobilized and far away.

"Oh," the man said, his thick eyebrows lifting as if he'd only just remembered something. "I thought it was wise to keep your hands out of my way, just in case my king wasn't imagining what you did to him." He grinned. "A wise move, evidently. What *are* you, anyway?"

Áed snarled, but it was no use. He'd have as much luck begging for mercy, which he didn't have any intention of doing. How had he gotten to this room in the first place, when he should have fought? He didn't remember, but then he closed his eyes and remembered how easily he'd slept. "You drugged my water."

Óengus shrugged. "I wanted to ensure that it was safe." That malicious smile crept slowly over his lips again and made them curl in a way Áed didn't think lips should curl.

"That is, for *me*." Óengus put his hands on his knees and bent over slowly. "I am the lord of this dungeon, my friend. My place," he breathed, and the stink of his breath, as sweetly disgusting as rotting food, made Áed's stomach turn, "is to bring justice."

Áed held his breath and did his best to look anywhere but the torturer's too-close face. Óengus raised an eyebrow, which looked like a fat, black caterpillar inching up his forehead.

The man examined his fingernails impassively. "Tell me, who is the child who came with you?"

"Leave him out of this." Áed jerked against the restraints, clenching his teeth. "Do you have him? If you've laid a finger on him, I *will* kill you."

Óengus didn't respond to his questions, merely regarded him with interest. "If I told you that, what would I gain?"

So this was to be emotional torture, too. "Fuck you."

Óengus laughed and turned to the table, where his fingers selected one of the fine silver implements. He laid a palm on Áed's bare back, and Áed couldn't move out from under his clammy touch. "Now, please try to relax."

"Leave me alone," Áed managed.

Óengus laughed again. "No." Twirling an instrument expertly, he held it up before Áed's face. It had a thin handle with a sharp loop at the bottom. "See this?"

Áed's gaze couldn't move away from the tool, and he couldn't summon a response.

"Some artists use tools like this for etching clay. It drags across the surface and removes a strip of material as it goes." He smiled wickedly. "But for clay, they don't have to be this sharp."

He stood slowly, still smiling, and Áed started hyperventilating again. "Wait," he said desperately. "Please."

He felt the cold metal of the tool before he felt the bite.

The pain was burning and wickedly sharp, but he bit his lip hard, trying not to cry out even as tears sprang to his eyes. The tool changed direction, slicing a thin strip of skin in another direction, and a shout broke free from his mouth. The torturer didn't pause. "Good. That was good."

Óengus worked his way from Áed's right shoulder blade, across his upper back, and then down along his spine. Whorls of red swarmed Áed's vision, and through the blistering haze of pain, through the screams that he hadn't summoned but that burst forth anyhow, he heard himself gasping, begging. Áed could feel his blood spreading over his skin, dripping down his sides and collecting in sticky puddles on the table.

He was becoming dizzy as the pool of blood spread, but the dizziness only made his heart pound faster, and he thrashed against the bonds as pain worse than any he could remember threatened to overwhelm him. His voice was leaving him, for he heard his own pleading less often and his screams cracked like breaking glass before they could make a sound, but he couldn't keep a thought in his head.

Finally, Óengus sat back and tossed the final tool, brilliant with blood, onto the table. Áed closed his eyes, but could not suppress his weeping. Every cry that wracked his body sent a spasm of agony across his mauled back, and each new wave of pain brought new tears. The torture-master waited patiently for the sobs to quiet.

"Please," Áed whispered hoarsely.

"Please what?" Óengus asked, sitting back. Drops of Áed's blood rolled down the man's wrists. "I can't think of anything I can do for you right now."

Áed could only close his eyes, trying to will his mind apart from the pain.

"Now, tell me," the torturer murmured, and Áed imagined throttling him, slowly and horribly. Then it occurred to him how much the movement would hurt. It was agony just to lie still on the table. "How does that feel?"

Áed's eyes flashed open. "How does it *feel*?" It was a struggle to form words. Parts of him were numb, but it was painful numbness, a disconnect between will and body.

Óengus remained still. "I ask," he said quietly, standing, and looked down his nose at Áed, "because I'm only about halfway done."

Áed choked and couldn't reply.

The torturer stooped, reached under the table, and brought up two cloths. He laid them on Áed's back and pressed, eliciting a moan of agony from his subject, then slowly sat down. "Hm. While this part will be over quickly, the *pain* it causes is far more severe."

"Why…" Áed gasped, breathless with pain and renewed fear.

"This," Óengus said softly, "is the reward for those who cross the king." He took from the table a small black pot. Like the other tools, he showed it to Áed. "See this?" He turned it before Áed's pain-fogged eyes. "This will fill your wounds. Scars fade, but tattoos do not. I am marking you as the beast that you are." He watched as Áed's breath hitched in his throat.

Áed couldn't stifle his howl as the torturer pulled off the cloths. Their fibers clung to his raw flesh and tore it away.

"Ready?"

Áed had no time to respond before Óengus dipped a finger into the pot of liquid and pressed it, blackened, into an open wound. The torturer repeated the motion, this time tracing the ink down the channel of the score.

Then the pain submerged Áed.

The *pain*.

He screamed, and the shards of sound flew out of his control. The sensation was otherworldly, cleaving his mind from his body as he writhed against his bonds and distantly heard one of his shoulders dislocate. Agony spread like fire, except that fire was warm and lively, and this was dark, deep, and drowning—it crushed him until he was barely a spark within his own body, overwhelmed.

His entire being was taken up, thrashing uncontrollably in an attempt to escape. Screams ripped his throat until it was raw, and then he screamed soundlessly, unable to defend himself from the pain that was splintering his mind, suffocating him, trapping him in his own body and spiraling him toward darkness.

⌇⌇⌇

CHAPTER EIGHTEEN

He awoke in the dark of his cell.

Groaning with pain, he shifted his weight to sit up, but his body was stiff and uncooperative.

Carefully, he brought a hand to his side.

He was shirtless, but ratty bandages wrapped around his torso, his arms, over his shoulders. They were wet with blood.

He hissed through clenched teeth as he slowly dragged himself to a seat, using the bars of the door to pull himself up. With his eyes closed, he rested his hands on his thighs while a wave of agony rolled over him. With it came night-black turbulence, and his mind heaved like churning water. He wanted to be sick.

"Áed!"

Áed started, and then cursed at the movement. Seething, he closed his eyes and waited for the hurting to subside. It didn't, and bile rose in his throat. "*Fuck*, Judoc." The wave in his mind was receding now, strangely, blessedly. Something in him separated from the churn.

"I'm sorry."

Áed concentrated on a slow, deep breath. The cold air entering his lungs gave him something upon which to focus, but the movement almost made him cry out. "S'alright."

Judoc took a deep breath that echoed down the hallway like falling water. "Óengus came for you."

Áed didn't answer. He faintly remembered his shoulder wrenching out of its socket as he'd struggled desperately against the bonds, and he lifted his arm ever so slightly to ensure it worked. The joint was tender, but everything else was so much worse that he could barely notice.

"Are you alright?"

He took a quick inventory, and then a shaky breath. He didn't feel like he properly inhabited his own body, like he'd slipped out somehow, and he recounted the truth with a sensation of peculiar detachment. "No, I don't think so. He, um…" Áed gave a short, humorless laugh, not sure where it came from. "He carved up my back." He tried to lift his arm away from his side, and bit his tongue with the effort. "And arms too, I think." He closed his eyes, though there was nothing to see either way, and caught his breath at the invasion of raw, unfiltered memories that threatened to drag him back under the black water's swirl. Óengus's tools had glinted in the candlelight, and the man's teeth had been soft with filth like moss. The bite of the restraints had cut into Áed's wrists.

Judoc's voice was heavy with empathy. "I am so sorry." There fell a pregnant pause. "I have evidence of that butcher's work on my shoulder. It heals, you know." He paused, and Áed imagined a shrug in the beat of hesitation. "At least, the physical wounds do."

The conversation lulled to a long moment of silence. Áed desperately needed it to continue, to hear Judoc's voice, to have a diversion to keep him afloat, but he could think of nothing at all to say. The freezing, stinging memories lapped at his consciousness, threatening him with *feeling*, and surely he would drown.

To his relief, Judoc offered a lifeline. "Áed, who do you care about? Think of someone, and you won't feel the pain so much."

That was a cheerful topic. Thoughts of Ninian brought dull, empty suffering where once love had flourished. Thoughts of Ronan brought tears to Áed's eyes and made desperation boil again as he considered that the boy, who Áed had raised from the time Ronan was little more than an infant, might be somewhere in this pit, maybe even in the torturer's chamber. He choked, couldn't answer the old man's question as another wave crashed over him, and he felt some inner light sputter. "How long have I been here?"

Judoc answered readily. "This is the third day. You've been unconscious for a while since they brought you back." How Judoc tracked the passage of time was a mystery that Áed hoped he would never have to learn.

Judoc seemed to have a much better idea of the night-day cycle than Áed. Hours passed, night came and went, and Judoc woke in the morning and called out to Áed to wake him as well. Áed hadn't slept. Food, evidently, came at 'midday,' whatever difference that made. Once again, nothing came for Áed but water, and Áed drank it carefully. He couldn't detect any sweetness, not like the first time, but he paced himself anyway, waiting to see if he grew drowsy. He didn't.

He fell into a pattern of sleeping and talking. Each morning, he woke a little hungrier and a little more feverish, but tried to extend his mobility by small measures. Painful as it was, he needed the sense of purpose the exercise brought. He'd managed, step by painful step, to wrestle on Cynwrig's sweater, which offered a familiar comfort. Nearly conquered by the effort, he'd lain on his stomach for a long while to recover, grimacing and panting, before he was capable of sitting up again.

When he slept—which, after the first night, he did often, for lack of anything else to do—it didn't take long before the nightmares began.

After the first one, he found himself crying, found himself shaking, found tears rolling down his cheeks. Then tears turned into awful, hoarse sobs that burst into steam in the freezing air. He couldn't stop them as they broke over him in waves, even as they made no sound but a rasp on his overtaxed voice, and the searing agony that gripped his back and arms only made the tears run faster.

He became aware of Judoc's voice calling to him through his misery, and he tried to calm himself so he could hear. He held his breath, forced the tears into hiccups.

"Áed!" Judoc was calling. "Áed, talk to me."

Áed took a breath and tried to gather himself enough to reply. "I'm here," he rasped, and he heard the deadness in his own voice. He wanted Ninian and Ronan and the gray flat in the Maze, and he wanted Ninian's arms around him and Ronan's simple fear of Máel Máedóc, he wanted the fires in the gritty streets, the worn-out armchairs, and the company.

"Áed," Judoc soothed. "Are you alright?"

Weakened by sobs, Áed took a moment to breathe and felt it rattle in his chest as though he'd cracked something deep inside. "No." He closed his eyes. He could not conjure a happy thought. "No, I'm not."

"Were you dreaming?"

Áed closed his eyes again, preferring the inside of his eyelids to the inside of his cell. "Yes."

"What was it?"

"Everything" he explained softly, trying not to strain his voice any further. It caught in his throat and gave out in the middle of words. "Judoc, what if I never get out? There's someone who needs me, he only has eight, and for all I know he's down here somewhere too, and before *that*—" His voice broke, and he coughed. "Before that, I lost someone, and I know I can never get him back, and I swear to the Gods, Judoc, I don't know what to do, and everything *hurts*."

"Áed," Judoc murmured, but Áed could barely hear him.

"There's nothing I can do, and nothing that I know except that I have to get out and I can't, and I can't even seem to find myself anymore. Maybe it's because it's so dark. Gods, Judoc, it's dark, and it's cold. I think I'm suffocating; I think that's it." He took a deep breath, exhausted by the words, and held his head in his hands. He felt hot and cold at once, and his skin felt inflamed where the torturer's blades had sliced.

"Tell me anything," Judoc said, and he offered the words like a hand for support, saving Áed from sinking. "I will listen."

"I'm scared, Judoc," Áed managed.

"I know," Judoc's reply floated down the hall. "I know."

⁂

Waking consisted of opening his eyes and nothing more, because it wasn't worth the effort to get up off the cot. Once Áed considered it, he supposed that opening his eyes wasn't necessary either, as everything looked the same either way. The next time he blinked, he left them closed.

Judoc hailed him with a yawn from down the hall, and Áed muttered a 'morning' with his eyes still shut. He left it up for Judoc to decide whether it was a good morning or not.

The old man seemed to be in high spirits, and he whistled

contentedly as he went through his morning routine, whatever it was. "I've got a good feeling about today, son," he said. His voice was chipper in contrast to their dismal surroundings and Áed's dismal mood.

"That so?"

"That so. Something good's gonna happen today, I know it."

"How's that?"

"I, my boy, am highly in tune with the fae. I ought to be. I've practically been stuck in a mound with the cunning bastards for seven years."

Judoc's ability to lighten the mood evidently worked even on the darkest of fevered stews, because Áed heard himself snort.

"I'm pretty sure this place is far from a faerie mound, Judoc."

"You wouldn't know," Judoc said sagely. "You've never been here on a festival night. How are you feeling this morning?"

He sighed. "I don't know." Every movement still brought whips of agony, and every thought inevitably turned to despair, but he omitted that from his response. It was probably clear enough in his voice, anyway.

The old man seemed to hear it, and his voice turned sympathetic. "It will pass."

"Thanks, Judoc."

Time plodded. Every heartbeat was a war between thirst and hunger, then hunger and pain, then pain and depression. Pain always won, but depression kept trying, probing around the outer edges of Áed's mind.

Judoc was right, though. There was something in the air, a change in the wind. It was all in his head and he knew it, but that didn't make it less real. His head was a strange place at that time, and it created a feeling of shivering purpose.

"Judoc?" he asked. "When will the guard come with water?"

"Oh, let's see," the man mused. "Another hour or so."

It was strange, but something quite like determination skimmed over Áed's consciousness at that. *Good*, he thought, not even sure he was really thinking. *Time to prepare.*

Prepare for what, he didn't know, but days in darkness—even weak, wounded darkness—had made him restless. The need for action was building against his ribs.

Only one action interested him.

How much worse he could make things for himself if he failed, or even if he succeeded, he didn't consider. For too much time had gone by, and it was time to find Ronan. He had failed to melt the bars of the cell, and he knew that if he tried again in his condition, the effort would fall pathetically short. Another way had to exist. His urge to pace his cell was met with stiff pain, so he slouched on his cot and played with tongues of fire on his ruined fingertips. He was getting better at controlling it, or perhaps he was too weakened to muster uncontrollable flames, but either way, he didn't think he would need very much power for his plan to work.

"You said it would be a good day, Judoc," he said thoughtfully. "I think at least it will be an interesting one."

"Oh? Is your back feeling better?"

"No." In fact, it was stiff and inflamed, and his movements felt heavy. But for the first time in days, a break appeared in the hopelessness. Not knowing how long it would last, Áed would take it. "But I'm thinking a little straighter."

"Ah! Well, that's an improvement! How will it make for an interesting day?"

"I'm not sure yet."

There must have been something in his tone, for when Judoc next spoke, his voice was low. "Are you planning something, Áed?"

"I don't know. I might be. I think maybe I should."

"Planning… what?" Judoc spoke carefully. "You asked about the guard. Tell me you aren't planning what I think you're planning."

Áed didn't reply right away. When he did, he spoke slowly. "There's nothing for it. I can't stay here another day."

It was actually possible to hear Judoc shaking his head furiously. "No. No, put that thought from your mind." There came a *clank* as the man leaned on the bars of his cell. "There is nothing you can do that I have not already tried, and you can tell how much success I've found. Do you know what they'll do to you?"

"I don't care."

Judoc was undeterred. "How much can you take, Áed?" A pause sank, as heavy as a stone. "There's an edge to this life. Get too close and you won't come back. So I ask you: How much more can you take? Another session with Óengus? Starving for weeks?"

Áed was silent.

As if it needed to be said, Judoc spoke softly. "They'll kill you. Please, tell me you understand that."

When Áed still didn't respond, Judoc called his name, but Áed only shook his head at the darkness. "I'm sorry."

"Sorry? Great Gods, are you mad?"

"I don't think so." Áed let his head hang heavy, let his back protest, and tried to find the pain encouraging. It meant he was alive, despite having already been buried. "If I don't try, I may as well already be dead."

"That's fool's talk."

"Is it? Am I living right now? Listen." He felt surprise at the conviction behind his words. "There are things I have to do. There's someone who needs me. What's more, *I* don't want to stay here for the rest of my life."

"It's impossible," Judoc exploded. "It's suicide. You *can't get out*, is there *any* way that could be clearer?"

"You don't *know* me," Áed burst savagely, and the old man hushed. "You don't know me, Judoc. You don't know what I've done, you don't know what I'm capable of. You have *no idea*."

Instead of a bristling retort, Judoc fell silent for several long breaths, and Áed closed his eyes and bit his lip. He hadn't meant to release his frustration onto Judoc. The bars of the man's cell clanked again as he leaned away from them, and, for another moment, the silence dragged on. "Well," he said finally. "Care to enlighten me?"

Áed laughed humorlessly. "Would it help to convince you?"

"No."

"Then no. I wouldn't." Áed pressed his knuckles to his temples, where the exertion of raising his voice had sparked a throbbing headache. "I'm so sorry. You've been nothing but kind to me, and I know you don't want me to leave you alone. I know I might not… well, I know it's dangerous. So, I'm really, really sorry." Swallowing, he let the decision wash over him. "But I have to try."

⁂

CHAPTER NINETEEN

WHEN THE GUARD'S LIGHT began to bob down the hall, Áed pushed himself to his feet. The procedure was familiar enough: the guard would come to the door, bearing the tray of water, and he would bend to slide it through the narrow opening between the floor and the iron bars.

The guard's torch dazzled Áed's eyes, and he squinted so that he wouldn't be blinded. Holding his crumpled hands behind his back, he summoned the ember in his heart and slowly let heat run through his arms until his palms were hot enough to shine. He kept his hands hidden from the approaching guard's sight.

The guard who brought the food and water was a ratty little man with a face paler than a termite's. He didn't have very much hair, even though he wasn't particularly old, and he walked with a lazy stoop and a slow, lopsided stride. Áed held his breath as the guard approached his cell, dragging the loudly-protesting cart of slop and water, and the scrawny man turned his back to reach for a tray.

It was what Áed needed.

Lunging with all the force he could muster, he grabbed the man's neck and yanked him backward into the iron door with a crash. The tray fell, the water splashed, and the tin bowl rolled off down the hall as the man gasped and tried to pull away. In response, Áed let more fire into his palms. Not too much, not enough to damage the spluttering guard, but enough that the man squawked. "Be quiet," Áed ordered. The world was spinning in the corners of his vision, but he would not show weakness. "And drop that."

The guard, in terror, let go of the knife he'd been edging out of his belt.

"Now," Áed said quietly through gritted teeth. "Using your right hand, unlock this door."

"But—but—"

Áed poured a little more heat into his hands, and the man choked. "Unless you want to lose your head, do what I say."

Shaking, the guard reached into his pocket and drew out the keyring, which jingled with his hands' frantic trembling. When he found the right one, he reached to the keyhole and hesitated. "They'll kill me."

"*I'll* kill you. Open the gods-damned door."

Without further protest, the petrified man did as he was told, and Áed pushed the door open with his shoulder. He was still holding the guard through the bars, so he carefully moved one hand at a time before kicking the door shut again and letting the heat in his palms fade ever so slightly.

"Well done. Now walk with me." Trying his best to hide the fact that he was using the guard for support, he steered him to Judoc's cell. In the light of his faintly-glowing hands, he could see the old man through the bars, as white as a ghost. Judoc's uncomprehending eyes were perfectly colorless, and his long, scraggly beard was not sufficient cover to disguise the expression of shock on its owner's deeply-lined face.

"Á-Áed?" he stammered. "What…"

Áed took a half-step toward the barred door, but to his

surprise, the old man backed away. Judoc's eyes were so wide with fear that they made perfect circles beneath his creased eyelids.

"No. No, get back!"

"What are you talking about?" He gave the guard a push. "Open that door, too."

But Judoc was shaking his head, and had backed all of the way to the corner of the tiny cell, hands clawing over the walls as if seeking a defense in the stone. "You've kept secrets!"

"What?"

"Don't say another word," the old man ordered. "Not another word."

"I don't—"

"What did I just say?" Judoc exclaimed with surprising vigor. "I know what you are! Great Gods, I was *glad* of you, I comforted you! You lying bastard!"

"Judoc!" Áed exclaimed.

But Judoc only pressed his wiry body into the corner. "They should have locked you up deeper. Stay away from me."

Any wounds that may have come from Judoc's words, Áed could not feel. His hands were trembling at the guard's neck, and though they stayed hot, Áed knew his weakness was evident. The spinning at the edge of his vision had turned to vertigo, and he blinked, trying to keep himself oriented. "So… so what, you're just going to stay here?"

"Yes."

"I don't understand." He shook his head and nudged his captive guard. "Unlock his door."

"Don't," Judoc begged, fixing his colorless gaze on the guard's face. "Please don't let that creature near me."

That creature. "Damn, Judoc," Áed said softly. "Alright."

He very nearly tripped as he steered the guard away,

but held himself as strong as he could. The guard was whimpering. “How are you doing that?”

Áed raised an eyebrow. “I don’t know.”

“It hurts.”

“Yeah? It’ll hurt a lot worse if you don’t do what I say. Where’s Ronan?”

The guard cringed. “Who?”

“Ronan,” Áed demanded. “He was with me when we were arrested.” At the guard’s blank expression, Áed gave him a little shake. “Come on. Young boy, dark hair. Green eyes. Where is he?”

“I don’t know! You’re really burning me, I swear, I don’t know!”

Áed took a deep, stabilizing breath, and the guard exhaled as the heat dissipated a degree. “Fine,” Áed said. “Then I need you to show me the way out.”

The guard made a guttural little moan, but he didn’t talk back. “Right. Alright. It’s this way.”

“If you lead me wrong…” Áed warned, and the guard shook his head.

“I know. I won’t, I promise.” He shrank away from Áed’s eyes.

“Just move,” Áed muttered. His voice had taken on a little tremor, both from pain and the strangeness that overtook him with the use of his fire, and he swallowed hard.

“You don’t look so good,” the guard ventured, and Áed scowled.

“Walk.”

If Áed closed his eyes, it was easier to ignore the tilting of the ground that seemed to ripple under his feet, but he had to see where he was walking. He could barely feel his back or arms; the nerves seemed to have died. It made it hard to move, like trying to speak with a numb tongue, but he knew that when the pain came back, he wouldn’t be able to hold it at bay. So he walked through his dizziness and concentrated only on placing one foot after the other.

The dungeon, Áed thought feverishly, was the sort of space that might be revealed if somebody were to drain the Sea. Such was its vastness and depth that at the top of every flight of stairs, no matter how far the dimness descended behind them, Áed felt no closer to the light of day. The divots in the steps where guards and prisoners had walked for hundreds of years caught his feet and made him slip, and more than once he gripped onto the poor guard to stop from falling back into the gloom. His vision faded to the point where he blinked, blind, at the spot where he was sure his hands still glowed. Then it snapped back, and the rush of clarity made his head spin. Nausea churned in his stomach, and his breaths came fast and shallow.

They stopped at the top of a staircase, and Áed's knees buckled. With no permission from his brain, his grip on the guard's neck loosened. The guard didn't move as Áed fought to stay upright, lost the battle, and collapsed to his hands and knees, but then the wiry man, out from under Áed's grip, warily stepped away. "Wait," Áed rasped. He tried to reach out, but his arm shook so badly that he could scarcely lift it. Seeing this, the guard took off into the blackness.

Áed's side hit the ground, forcing the air from his lungs. The cold stone wasn't unpleasant, and Áed's will to fight the darkness faded quickly as pain, reborn at the impact, clawed into his tortured form.

He gritted his teeth, fighting to keep himself conscious.

Moaning, he slowly brought an arm under him and pushed himself to a stiff, semi-paralyzed seat. He needed to move, he knew this, but his unwilling guide had fled. Surely, if he just continued up the stairs, he would reach the level of the ground, but he could barely wrench his body off the stone.

The wiry guard had doubtlessly gone to tell somebody

about Áed's flight. Áed had to get up.

Taking a deep breath, he shoved himself to a seat, tried to ignore the stars that winked into existence to whirl around him, and almost threw up. Steadying himself, he got his legs under him and rose to his feet, where he stumbled and fell against the wall. His ears were ringing so loudly that he couldn't hear himself coughing.

His stomach heaved, and he dry-retched. The rough wall was the only thing between him and falling again, and he braced himself on it as best he could—he knew if he fell again, he wouldn't get back up. He'd been able to stand, and that was good, so he took a step toward the next flight of stairs.

It was easiest if he took the stairs at a half-crawl, hands on the upper steps and feet on the lower. It was also less likely for him to fall, and so he progressed that way until the flight ended. Then he used the wall to claw himself upright, hobble around the corner, and mount the next flight. The stairs stretched on and on, encased in their shaft of stone, and it felt as if the walls were leaning inward toward him as three more flights he climbed.

And then the stairs ended.

A door nestled almost cozily into the top of the stairwell, a door not of metal but wood, and though it was locked with a heavy chain, Áed needed only to stumble toward it and press his hands to the wood for the problem to disappear. The smoke didn't bother him as the door caught fire and poured sparks into the air, and Áed didn't even wait for the fire to die before he shoved at the fragile, glittering-black remains and stepped through the flames.

Áed recoiled as blinding light assaulted his eyes, so stark compared to the pitch-darkness or even the firelight, and stopped himself from stumbling back into the dungeon by clutching at the smoldering remnants of the door.

He'd come into an alley, and the palace folded around him. At the end of the alley, people passed, and carriages clattered forth and back along the street. Áed wouldn't blend in, he knew that, not with blood soaking through the back and upper arms of Cynwrig's now-filthy sweater, but there was no place else to go. Bracing himself on the side of the palace, he stumbled haltingly toward the street.

It wasn't long before he began to draw stares. People whispered, just loud enough to hear, and most stayed well away.

Entirely disoriented by the light and the colors of the street, a wave of vertigo sent Áed staggering away from the wall before crashing into it again. Whenever he tried to take a step, the paving-stones bucked beneath his feet, and he felt as though serrated blades were ripping through the flesh of his mauled back and arms.

"Hey! Mate, you okay?"

Áed looked up and blinked around before squeezing his eyes shut at the surge of nausea that rose. Through his eyelids, he watched a shadow fall over him.

"Whoa, there. You alright?"

Áed opened his eyes for a fraction of a second, long enough to see a rather heavyset man in a brown jacket leaning over him in concern. It was only when he registered that the man was above him that Áed realized he'd slid to his knees. "A fight," Áed managed, saying the first thing that came to his head. "Got in a fight…"

"*Lost* a fight, by the look of it. Agh, you're bleeding!"

Áed nodded.

"Looks to me there's somewhere you gotta go. That right, mate? I drive a cab." He pointed across the street to where a tan horse stood, nickering, before a carriage. "I've picked up all kinds. Fighters, drinkers. Nothing new to me. Cheap fare, and mate, you need a ride."

"I don't…" Áed couldn't keep a thought in his head. "I don't have any money."

The cab-driver looked him over with a hint of pity. "Where you gotta go?"

He could think only of Boudicca's flat; it was all he knew. It was the first place anyone would look for him, but he had no other choice. "Apothecary," he said. "Apothecary by the bonfire."

The driver nodded slowly. "Down the road from the Festival fire, right? The place run by the magicky healer and the old lady?"

Áed swallowed hard, but his throat was dry. "Yeah."

"Agh," the driver groaned, rubbing at a nonexistent beard. "Damn it all. Mate, I came over lookin' for a customer." He pressed his lips together. "But I think you might need a ride more than I need the money. I say, you're bleeding pretty good."

Áed put a hand to his back, and it came away red.

With a burst of a sigh, the cab-driver reached for Áed's hand and helped him to his feet. "Did you do this to your hands by fightin' too? I tell you, people like you are good for business, but you're gonna get yourself killed."

"Second time I've heard that today," Áed mumbled.

"Come on then," the driver encouraged. "Agh, you'll bleed in my cab. Now, why'd I have to be born with a conscience, eh?"

For all his complaining, he was good-natured enough as he helped Áed into the carriage, and Áed thanked him.

"Don't mention it. Try to keep your blood off the leather, alright? Better yet, just keep it inside you. There's a good man." He closed the door, and Áed slumped against it as the driver clambered into his seat and snapped the reins. The White City began to bounce by, its lovely ivory buildings trimmed with boxes of flowers, and people on the streets went about their daily lives, oblivious to what happened in the dungeons beneath their feet.

The driver slowed as he neared Boudicca's shop, and, once they were before it, he clucked his tongue so that the dun horse stopped. "Thank you," Áed said again as the driver jumped down to open Áed's door. "I think you've saved my life."

"Well, that isn't something I do every day. C'mon, I'll give you a hand." He helped Áed out of the carriage and supported him to the stoop. "Best of luck, mate." He tipped his hat. "I wouldn't recommend fighting that bugger again." Then he jogged back to his cab, stroked his horse's nose, and vaulted back into the driver's seat.

The door was unlocked, though it took Áed a couple of tries to get enough grip on the knob to turn it. It creaked as he opened it, and Áed hobbled into the apothecary. For a moment, he felt safe, and the realization of what he had done rang triumphantly in his bones. Then he cursed under his breath; he'd forgotten about the stairs.

After all of the dungeon's flights, he didn't have anything left. He could scarcely lift his hand, and it took all of his will to shuffle toward the forbidding steps. How he'd come so far was beyond him, but one flight of stairs, shorter than all of the stairs he'd climbed before, was the only thing that stood in his way from the closest thing he had to home. Boudicca would help him find Ronan, he was sure of it, and if she couldn't, then he would do it himself. Slowly, impossibly, he moved one foot up, and then the other, and, his weight on the banister like it was a lifeline, he dragged himself up the steps.

By the time he reached the top, he could barely recall his own name. He stumbled over to Boudicca's door as blackness bled into his vision like swirling ink, and he caught himself against the wood as if it had risen to strike him. He couldn't muster the power to knock, because his body was ignoring him, and when the door swung open, he tumbled lifelessly to the ground.

CHAPTER TWENTY

HE WAS LYING ON A COUCH with a blanket draped over him, and so he waited for the dream to turn sharp and flay him, because that was what good dreams did. But nothing happened except that something cool and wet touched his lips, and his eyes fluttered open as water filled his mouth. He hadn't realized how thirsty he had been until the water stopped coming, and he wanted more.

"*Áed.*"

He blinked, trying to find who had spoken, but everything was remarkably blurry, as if he saw the world through frosted glass.

The voice turned away from him. "*He's waking. Quickly, get me some more water.*"

Footsteps pattered away, then back, and then the glass was at his lips again and he drank desperately.

"*Áed, can you hear me?*" Something soft patted his cheek, and he strained his eyes to see. A bit of clarity was returning, enough to see someone leaning over him. "*That's it,*" the voice coaxed. It was a woman's voice, soft as down. "*That's right. You're safe.*" The voice turned from him a second time. "*Ronan, come here. Come here, let him see you.*"

Áed took in a quick breath. He couldn't see properly, something was wrong, but he cast his eyes frantically over the blur. "Ronan?"

A little figure bent over him as the woman gasped softly. "Áed!" A small hand took his own. "Yes, it's me! I'm here, right here."

The woman brushed her fingertips over Áed's cheek, and he realized there were tears there. "I thought…" He couldn't finish. Breath shook in his chest, and his eyes fell closed again.

"Boudicca," Ronan said, and his little voice trembled. "What's happened to him?"

The question made Áed frown, although he couldn't immediately think of why. Something hurt, and he exhaled shakily.

Warmth touched his skin, and Boudicca gently pressed a hot cloth to his forehead. "I don't know," she said, but her tone made Áed think that she had an idea. "Stay with him, Ronan. I'll be right back."

Ronan took her place, and Áed turned his head to see better. His sight was coming back a bit, and he saw the boy's face held desperate worry. But he looked whole. No pain fell behind his eyes. "What happened?"

"You don't remember?" A note of fear entered Ronan's tone.

Áed did remember, or at least, he was starting to. He didn't want to think about it, and that wasn't what he'd meant. "What happened to *you*?" He swallowed. "I didn't see where they took you…"

"Cadeyrn let me go," Ronan said, taking Áed's hand again. The contact felt good. "He said I reminded him of his son, and I was too little to put in jail. And the king was…" He licked his lips. "Well, you know what the king was. In the chaos, Cadeyrn told me to go, that nobody would notice."

Relief washed over Áed, so potent he almost fainted. Ronan had never been in the dungeon. He had never smelled Óengus's putrid breath or felt the bite of his instruments, he had never been trapped in that infinite darkness. The golden-eyed guard had a soul, and Ronan was safe.

Boudicca slipped back in carrying a bowl, and she knelt on the floor beside the sofa. "Áed," she said gently. "Can you eat?"

He wasn't sure. His stomach was hot with nausea.

"I have some broth here. Could you keep that down?"

He nodded minutely, but his arms didn't obey when he tried to accept the bowl. Boudicca put it at his mouth instead, and he drank.

When he was finished, Boudicca sat back on her heels and put the mug on a side table. "Are you feeling a little more lucid?"

"Yes." The word came out as uneven as sandpaper.

"Can..." She hesitated, and Áed noticed that there was something different about the way she was looking at him. It was strange, as if he was unknown to her. "Can you tell us what happened to you?"

"I think," he started, and then he bit his lower lip and commanded his voice to rise above a bullied whisper. "I think it would be easier to *show* you."

⁂

Áed knelt on the ground, seated on his heels, and he braced himself on the edge of the sofa. A few hours had passed since he'd first woken, as he had fallen asleep, a natural sleep, for a while. His mind was clearer, especially after he had a few bites of proper food, but while that was an improvement, it also made the memories all the more clear. He still felt fevered. Boudicca drew a deep breath and blew out her cheeks. “Ready?”

Áed braced himself. “Yeah.”

“Right,” she breathed, and from the tension in her voice, he knew she was nearly as nervous as he was. She pressed the scissors gently to the edge of the bandage at his side and began snipping upward, careful not to nick his skin. He realized that he was holding his breath, and slowly exhaled.

He sucked a breath through his teeth when she began drawing the bloody bandages away, and she paused and waited for him to be ready. “Sorry,” he said hoarsely. “Keep going.”

Carefully, she lifted the cloth from his back.

Ronan made a peculiar choking sound.

Boudicca swallowed hard. “Oh my.”

“How bad?” Áed asked quietly, and it seemed to occur to them at once that he didn’t know.

Boudicca, eyes still fixed on his back, took Áed’s elbows and helped him up. She supported him as they moved. “Come with me.”

She led the way to one of the bathrooms and positioned him so that his back faced the mirror before leaning out of the door to take a smaller mirror from the wall of the hallway. She held it up in front of Áed, tilting and positioning it so he could see his back.

Lifting his eyes, he blanched.

The first thing he noted was the color.

The horrific ink was blue-black, crawling over his back and standing out from the dark red edges where scabs had broken and reformed. In the rare places where his skin remained undamaged, its color was mottled with sickly, purple-and-yellow bruises that bloomed over his flesh like macabre flowers, and everywhere, it was reddened and inflamed with infection—no wonder he felt so feverish. The gruesome web of indigo-black lines sprawled deliberately through it all, ghoulishly artful.

It was the most stunning and abhorrent thing he had ever seen.

His voice failed him.

He managed to tear his eyes away when Boudicca's arms began to quiver from supporting the heavy mirror, and he looked at her, agape.

Pressing her lips together, she set the mirror on the counter and turned back to him, folding her hands tensely behind her back. Áed remained motionless as he stared at the wall, too shocked even to breathe.

There was something despicable about the fact that it was, undeniably, art. If they had been thoughtless gashes, gouges meant only to cause him pain, somehow that would have been easier to stomach; the idea that he was solely a medium for his torturer's creation was unbearable. He'd been marked.

In a daze, he shuffled back into the living room and sank onto the couch, followed by Boudicca in her coral-red dress. Ronan trailed after her, and Boudicca perched timidly on the arm of the couch.

Áed looked up at her, dazed. It seemed pointless to feel anything at all. "Let's just do my arms."

Boudicca blinked, worried by the lack of luster in his voice, and then nodded. "Of course."

She gingerly tugged on the bandage, found the end, and unwound the bloodstained strips. Áed watched her face during the process because it was far better than watching the bandages, and he noted that she carefully kept her expression serene and inscrutable. When the final layer of cloth fell away and the bandage fluttered to the floor like a loathsome ribbon, she did not gasp.

Ronan, however, predictably did, and Áed looked down. He was too deadened to feel anything at what he saw.

This design was simpler, but it was no less deliberate, and no less revolting. A thick, indigo-black band half-encircled his arm in the shallow valley where his shoulder muscle met his bicep, detailed with curving spines. Beneath the first band were finer curves, unadorned with anything but the blue-black ink and hints of his blood.

He took it all in with a quick nod and looked away. "Right. Next one."

Boudicca regarded him with concern, pausing with the scissors still in hand. "What is it doing to you to see this?"

"Nothing. I'm fine."

"That's not true."

"I don't know what you want me to say."

A vertical crease formed between her brows, enough to let Áed know that she would persist. "The truth."

He blinked. "The truth?" She nodded gently, and he swallowed. "I wish my body were as numb as my mind right now.

Her reply was silence, but she squeezed his hand. As she gingerly pulled away the second bandage, she sighed heavily. "Same thing. Gods, it's so detailed."

Áed choked as the remark erased the flat around him, and for a moment, he was back in Óengus's chamber, bucking against the bonds. Boudicca put a concerned hand out to steady him, and Ronan started forward as Áed's face contorted, and Áed bowed his head so they wouldn't see the distress on his face. Fear flooded him, ebbed too slowly, and left his skin tingling.

"Áed!"

He took a shaky breath and looked up. Boudicca's eyes were round, and Ronan had covered his mouth with his small hand. "Sorry," he mumbled.

"Are you alright? What just happened?"

"Nothing. I'm sorry, I'm fine." He'd already blacked out

when the torturer had tattooed his arms, and the memory of pain dragging him down into darkness echoed still in his wounds.

Boudicca closed her eyes for a moment, exhaling steadily through her pursed lips. "Let me redress your back and arms, and then we'll figure out what to do." She stood, gaze still fixed on Áed. "This was the work of Óengus, wasn't it?" When Áed couldn't answer, she went on. "Cynwrig's told me about him. I recognize this from his descriptions, this is what Óengus does. That's what happened to you."

Áed nodded. He felt a little ill somewhere deep in his desensitized mind. "This marks me as a criminal."

"You're not," Ronan murmured. As Boudicca slipped into the kitchen, the boy knelt down next to Áed, and his green eyes roved over the face of his guardian. "Áed, I was so scared. They dragged you away, and we didn't know where you were."

"I was in the dungeon," Áed said quietly. "Ronan, I can't explain how relieved I am that you were never there."

Ronan scooted a little closer, but he was careful not to touch Áed's tattoos. "How did you get out?"

Áed squeezed his eyes shut, remembering the endless stairs and the suffocating certainty that he'd never reach the top. He remembered Judoc's fear, and though he didn't blame the old man for distrusting him after seeing his fire, being called 'that creature' stung harshly. He remembered the feeling of the guard's clammy skin slipping out from under his crooked palms and the impact of the floor as his knees buckled. "It doesn't matter, *ceann beag*. I'm out."

"Did you…" he bit his lip. "Did you have to kill anyone else?"

Áed shook his head. "No, I didn't kill anyone else." How he wished he could wipe the memory of Morcant's demise from Ronan's mind. "I never meant to kill Morcant, you know that, and I never want to hurt anybody again." Singeing the guard's neck a little didn't count; he'd done no real damage.

"What about—" Ronan made a little gasp. "*A thiarcais*, you don't know."

"Know what?"

"Seisyll."

The king. Áed had badly burned him, that was sure, but... "What about him, Ronan?"

The boy looked away. "He's dead."

"No."

Ronan nodded reluctantly. "He died three days after." He didn't finish, but they both knew after *what*.

Áed closed his eyes and pressed his thumbs into them. He wanted to ask if Ronan was serious, but he knew that the boy wouldn't lie, not like that. Áed hadn't been able to stop it when the fire had come and had pushed Seisyll away automatically. And now the man was dead.

Boudicca emerged from the kitchen with a tray of bottles, and Ronan looked up at her, chewing on his lip. "I told him Seisyll's dead. I don't think I should've."

With a quiet exhalation, Boudicca set the tray down. "That might have been a little much, Ronan."

The boy looked at his feet guiltily. "I'm sorry."

"Hey," Áed said, and Ronan looked to him. "It's not your fault. I'm the one who..." His voice stopped in his throat, and he covered his face. "I can't even say it."

Boudicca selected a couple of bottles. "Áed, here's what we're going to do. We're going to patch you up, and then you're going to eat some more, and then you're going to sleep. We aren't going to talk about Seisyll. Alright?"

Whether or not he agreed, Áed knew better than to argue. He was weary to the centers of his flayed bones.

"And then," Boudicca added, "Cynwrig will come over, and he'll tell you a little more than I can."

"Sorry," Áed said. "Did you say *Cynwrig* will come over?" Seeing the General again was something Áed wanted to avoid.

Boudicca nodded. "Don't worry. You're safe, and he'll not touch you."

"How can you promise that?"

She hesitated. "He has no reason to bother you," she said finally. "You can trust me. You're safe, you and Ronan both."

Áed did trust her. Beyond that, his exhaustion filled him too deeply to delve into the issue, and his whole body was relaxing as Boudicca, whispering unfamiliar words, dabbed salve on his wounds. Boudicca pressed both of her palms onto Áed's back, keeping the rhythm of her quiet chant, and Áed felt the pain ebbing away.

He couldn't decide any more. He would do what Boudicca said.

⌇⌇⌇

CHAPTER TWENTY-ONE

THREE BRISK KNOCKS ON THE DOOR heralded Cynwrig's arrival, and Boudicca swished over to answer. Áed, who had been sleeping, sat up slowly on the couch, and apprehension dripped into his veins like ice water.

The General's presence filled the room with purpose, as if his confidence could change the very air, and Boudicca moved aside to let him in. Áed was torn between standing to lessen his height difference and sitting because he ached all over, and decided to stay seated. The dread that rushed through him made his heart beat fast, though it surely would soon be meaningless.

To his surprise, Cynwrig's expression flickered when he saw Áed on the couch, and Áed couldn't tell if it was pity or disgust. Whatever it was, it made the General's face look less hostile, but then it fell back into its strict calm.

Boudicca closed the door with a click and folded her hands in front of her. "Áed, Cynwrig is going to be very civil." She turned to her brother. "Isn't that right, Cyn?"

Cynwrig raised an eyebrow but nodded.

They sat around the radial table, Áed carefully leaning

away from the back of his chair, and the General folded his hands on the patterned wood and regarded Áed thoughtfully. "So," he said. "You're out."

Áed nodded.

"Did someone release you?"

"I did." He leaned forward and matched Cynwrig's pose, except that it was too hard to intertwine his fingers like the General had. They ought to get right to it, he thought: no use postponing the inevitable. "Ronan just told me a few hours ago what's happened." Cynwrig's icy eyes flicked between Áed's shifting red ones, and Áed swallowed. "Boudicca says that you won't arrest me, so…" He glanced to Ronan, wishing the boy couldn't hear. "Without arresting me, I can only imagine that the justice is to be immediate."

Cynwrig pressed his lips together before he spoke. "It would be."

Áed maintained eye contact. "Please," he said. He didn't have much of a fight to put up, but he would have to try, and it would be messy. Even with his fire, the General probably wouldn't have too much difficulty slaying him where he stood. "Not in front of Ronan."

But there was no creaking of chairs, and Cynwrig didn't stand. "Áed, I'm not here to kill you."

Áed didn't allow himself relief. "Then why are you here?" He pushed his hair back, stared at the ceiling. "The king is dead. Why are you here?"

Very patiently, Cynwrig let out his breath. "From what I understand, you didn't act with malice."

"That matters?"

The General only shrugged, casting a glance at Boudicca. His sister shook her head minutely. "There are extenuating circumstances," Cynwrig said evenly. "And several things we need to address." He leaned forward. "Firstly: You summoned fire to your hands. How?"

Áed, obeying his deep instincts as he looked over the General's face, decided to play dumb. "What?"

"King Seisyll said that you brought fire to your hands and attacked him."

Áed shook his head. "That's… no. Seisyll was wearing a long cloak, and there were burning torches all around the edges of the hall."

The General scrutinized Áed's face, but he couldn't discern the lie. "That is plausible."

Áed leaned carefully forward. "I still don't understand what's going on. What 'extenuating circumstances'?"

Boudicca's lips were flat against each other, but she said nothing while Cynwrig's forehead crinkled. He was young yet, but Áed could see the crease in his brow from years of forming that expression. He ignored Áed's question. "I understand, too, that you tried to extinguish the flames."

Too late, yes. "I tried."

Cynwrig nodded. "It is as I said. I am here to neither arrest you nor put you to death. But the facts remain that the king is dead, you have escaped from prison, and the August Guard is maintaining order."

"I still don't understand why you're telling me this."

Again, Boudicca shook her head subtly, and Áed narrowed his eyes.

"What *aren't* you telling me, then?"

"Áed," Boudicca said. "You've been in prison nearly a week, and you've been tortured badly. On top of that, your escape left you in such a way that if you weren't—" she stopped herself short and took a deep breath. "I'm just saying that a different person might not have lived. There's nothing so important that it needs to be said right now." She nodded at Cynwrig. "My brother is here to assure you that you are safe and to provide a few details about the current circumstances. This done, he'll leave."

She was convincing, but not quite enough. Áed shook his head. "There's something else. You've been looking at me strangely."

"No," she said. "Why shouldn't I look at you strangely? You're a wreck, Áed."

"Please," he said. "Just tell me what it is."

Next to him, Ronan was furiously chewing on his lip, his little face ever so slightly pink, and Áed sensed a weakness. He knew very well the boy's inability to keep secrets, and clearly Ronan was in on it.

"Ronan?" he asked, and Boudicca groaned softly. "What aren't they telling me?"

The boy's enormous green eyes flicked desperately to Boudicca, who, a beat too late, shook her head. "Nothing important, Áed, I swear it."

Ronan blinked three or four times, fast, and Áed sensed he was getting close.

"It's okay, *ceann beag*. You can tell me."

The boy took a deep breath, and Boudicca tensed. "Boudicca said not to tell you until you felt better."

That was suspicious. "Tell me what?"

He could see Ronan cracking under the pressure and waited a moment, just looking at him.

It was enough.

Speaking all at once as his color suddenly faded, Ronan blurted, "Seisyll named you heir."

The blood drained from Áed's face, and he forgot how to breathe for a moment. Boudicca threw up her hands as Ronan pressed his fist to his mouth, curling his knees to his chest remorsefully. Áed shook his head. "*What?*"

Cynwrig nodded with some chagrin. "That is the truth."

Áed gaped at the General, actually glad that the man disliked him enough to be honest. "How?"

"It happened," Cynwrig said blandly as his sister glared

at him, "that the late King Seisyll claimed you as his son."

"*Why?*" Áed demanded, stunned. "I set—he thought I set him on *fire*!"

"That is exactly why," Cynwrig replied. He took a deep breath. "Seisyll's mental state was never completely balanced. Did he show you the burn on his arm?"

Áed nodded mutely.

"He says he received that from a woman in Smudge on one of his *outings*."

Something clicked in Áed's head, and his mouth fell open. *I have seen your eyes before,* Seisyll had boasted. *Full of fear and fire.* In Áed's memory, the king's mouth slid into an uneven smile. *I didn't realize you would come of it. I always wanted this…*

"Oh, Gods," Áed mouthed.

The General sighed heavily. "He believes you to be his son by a woman he raped in Smudge some seventeen years ago. He's always been desperate for his own blood on the throne. The Council of the King was ready to overturn Seisyll's ruling after the king's death, but their minds were, unfortunately, changed." He cracked his knuckles bitterly, pressing on each joint with his thumb. "So instead of a more qualified candidate, we have you. Cadcyrn, however, refused to reveal where you were. He *should* have executed and disposed of you, so I suppose he thought he was protecting his position if we couldn't prove that he hadn't." Finally, the General cracked his thumbs, and Áed cringed. "Which is why nobody came for you."

Áed's head was a swirl. "This is unbelievable."

Boudicca rubbed at the inner corners of her eyes. "Great job, everybody. Áed, you do not have to think about this right now. The August Guard is keeping order, and there isn't any haste."

"I'm assigning a guard to the apartment," Cynwrig said. "Haste or no, you are the heir to the throne, and those who don't approve can be dangerous." Áed couldn't tell whether or not the General included himself with those people. Perhaps it was only his discipline that kept him from offing Áed there and then. "For now, I'm staying the night."

Groaning, Áed stood. Boudicca's medicine and magic masked much of the pain, making a distant corner of his mind marvel gratefully. "Boudicca, I know it's a lot to ask since you've done so much, but could I stay the night again?"

"Of course you can. The guest room is practically yours and Ronan's now."

He wasn't sure if he'd be able to sleep with everything whirling around in his head, but the thought of the wide, soft bed with its smooth sheets and warm quilt sent a tremor of anticipation through his body. "Thank you for everything, Boudicca. And Cynwrig…" Guilt rolled over him, whether Seisyll deserved his remorse or not. "I am sorry about what happened. For whatever that's worth."

⁂

Áed made his way to the bathroom while Ronan settled down to bed. He still hadn't had a chance to clean the dungeon's grit and sweat off of himself, and he didn't even think that he'd be able to close his eyes before he cleared the last of the foulness off of his skin. He took his time, carefully cleansing the residue from every pore and fingernail.

His footsteps were quiet as he shuffled to the guest room, feeling ever so slightly improved. The candle on the chest of drawers bathed the bedroom in warm light, the window-curtains hung limply, and Áed's letter was folded on the dresser. Áed could hear the boy in the closet, shuffling around, and his head popped around the corner as Áed closed the door quietly. Áed noticed that he had a new fullness in his cheeks that replaced the gauntness that had lurked there before, and his dimples were a little deeper as his little face broke into a timid smile. "Hi, Áed."

"Hey, mate." He sat down on the edge of the bed, and Ronan tossed him some clean clothes before disappearing back into the closet to give him some privacy while he put them on.

"Um," Ronan's voice came from the closet, and he emerged and plopped himself onto the bed. He swallowed, glancing down at the quilt and fidgeting with a crease in the colorful fabric. "I don't know if it'll hurt too much, but, uh…" He looked up abashedly, his green eyes not meeting Áed's. Rather, they took in the rest of him, skimming over the bandages, his arms, his hair. "I haven't really hugged you yet."

Áed blinked as Ronan looked down. "Aw, mate." The genuineness melted him completely. "Of course."

Ronan turned and buried himself in Áed's arms, pressing his cheek into the crook of Áed's shoulder and neck. It was clear that he was trying to be gentle, but Áed still had to suppress a wince as Ronan wrapped his arms carefully around Áed's back and curled his knees up the way he always had when he was little. In the stillness of the room, Áed thought he could feel the boy trembling. "I missed you," Ronan mumbled, his face still buried in Áed's shoulder.

"I missed you too, *ceann beag*," Áed murmured, rubbing little circles on Ronan's back and looking up to the cream-colored ceiling. "So much." The boy's warmth was filling, and his weight comforting.

Ronan sniffed, and Áed realized that the slight trembling was that of a boy holding back tears. A drop of moisture fell onto his neck, and Ronan buried closer. "I didn't know what was happening to you, and I was so scared."

"I know," Áed murmured, still rubbing Ronan's back soothingly. The role was familiar, even if the circumstances were not—comforting Ronan was, and always had been, his job. "I'm here now. Not going anywhere."

Ronan squeezed him tighter for a moment, making Áed flinch, and the boy eased his grip. "I want you to be okay."

"I will be, *ceann beag*. I'm not right now, but I will be. I promise." He pulled back as Ronan sighed, and Áed scrutinized the boy's face carefully. "I'm still worried about you, though."

Ronan blinked, his brilliant eyes confused, as if Áed could be talking about someone else. "Me?"

"Yeah." Áed crossed his legs as the boy slid off his lap. Ronan looked healthier; his cheeks were fuller and there was color to his face, but that wasn't necessarily an indication of what lurked beneath the surface. "I mean…" Áed exhaled through his nose, gathering himself. "Ninian died. And then we ran off to the White City, where we were arrested, and everything else happened." He shrugged gingerly, his back still smarting where Ronan's arms had rested. "You've been really strong, but I want to make sure you're hanging in there."

The younger boy sighed. "I'm okay."

"Really?" Áed wheedled. He sensed reluctance behind Ronan's words.

Ronan huffed quietly, resting his elbows down on his knees. "Well, I *will* be."

That brought a hint of smile to Áed's lips, and he put a hand on Ronan's shoulder. "Come on, *ceann beag*. It's late."

Áed eased himself carefully into bed as Ronan wriggled between the sheets and curled into a ball. Áed turned and blew out the candle, releasing a wisp of sweet-smelling smoke into the room before he settled in.

The quiet lasted about seven seconds before Ronan spoke.

"Hey Áed?"

"Hmm?"

There was a pause, and the smaller boy shifted in the dark. "Do you really have to be the king?"

Áed groaned and rolled over. "Please, I don't want to talk about that."

"No, no…" Ronan hurried to amend what he was saying, his little voice fluttering around in the dark.

Áed pulled the blankets over his head, savoring the close warmth against his body, which seemed to have been imbued with cold. "It's been a long day, mate. We can talk tomorrow, okay?"

"I know, I know, but please just listen for a moment."

"Later. Seriously."

Ronan knew that tone. He had to know it, just as Áed knew it as soon as it left his mouth more sharply than he'd intended. That was the tone that meant for Ronan to cut it out. To stop whatever he was doing, and stop it *yesterday.*

Ronan ignored it.

The boy sat up in bed, pulling the quilt with him and robbing Áed of its warmth. "No, Áed. I mean it."

Áed sat up too, feeling his fuse burning down with the spines of pain over his skin. He didn't feel irritated, not really, but he was heavy and weary and wanted nothing but sleep. "I'm being serious, Ronan. Stop."

"Áed—"

"I am going to sleep now. Please just do the same."

"Áed!"

"I don't want to talk about it!" He knew that his voice was louder than he'd meant, but he couldn't take it back. In the darkness, he could tell that Ronan's lips were pressed together. "Oh, don't give me that look," he grumbled, and carefully lay back down. "Goodnight, Ronan."

Ronan did not lie down. "Come on, Áed," the younger

boy said softly to the dark. "Just listen. Please?"

Áed resorted to pleading. "I'm trying to sleep, *ceann beag*. I'm sorry, mate, I just can't do this right now."

Ronan was quiet for a moment, and for a split second Áed relished it, breathing in the quiet. Then Ronan spoke. "I don't want you to be king," the boy whispered.

Áed didn't speak. The words were taking longer than usual to sink in given his exhausted state, and Ronan seemed to draw confidence from the pause.

"You don't want to, do you?"

"I don't know." In truth, whether or not he *wanted* the throne had not crossed his mind.

"Wouldn't it be better if we just found someplace to stay where it was quiet? I'd like that so much. You've seen such awful things, and we came to be safe. Not for this."

"*Seen* awful things, mate?" He was actually glad he was facing away from Ronan and the light that shone in his eyes. Áed gestured exhaustedly to his body. "This *is* an awful thing." He let his hand drop onto the pillow. "Ronan, I need time. I'm sorry, *ceann beag*, I can't think about this right now."

Ronan was finally quiet, defeated, and Áed realized how much emotion was wrapped in the boy's tense, whispered words. The Áed from before all of this would have felt something, anything, in response.

But he hadn't.

It was in that moment that Áed thought the person he used to be was gone.

Surely that Áed died on a cold table as knives pierced his flesh and poison filled his wounds. That Áed had died alone in a cell of pure darkness, buried like a skeleton fathoms below the ground.

⌇⌇⌇

CHAPTER TWENTY-TWO

HE AWOKE BEFORE THE LIGHTS turned on, bathed in cold sweat. The remnants of a nightmare lingered in his vision, silhouetted brightly against the dim room even when he opened his eyes, and he snatched at the memories before they could float away. He couldn't catch them.

He sat up, unnerved, and quietly headed into the kitchen. The darkness felt too close, as if it was holding itself to him like a second skin.

Ronan's words from the night before circled in his head, nibbling at his conscience. Whatever his own desires might prove to be, once he was sure of them, what business did he, Áed of the Maze, illiterate, broken and tired, bastard son of a madman, have being the leader of anything?

At the same time, it was an opportunity. How many times had he prayed to change things for the better? He'd settled on raising Ronan kindly, on bringing goodness to just one more person, but if he could do more…

He jumped at footsteps behind him, and whirled around too fast. He caught himself on the edge of a chair and gritted his teeth as Ronan held up his hands defensively. "Sorry. I didn't mean to scare you."

"Ah," Áed groaned, straightening with some effort. "I'm alright."

"I heard you get up."

"Nightmare, is all. You can go back to bed."

"I think it's almost morning."

Áed sank into the chair, hissing. "Ow."

"Are you sure you're alright?" Ronan perched himself on the arm of the overstuffed chair, which creaked under the imbalance. "Maybe I can find some of Boudicca's medicine for you."

"I'm fine."

Ronan sighed quietly. "About last night…" He shook his head, and crazy sprays of his hair stuck up every which way.

"I'm sorry I snapped at you. It's not what I intended." Áed leaned his head back into the soft cushion of the chair and closed his eyes. Sleep had done nothing, and he was completely exhausted.

Ronan took a deep breath, and for a moment, no one spoke. Ronan's presence lifted the weight of the darkness and made Áed less lonely. "What was it like in the dungeon?" Ronan asked after a while.

"Dark. Cold."

A long, companionable silence settled in as Ronan thought this over, and the sun began to tinge the very edge of the sky with mournful indigo. Áed had never thought of a sunrise as sad before, but it really was; the colors were dark and muted, as deep as the night they followed. Even when the sky began warming, with colors like the insides of seashells, it was melancholy that light replaced the stars. He should have been glad of the light after so long in darkness. He should have been grateful for the faint warmth that the spring day would bring. Instead, he almost felt that, though the darkness was awful, the difference between it and the light wasn't significant enough to matter at all.

There came a groan from the couch as Cynwrig, who had stayed the night as promised, sat up, and both Áed and Ronan looked over. The General yawned, stretched, and then slouched over to rest his elbows on his knees. "Morning," he grunted thickly.

Áed nodded in reply. "Another day."

A little later, Boudicca emerged from her room, and she smiled at him, her eyes concealing her thoughts. "It's early yet. How are you feeling?"

He glossed over the question. "I've been better. What's the plan for today?"

Boudicca's face turned startled. "Beyond staying here and resting?" she asked, obviously confused.

"Yes. No. I don't know." He couldn't think. "I can't do nothing."

"You aren't doing nothing," Boudicca hastened to assure him. "You're healing."

Well, perhaps his body was. His mind felt on edge, not quite at rest, not quite moving. All that was familiar had been overturned, and there were pieces to pick up. His hands, ever broken, couldn't stay still.

Ronan could sense his agitation. Áed knew this because the boy abandoned his spot on the armchair and took a few steps nearer, and Áed welcomed him under his arm. That, at least, would never change.

Boudicca, he noticed, was still looking at him the way she had the night before, as if she didn't quite know who he was. He supposed that was fair. But her expression unnerved him, the way her eyebrows knitted just slightly and the inner corners of her eyes pulled in so that she seemed guarded to him. There was something she didn't understand, something about Áed she was puzzling over, but she didn't ask, and Áed didn't answer.

The day opened up, and Cynwrig left to order a guard to

the flat. There was nothing to do but think, but since Áed didn't want to think, he sat by the window and watched people pass who were happy and whole. His mind was circling without his conscious guidance, like a waterwheel that dipped into the recesses of his memory and splashed what it gathered over his view of the sunny street. If he chose it, he was to be the king of that street, those people, and all the streets and people he'd seen before.

When that thought arose, he let out a little breath.

There would be good to come from taking the throne. He, most certainly unlike any of Cynwrig's 'more qualified' contenders, wouldn't neglect the Maze any longer. He'd seen all too clearly the effects of that negligence accumulating like dust over the centuries, and the Maze, hateful though it was, had played its part to shape him. He would care for it if he could.

Of course, he couldn't be entirely objective, not with Ronan's plea in his head. Áed had already taken away Ronan's lifelong home, and before that, they both had lost Ninian. With the fear of losing Áed still too fresh in the boy's eyes, it seemed barbaric to ignore him.

Áed shook his head. Boudicca was right, there was no haste.

The street slowly emptied as the light became leaner and the White City's citizens slipped indoors. Footsteps from behind told Áed of another presence, and he carefully turned to see Boudicca pulling up a seat next to him. "So," she said.

"So."

She pursed her lips, her face as inscrutable to Áed as an open book. Even so, he easily felt her discomfort pouring off of her. "You've been here a while."

"Yeah." He shrugged gingerly. "It's a nice view."

Her nod was an afterthought. "Listen, Áed," she said,

smoothing her skirt nervously over her knees. "We should talk."

"Sure." He shifted so that he faced her with more attention. "What about?"

She opened her mouth, then closed it, clearly nervous to continue. "Well—"

The door-handle turned, and Boudicca jumped up. Áed frowned at the mixture of disappointment and relief that shifted over her face. "Boudicca," he asked, "are you alright?"

She nodded quickly. "Cynwrig's back. We'll talk later."

The General came in, and Áed pushed himself, wincing, out of his chair. Cynwrig slipped a hand into his pocket and pulled out a cigarette and a match. "There's a guard outside, and there will be one until you move into the palace." He fixed Áed with a curious stare. "Assuming, of course, that you accept the responsibility."

"I haven't been able to think about it," Áed lied.

Cynwrig shrugged and lit his cigarette, drawing a frown from Boudicca. His features weren't spiteful when he cast his cold eyes on Áed, but his face held a look of lingering disappointment. "What would quicken your decision?"

Áed didn't know. To accept his heritage was to betray Ronan's trust for what felt like the hundredth time since Áed dragged him from the Maze, but it also represented the chance to do right. What was more, to take the throne was to reclaim some control over his life. He needed that. "I need to know more," he confessed.

Slowly, the General nodded. "Yes," he mused. "You do."

⌇⌇⌇

CHAPTER TWENTY-THREE

FOUR AND A HALF DAYS HAD PASSED since Áed had collapsed back in Boudicca's flat, and the mood of the marketplace through which he and Boudicca now walked was uneasy. The open revelry of the Festival of Fire had passed, and along the street, the August Guard maintained well-starched stiffness while their sharp eyes combed through the crowds.

Cynwrig had encouraged this outing in response to Áed's need for information. What better way, he'd explained, to learn the city than to act as one of its people? Áed had harbored no opposition to the suggestion, not as the days dragged on and Boudicca's comfortable flat grew slowly more stifling.

Boudicca had initially refused to let him leave. Insisting he still needed rest (which he did), she ordered him to sleep if he could (he couldn't), and provided him with ample food. On the fourth day, however, he'd convinced her that house arrest was unnecessary. She'd changed his bandages again, reported that his wounds were healing well, and reluctantly agreed that she would accompany him into the city.

The market, though subdued by the August Guard's supervision, still sparked with life. No vendors shouted their wares—nobody wanted to draw attention to themselves—but people flowed around the stalls like water, touching, haggling, smiling, arguing. A few children darted through the crowds, little hands snatching at unguarded wares only to be shooed off by peddlers, and they giggled and tripped and chased each other so that they stood out from the wary adults.

Boudicca paused, and Áed stopped with her as she turned to a nearby stall. She had been pausing periodically, and together they stepped apart from the quickly-moving crowd. To blend in, they had to keep up with the flow, but Áed wanted to drink in the details. As Boudicca pored over skeins of colorful yarn and ran her fingers over spools of thread, Áed paused nearby as if waiting for her and cast his eyes over everything: a sign that hung askew over the entrance of a building, a window-box trailing violet flowers with tiny green leaves, a window whose glass shaped a gnarled tree. Farther down the street, an upended carriage split the swiftly-flowing foot traffic, and its broken wheels turned slowly in the wind.

Thanking the vendor, Boudicca tucked a new skein of poppy-bright yarn into her handbag. Unlike the rest of the crowd, Boudicca moved with her head held straight, looking forward confidently with her chestnut hair spilling free and glossy down her back. At first, Áed had thought that was risky, but as he observed the gazes of people who passed, he realized that her beautiful, unhooded face drew attention away from her nondescript companion. Besides, a guard trailed the two of them like a shadow, keeping watch for danger.

"Boudicca!"

The call came from behind them, and they turned to

find a man of about Boudicca's age jogging toward them. Boudicca broke into a friendly smile. "Finnan! How are you?"

"Well enough, well enough! And yourself?"

Boudicca chuckled and rolled her eyes. "What with everything going on, I suppose that I've been a bit anxious."

The man called Finnan nodded understandingly. "You can always come by if you need anything."

Boudicca smiled. "You're a good man." She looked down the street. "How's business? I haven't seen many people stop by the tavern."

Finnan shook his head. "It's rather poor. But with things as they are, I'm not surprised." He shrugged. "The Council of the King isn't used to keeping more than the city's usual order, and given that *nothing* is usual about this, I'd guess they're struggling a bit. Nobody even feels safe enough to get a drink, I suppose." He gave the two a conspiratorial smile and leaned a little closer, rubbing his ungloved hands together against the chill. "If I may ask: you never did admire Seisyll much, did you?"

With a wary glance around, Boudicca shook her head.

Finnan's eyes, the deep blue of a morning sky, brightened. "So then I can ask what you think of all the current goings-on. The heir and all."

Áed felt himself redden, certain for a moment that the man saw through him, but Boudicca only flashed Finnan an easy smile. "You always were a gossip," she teased.

Finnan rubbed his hands together. "I've *got* gossip. You know how the heir's supposed to be dead? You'll never believe what I heard. Torin, the butcher, heard from Cian, who heard from Treasa—she owns that brewery on the corner by the palace—that she saw some cab-driver pick up a fare out of an alley of the palace." He paused to take a breath, and his eyebrows rose as he gained energy. "Said she'd been there all day, and she never saw the boy go *into* the alley, only come out, and when she went into the alley to look, there was this door, which I suppose leads to the dungeon. And it was *all burned out*, like he'd set it on fire to escape." Finnan held up a finger, coughed once into his fist, and plowed on. "Said the fellow was in real bad shape, too, beat to hell. Said he looked just like a boy who got dragged into the palace a week or so ago, and she'd heard from Caoimhe, whose wife's in the August Guard, that that boy was there because he was from Smudge. And the heir's supposed to be from Smudge, so…" He stopped for air, looking at Áed and Boudicca expectantly. "So she thinks maybe he never got killed." He grinned as Áed swallowed hard. "How about that?" He winked to Boudicca. "And as for my being a gossip, I'm hardly the only one talking about it. In fact, it's all *anyone* can talk about."

"What if it's true?" Áed asked. He hadn't intended to sound interested, but a bit of a sparkle came to Finnan's eyes. It was clear he fancied the speculation. "I mean, what if Seisyll's son actually took the throne?"

"Well," Finnan replied. He folded his hands behind him and leaned backward, and his face was ripe with intrigue. "I suspect that if that day comes, Suibhne won't be quite the same again, will it?"

⁂

When Finnan said goodbye and set off down the street, Boudicca and Áed wandered down a side street that constituted just one arm of the sprawling market. Boudicca stopped at a spice merchant and fingered the sweet-smelling leaves, unscrewed caps from jars of earthy powders, and examined glass vials of different extracts that sparkled in the sun. A vegetable booth laden with fat, colorful fruits was next, and then they paused at a table that was heaped with cut flowers.

It seemed there was a booth for everything. They passed a bakery stand, an oily vendor of scrap metal, a peddler selling glittery, light-catching jewelry, and another selling every variety of textiles. There was a stand for honey, a stand for glass, a stand for books of all sizes and bindings. Soap, knives, cured meat, herbs, candles—the market lacked nothing. Áed could barely take it in.

"Alright," Boudicca said, tugging Áed by the elbow into the hollow of an alley. She hiked her bag more firmly over her shoulder and crossed her arms against the chill in the air. "How are you feeling? Can you last another hour?"

In truth, he was exhausted and aching, but Boudicca sounded excited. Besides, the market was interesting and alive. That struck a stark contrast to what he knew he would find if he dared to close his eyes and sleep, so he shrugged gingerly. "I'm fine. We don't have to go back yet."

She nodded and smoothed her hair over her shoulder. "What I want to show you is best seen at night."

That piqued his curiosity as Boudicca stepped back out onto the bustling street. "And what's that?"

She looked over her shoulder as he started after her. "We're going to see No-Man's-Land."

No-Man's-Land. The words echoed through his head as they hailed a carriage to take them farther from the heart of the city. The name made Áed think of gangs and the turf wars with which he was all too familiar; in the Maze, No-Man's-Land was the strip of neutral territory that separated warring parties. The White City, however, didn't seem to have gangs, and so he didn't know what the phrase could refer to.

Boudicca, meanwhile, provided a torrent of facts about landmarks they passed. Áed found himself being involuntarily educated about the oldest building, a new cistern, the history of this, that, and everything in between. When he wearily leaned his forehead against the window, she seemed to take the hint, and from then on, she limited her commentary to information she deemed strictly necessary.

A headache was beginning to build in the base of Áed's skull as the cab drew to a stop. Permitting himself a little groan, Áed flicked the handle and leaned his door open, and Boudicca raised an eyebrow at him as he slumped against the side of the carriage. "Are you alright?"

"I'm fine."

"Of course you are," she sighed, not fooled. "I promise this'll be worth it, and then we'll head home."

"Sure." He looked around in an attempt to discern where they were. It was someplace he'd never been before, but that could be said of most of the city. "What is this place?"

"The coppersmiths' guild," Boudicca replied as the carriage started away with a clatter. "Northwest of the palace, if that helps." She took his arm even though he hadn't offered it, and her touch lent a welcome warmth as she led him down a side street. The flawless pavers became rounded and uneven, and the windows of the buildings veiled themselves in a scrim of grit.

Áed was certain that Boudicca hadn't brought him all this way to see the coppersmiths' guild, and he debated asking exactly what she was planning. Eventually, he decided against it. She was being secretive, like she was waiting to surprise him. Despite not wanting to be surprised, he lacked the energy to argue.

Forge smoke hung in the air and adhered to the pearl-white bricks. The sounds of hammering and the flickering of firelight emanated from some of the buildings' windows, and every now and then people working inside would move across the light to cast giant shadows on the walls of the alley. Behind them, a burst of flame rose periodically into the sky as somebody manned a forge's bellows.

From the gloom at the end of the alley, there materialized a tall, curling gate, greenish with the patina of old copper. It was decorated with dull, symmetrical coils, and Áed fancied that despite its elegant construction, it appeared gloomy against the unusual grayness of the buildings.

Boudicca swung the gate open and held it for the both of them, and it closed with a raucous *clang* behind them. Boudicca quickly turned around. "Right," she instructed. "Close your eyes."

She took his wrist and guided him. They didn't walk far, perhaps twenty steps, before Boudicca gently stopped him with a hand on his chest. "Okay," she said, and her voice was touched by awe. "You can open them now."

When he obeyed, he could not immediately comprehend what he was seeing.

The wall of the alley and the ground in front of him had vanished, and his first impression was that of being suspended in mid-air. He looked around, and realized that they were no longer enclosed by buildings on both sides. Instead, the two of them faced empty air separated from them by a thin, blue-green railing.

Áed took a step toward the railing, working to comprehend what filled the space where the buildings had been.

In vastness, he could compare it only to the expanse of the Sea, but that comparison fell magnificently short, because the Sea did not vary. He and Boudicca stood on the edge of a precipice, a cliff of umber dirt, and where the cliff met the flatland, a heath spread out before them in a colony of whispering grass. Farther away than he'd ever imagined was possible, a ring of low mountains enclosed the grassland protectively, and they were hazy with distance.

He stepped back from the edge when the wind blowing

from below made his eyes water. "So," Boudicca said, and he knew that nothing was going to follow. She was waiting for him to speak.

"This." He could barely get words out. "This is No-Man's Land?"

"It is."

There were so many questions in his head that he couldn't isolate just one. At length, he managed, "How?"

Boudicca's reply was a shrug and a blink. "I don't know."

"Does it *end*?"

"Nobody knows."

His gaze drifted over the massive landscape, spellbound.

"Look," Boudicca murmured, pointing out over the precipice, and Áed realized her arm was glowing with orange warmth. "This is the magnificent part." Following her instruction, he looked.

And the sky slowly lit on fire.

That was his first thought as he looked out over the low mountains: that the sky, with some strange lightning, had ignited itself and was flaming away. It was a sunset such as he'd never seen.

Streaks of quiet light swabbed like paint over the sky, and the clouds, thin over the mountains, had their tendrils cloaked in sheets of orange and red, yellow and pink. Beams of retreating gold highlighted ripples in the clouds and hung illuminated curtains onto the sides of the hills. The grassland swayed, absorbing the fine, warm light, and turned bluish in the shadows as the colors slowly dimmed.

He watched, entranced, as the light withdrew first the oranges, then the reds, and finally the pinks from the sky, creeping over the hills and leaving in their place a faint lavender. Patiently, even the lavender bled away from the vast panorama and left the lands in darkness.

If he'd been breathless before, it didn't compare to the

way he felt at that moment, staring out over the hunched silhouettes of the mountains.

"Well?" Boudicca prompted.

Áed just shook his head, still awed. "It's so *big*."

She leaned against the railing. "I know. Suibhne's been growing into it for centuries, but it seems there's just as much of it now as there always has been. Look over there." Her finger indicated the way, and Áed looked. "There are farms to the north, and they make a sort of barrier between the city and the wild. But here, and all to the south, No-Man's-Land comes right up to the edge because of these cliffs. That's why I thought I should show it to you from here."

"Has anybody tried to explore it?"

"Oh, yes, certainly. Cynwrig has. He says there are animals in the woods, and lakes, and streams so clear that you might think they were made of diamonds."

Áed braced his forearms on the railing and let the wind blow his hair back from his face. "Was Seisyll the king of this, too?"

Boudicca understood the subtext of his question. "Formally, if you took the throne, No-Man's-Land would be yours. But it's far too wild to govern, and as far as we know, it's uninhabited anyway." She let him stare at the darkened vista for a few seconds more, and then she took his elbow. "Come on. Let's go home, alright?"

Áed drank in the view for a couple more seconds, and then let Boudicca lead him away.

⁂

His sleep that night, though the exertion of the day had filled him with the kind of exhaustion that made his very bones feel heavy, was not restful.

Nearly the moment his mind slipped into sleep, the shadows in his head hardened, and their soft edges grew razor-sharp in the quiet before dreams. Even before his eyes began to flicker behind their lids, before imagined sounds slid into his ears, those shadows carved their way through his mind.

When the dream came, it was splintered and washed-out, broken as it churned up from the depths.

In it, he heard shouts and cries and soft words, as if he were listening to the sound of memories playing over each other. He heard Ninian's voice in the tangle and searched longingly for him, but then he heard the fry of Óengus's vile purr and recoiled. Boudicca spoke too, and Ronan, and he could hear the guard whom he had burned, and the grating voice of Áed's adoptive mother. There came a scream and he jerked, and it was followed by a hungry moan and a weak, exhausted cry.

"*What's the matter with you?*" his adoptive mother screeched. "*Put it out!*" Étaín's hand whistled toward Áed's head, and then she drew back. "*Wicked boy!*"

"*Get away!*" His own voice echoed in his head, a frightened phantom acting out a scene that he did not consciously remember. "*Please!*"

"*You have no power here! Nothing, do you hear me?*"

Áed's voice was desperate. "*Just get away.*" Firelight flickered into his awareness, and it was his, and Étaín was angry. "*Don't touch me!*"

"*I told you to make it stop!*" Étaín's face twisted. "*I* will *stop it for you.*"

"*No!*" A quiver had entered his voice, and it was afraid. "*No, please! No! NO! Oh, Gods—*" The swirl of colors in his mind grew dark, and his own voice broke off into a series of screams, gasps, and broken words. Étain cried too, bitterly and angrily as she shouted and his mind flooded with the sound of it, and he could feel splinters of pain cracking through the bones of his hands as he screamed in his head.

He sat bolt upright in bed, sweat dripping between his eyes.

He was panting for breath like he'd been running, and he could feel his heart galloping madly in his chest as he tried to blink away the dream. His hands were crumpled and tingling. Spikes of pain stabbed up and down his body, and he knew from the twisted bedspread that he'd been thrashing.

In that moment, longing for Ninian crashed over him. Ronan was too young to be burdened with the crushing significance of the nightmare, and Boudicca seemed too unfamiliar, and so the sharp remnants of the dream trapped him. He felt Ninian's absence as though his chest was a hollow cavity filling with the brackish swill of nightmares and loneliness and crippling responsibility, and a small gasp flitted into his chest, trying to fill the unfillable. He choked on it, suffocated, and then his defences failed and he wept. Sobs tore through him and shattered as he shook; he pressed his forehead to his knees, searching for comfort in something solid, but it was to no avail. At that moment, he was small and alone, and the cracks inside him were deep and wide. He was broken, he was *ruined*, and the pieces had not at all healed.

He was grateful when he heard the sound of the door open and felt Boudicca's arms encircle him, if only because it kept him from falling apart there and then. She sat on the bed next to him, tucked her knees up, and let him lean on her while she cradled him. Her hand was on the side of his face, her chin on the top of his head, and his tears soaked her bosom as she held him together. "Shh, shh," she whispered gently, and the sound was like a heartbeat, soft and stable. "It's going to be okay."

"It won't—"

"It will, I promise it will. Áed, it takes time."

She brushed his hair from his forehead and swayed with him while he shook. Her arms were strong and warm, and he clutched at them like he was drowning.

"Breathe," she murmured, and he tried his best to obey. Air entered his lungs in ragged gasps while she traced circles on the nape of his neck. "Good," she soothed. "That's good, keep doing that."

When he had his breathing under control, glad for something to focus on, she leaned back ever so slightly and examined his tear-streaked face with an expression of protective concern. "Boudicca—" he choked. His back and arms hurt as if someone had taken a scythe to them, but he had no capacity to care.

Boudicca's soft fingers gently dabbed the tears from his cheeks. "What happened?" she asked quietly.

"Nightmare."

She sighed and took his left hand in hers, where she worked her fingertips in tiny circles on his ruined palm as if divining the content of his dream.

He was suddenly certain of the truth revealed through the terror: A memory had been resurrected, and it clawed at his heart, begging to be released. "I remember," he blurted. It was all he could manage at that moment, and he flexed his hand in hers. She stared at it, and understanding dawned in her face. "I remember."

CHAPTER TWENTY-FOUR

HE SAT AT THE RADIAL TABLE, STARING at the honey-and-mahogany-colored tiles of inlaid wood. A mug of steaming tea sat near his best hand, but it was too hot to drink. Boudicca had shooed Ronan off to Gráinne's with instructions to give her and Áed some time alone; Ronan had looked concerned to see Áed's red-rimmed eyes and pale face, but he'd obeyed Áed's quick, firm nod.

Boudicca sat across from him. She leaned forward while a furrow sidled between her eyebrows, and Áed avoided her gaze. It unnerved him.

"I had ten years," he began. "I don't know why I didn't remember if I had as many as ten. I wouldn't think I'd just forget." He rubbed his hands over his face, gathering himself.

"Trauma," Boudicca said softly. "The mind hides what it doesn't want to remember."

"I can see why," Áed murmured. "I really don't want to remember."

"I know." She put her hand on his across the table, and her perfect nails shone dully in the sunlight. The warmth and soft weight of her touch gave him the strength to keep speaking.

"I lived with a woman named Étaín," he said quietly. "My mother left me on her doorstep."

Boudicca's hand was still on his. It comforted the turbulence in his head, and he allowed the sensation to fill his awareness.

He used his knuckle to trace the rim of the mug, and the light from the window puddled on the table. "I resented her." He stared, not looking, at the edge of the table. "Boudicca, can I trust you with something? A secret?"

She nodded. "Of course you can. Anything."

Áed nodded, and, with the hand that Boudicca did not touch, held his palm up. The ember in his heart pushed warmth through his veins, and he allowed a flame the size of a crabapple to gather in his hand.

Boudicca's mouth slowly fell open.

"I don't know what this is," Áed confessed. "I don't know how I do it, only that it feels just like breathing. Easy. *Good.*"

Boudicca couldn't reply, and Áed pulled the fire back inside him and laid his palm on the table again.

"My fire, whatever it is, I had it then. I remember that now. I suppose that means I've always had it, but I only found it again after Ninian died." He still stared, unseeing, at the edge of the table. "Étaín was afraid of it. Hated it, hated me, really. But I couldn't make it stop, or maybe I didn't want to." He closed his eyes as the dream flashed back, but that only made it more vivid. "She tried to make it so I couldn't do it anymore. She didn't want to discipline me, she wanted to *damage* me, so she… she broke my wrists against the edge of the table." He rolled his right hand and felt the familiar needles. "She kept hitting them, again and again, and I think there was something else, a bottle maybe, that she smashed them with." He paused. Boudicca's hand tightened on his, and he drew a breath. "She threw me out, after that."

Boudicca broke her silence. "She threw you *out*?"

Áed nodded grimly. "I terrified her."

"So what did you do?"

He pushed the heels of his hands into his eyes and tried to think. "It's hazy. I don't remember. I can remember crying and vomiting, but I don't remember anything after that. Not for a while."

"Gods," Boudicca murmured, and he turned his eyes to her. Her face looked repelled, horrified, but her fingers pressed solidly into his hand. "Áed, that is the worst thing that I have ever heard."

"There are people who've had worse."

"I can't imagine how."

"Oh," he said slowly, "I can." He shook his head as she looked on blankly, and tried to explain. "I met Ninian. He cared for me, and he told me I was strong, and brave, and good. And then we found Ronan, who I could protect, and he loves me and needs me. We created our *own* family. We *loved* each other." He blinked, looking into his tea. "There are people, so many people, who are far less fortunate than I am."

Boudicca took a deep breath and stood, her coppery dress shimmering like sparks. That funny expression was back on her face, and she looked like she wanted to say something. She bit her tongue, and finally shook her head. "Let me get you some breakfast," she said quietly. "It almost hurts to look at you, you're so thin."

He cracked a wan smile at her as she bustled into the kitchen. It was clear she didn't know what to do with him, and there lay the humorless difference: Boudicca, full of naught but the best of intentions, couldn't relate to his history. Ninian would know what to say. His absence was a more brutal wound than the gouges in his flesh, but Áed had already completed his vigil. Ninian was gone.

Áed pushed himself up and followed Boudicca into the kitchen. She turned around in front of the stove and gave him a smile, to which he nodded in return.

"Áed," she said softly. "You look embarrassed."

There *was* something stirring in him, an unwillingness to be seen when his body was so flawed, and when he felt so emotionally crumpled. He shook his head slowly and looked up at her beseechingly, begging her to comprehend. "I don't understand why this happened. I don't understand how I'm supposed to keep myself from breaking down, or how I'm supposed to take care of Ronan, much less lead a kingdom." Boudicca's face was sad and quiet, and Áed closed his eyes. "In the Maze we just *survived.* And now I have the luxury to *feel*, and I'm breaking."

Boudicca didn't immediately speak, but she gently wrapped both of his hands in hers and lifted them up in front of her, making them a focal point. She was close to him, and didn't seem to mind. "Áed," she said, her voice was as soft as a breath of wind. "Perhaps this isn't the best time, but there's something I have to ask you."

"What's that?"

She regarded their hands instead of Áed, and couldn't meet his eyes. "I found your letter," she said. "While you were in the dungeon. You'd left it on the dresser." She exhaled, lips barely parted. "Do you know what it says?"

Áed looked down. "Yes. Well, mostly, I think." Ninian hadn't told him all of it. He knew that now. "But I think I'm missing some important parts."

Boudicca nodded and gave his hands a squeeze. "I'm going to get it, alright? You need to know."

She slipped out of the warm room and down the hall, and returned with the scrap of paper that looked even more delicate in her hands. All Áed felt was emptiness. He couldn't imagine that what it had to say could be important enough to change him.

Boudicca cleared her throat and straightened her shoulders, and the little movement rippled through the fabric of her dress and made her skirt look fiery. Her face however, almost ashen, was anything but. "I'll just read, then." At Áed's nod, she began.

Áed—

I owe you an apology. What ought to have been a gift to me is a burden that I will not carry, and for my selfishness, I am sorry. My actions are not of your doing.

Áed's throat was tight, but not from his mother's words: He knew this part by heart, and he could not hear it spoken without hearing Ninian's voice.

I should like to explain myself. I don't need forgiveness or a reason for my choice, but I want to be heard nonetheless. Child, you are the son of an animal, a glittering, half-mad animal whom I could not deter. I never expected any man to be so bold with me. Perhaps I resent you. I think I do. So I will not bring you with me, but leave you to become my revenge the way I know you will. You are as much my child as the dazzling animal's, after all.

"Boudicca," Áed said hoarsely. He didn't want to be anybody's revenge, but it was too late for that, wasn't it? Seisyll was dead. Ninian's voice was in his head, memory echoing the words Boudicca spoke, and Áed pressed his hands to his temples. "Please, stop. I don't want to hear this."

"I'm sorry, Áed," Boudicca replied, but Áed noticed her hands quivered a little on the paper. "I think it will make things clearer."

I suspect you will come to hate me, she read. *I understand. I do hope that nothing truly hurts you, and that you aren't alone.*

Boudicca took a breath to continue, and Áed bit his lip.

They had reached the point where Ninian had stopped reading. Áed could remember his love's violet eyes flicking down the page, his long fingers folding it up and handing it back. "That's it," Ninian had said.

He'd lied.

There are things you should know, Boudicca went on, her hands worrying at the edges of the paper, *because I'm sure there will come a day when you need an explanation nobody will be able to give. Your father was an animal, yes, and a human one. But your mother, child, is no such thing.*

Áed swallowed hard and found the counter to brace himself.

I'd come to this realm on a festival night, and found that I couldn't leave it while I carried you. Now, I return to my home. I don't believe it's a home you can ever be a part of, not any more than you can truly belong here. Boudicca paused and stared at the next line for a few seconds. *You, my son, have my blood.*

And that blood is fae.

For a beat or two, there was silence. "*In ainm dé,*" Áed finally muttered.

Boudicca ran her tongue nervously over her lips.

Áed pushed his ruined fingers through his hair and couldn't tear his eyes—red, of course, because of all the colors, he'd never met another person with red eyes—from the letter in Boudicca's hands. "I had the right to know that." Ninian hadn't told him. Ninian had made the decision not to tell him, and Áed had believed the lie. He'd believed the lie because Ninian had earned Áed's trust, complete and simple, and for all Áed's ability to read a human being, he'd never thought to look for deception from his love.

"Áed," Boudicca started, setting the letter down, but Áed turned away.

Étaín had broken him for what he was. That inhuman side of him had killed two people. "Ninian should have told me," Áed murmured. "Boudicca, do you think if he had, if I'd known, I'd have learned to control it? I'm getting better now, but it's taken me too long, and look what's happened."

Boudicca shook her head and dropped her eyes to the floor. "Áed, we'll never know. But… I understand why he didn't tell you." She shrugged weightily in response to his questioning stare. "*I* almost didn't tell you. The fae are unpredictable and dangerous, and I'm sure that deep down, Ninian hoped that part of you would never surface." Her face was sad. "Maybe he thought that if he told you, if you recognized it, you would change." She spread her hands. "And he didn't want that, because he loved you."

Áed hid his face in his hands. This, of course, was what Ninian had used his last breaths to apologize for. But perhaps his love had been right. Áed *had* changed. "Thank you," he mumbled to Boudicca. "For telling me."

She crossed to him and carefully put her arms around him. He rested his forehead down on her shoulder, and she didn't shy away. "After you eat, you should sleep some more. Half-fae or otherwise, you need it, alright?"

He quailed at the thought of the nightmares sleep would bring. "I don't think I want to."

Boudicca sighed. "I know."

⸙

When he woke, it was nearly mid-afternoon, and he felt hazy and quiet. For a while, he just laid there and admired the grayish light on the walls that slanted in from the window. He heard muted taps on the glass and recognized it as rain; it pattered away, unhurried, and the drops cast hazy shadows against the opposite wall. Muffled thunder growled above the flat, and the rain made a gentle hiss that filled the air with dampness and renewal.

Miraculously, he had not dreamed, but he felt a little hollow, a little new, and rather destabilized. His understanding of what it meant to be 'Áed' had shifted, and he waited for it to settle. It seemed wont to do no such thing.

He padded out into the flat, where Boudicca was reading a book at the table, and she looked up at his approach. "How did you sleep?"

"Well, actually," he replied, taking a seat across from her. "I was surprised."

"Good." Silence fell for a moment, a peaceful, rainy silence. "We ought to take it slow today, I think."

Áed nodded in agreement and tapped Boudicca's book. "Perhaps you could begin teaching me to read for myself." So much would have been different if he had learned earlier.

"That's a good idea." She stood and crossed to the bookshelf. "That's a very good idea."

⌇⌇⌇

CHAPTER TWENTY-FIVE

RONAN CAME BACK FROM GRÁINNE'S as Áed was struggling through the alphabet. Ninian had made reading seem effortless, but even under Boudicca's guidance, Áed had barely managed to remember the order of the letters. They were foreign, and it was strange to think that they represented sounds. They didn't *look* like the sounds they embodied. They were too round, or too sharp, and certainly too complicated.

Ronan, after giving Áed a concerned look, ambled over to the table and examined the page of Áed's letters. "Are you learning fast?"

Áed's hand was cramping from trying to write, even though Boudicca had wrapped the quill in layers of paper to make it easier to grip, and he shook his hand out under the table. "I don't think so."

"What has she showed you so far?"

"Just the alphabet."

Ronan's beryl eyes narrowed as he scrutinized the page. "These don't look anything like the words on the books."

Áed snorted. "It's hard to hold the quill." Ronan picked

up the quill and started drawing on the back of Áed's paper, and Áed watched, interested. "What are you making?"

The younger boy thought about it, frowning. "A horse."

"A horse? Isn't that hard?"

Ronan penned a crooked oval and added some scribbles to the front and posterior, then four lines at the bottom. "A little."

Áed smiled for him. "I think it's great. Why don't you show Boudicca and ask her if she can tell what it is?"

Grinning, Ronan danced into the kitchen, and Áed eased forward to rest his forearms on the table. He sighed, shaking out his hand again. It felt good to be doing something. He would study the letters until they were his, and then the words until he'd mastered them, too. He'd teach Ronan. As he finished the thought, Ronan trotted out of the kitchen and sagged dramatically into the chair opposite Áed. "She thought it was a cow."

Boudicca leaned around the corner out of the kitchen. She flashed the boy a smile and walked over to place a cloth-wrapped package on the table. "Here, Ronan, you just reminded me. This is for you."

Ronan broke into a smile. "It is? What is it?"

"You have to find out." Before Boudicca got another word out, Ronan was up from the table and wrapping his arms around her. Boudicca patted his back, smiling. "Oh, that's sweet, Ronan."

"Thank you!" Releasing Boudicca, the boy bounded over to the table and scooped up the package. "Can I open it?"

"Of course, it's yours."

Beaming, he flew into the wrapping, and then looked with interest at the small leather pouch it had obscured. Ronan's small fingers found the mouth of the bag and slipped it open. Inside, something rattled, and he poured some of the contents out into his palm. They glinted in the candlelit room. "What are they?"

"Marbles," Boudicca answered. "I bought them in the market for you."

Ronan was enchanted. "Marbles." He let one roll off of his hand, and it bounced on the table and clattered to the floor. Áed scooped it up as it rolled toward him. "They're so pretty!" Ronan exclaimed delightedly.

"They're for a game. I'll teach you how to play, once it's light out."

Áed examined the marble in his hand. It was smooth glass, but not clear. Transparent swirls of sanguine and pale blue laced its surface so that it looked almost sugary, and Ronan was right. It was beautiful. "Here, Ronan," he said, and tossed it back. "Those are wonderful."

Boudicca smiled. "It seems right, doesn't it? He should be able to play."

Áed agreed. Ronan didn't need to worry about safety or hunger any longer, and Áed was happy to give him a playful childhood.

After dinner that night, for which Cynwrig joined them, Ronan vanished into the bathroom, the General took a book from the shelf and staked a claim on the couch, and Boudicca stood for a moment, stretching. The energy in the flat was in transition as each person settled into their own activity, but Boudicca and Áed still inhabited that curious limbo that exists before one commits to a pastime. It seemed as good a moment as any. "Boudicca?"

She looked up. "Yes?"

"You'd know best if it's wise, but I thought that maybe you could take my bandages off for a little while." They were a reminder of what had happened right along with the stubborn pain.

She straightened. "Not a bad thought. Let me get some supplies, and we can work in the bathroom."

He made his way to the bathroom and clumsily unbuttoned his shirt, sliding it gently off his shoulders. The bandages appeared free of new blood, and only the old blooms marred their whiteness. That seemed like an improvement.

Boudicca opened the door and stepped in to the room. "Right," she mused quietly as her hands gently found Áed's wrists and nudged him around so that his back faced her. Then he felt her fingers carefully pulling away the edge of the bandages. "Does that hurt?"

"Not too much."

"I'm going to take these off slowly. Let me know if you need me to stop"

He flinched as the bandages parted company with his back and arms, and cool air brushed over his exposed skin. Boudicca sighed. "Well, everything *is* healing."

"Good." He hesitated for a moment. "Healing with that ink inside?"

Boudicca stood behind him, but Áed saw her slow nod through the mirror. "They really are tattoos."

He sighed heavily. "Stupid of me to hope."

There was a quiet clink as her nails tapped the bottle of ointment, and a beat of silence. "I don't think it's stupid to hope." She drew in a breath between her teeth. "Ooh, that still looks bad. Stay still, this is going to burn for a second."

Sure enough, the potion made him grit his teeth as she dabbed it on the afflicted place with a cloth, but the pain faded quickly into coolness.

Suddenly, Boudicca froze, and Áed's stomach twisted in reaction. "Quiet," she whispered as he turned around, holding out a hand to arrest his motion. He stilled, listening, but at the sight of her suddenly-focused face, he heard only his heartbeat pounding in his ears.

"What is it?" he hissed, but she waved a hand at him.

"Stay here."

She closed the door to the bathroom as she left, leaving Áed straining to hear. Boudicca's footsteps crossed to open the front door, and then her voice penetrated the wall. "Oh, goodness! I wasn't expecting you!"

Áed sagged in relief that her tone held no fear, but instinctive wariness kept him alert. Reaching down, he snagged his shirt and drew it over his head, ignoring how it brushed on his exposed wounds.

"What are you doing here?" Boudicca's voice went on, and was answered by a smooth baritone.

"I thought I'd check in, see how you were faring. Say, why is there a guard out here?"

"Cynwrig's with me, that's his man. Oh, here, come in."

"Thank you dear. Ah, that's better, now." The door closed, and footsteps crossed to where Áed thought the radial table would be. "I did think that wherever you were, your brother might be, too. It seems I was right. Cynwrig! I'm glad to see you well!"

"Well enough, I suppose," The General's assured voice came. "Better now that the August Guard is in order, we had some chaos in the beginning."

"Oh certainly, I know it's all been horrid. But you're well. Oh, come now, won't you stand for me?"

The couch creaked as Cynwrig shifted off of it. "My apologies, Father. It's been a taxing time."

Áed's eyes narrowed, though it should make sense; Boudicca and Cynwrig's father—or stepfather, he remembered—was worried about them, and had come to check on their safety. Still, an uneasy tingle coursed from Áed's heart to his fingertips, bringing with it a touch of heat.

"That it has, that it has. Let's have some tea, shall we?"

He heard Boudicca move to the kitchen, and her stepfather kept talking.

"Come and sit down, Cynwrig, I've been worried over you, you know. Not on the couch, at the table."

"Father," Boudicca's voice interrupted from the kitchen, "Do you have news?"

"News? News about what? I've got heaps, my girl, you'll have to be more specific. I assume you mean what's afoot at the palace?"

"Naturally."

"Well," the man said with some satisfaction. "It's all very interesting, I'll tell you. I hear Seisyll's son's an interesting fellow."

Áed heard Boudicca draw in a quick breath. "How do you know? I thought he was meant to be dead."

"Dead! Heavens, no." The deep voice chuckled. "I haven't personally met the boy, but I know someone who has. He's been seen in the city, too: He's got two bad hands and eyes like fire. Quite unnatural. Now I ask you, what kind of creature can hold fire in his hands without a burn?"

"Isn't that what Seisyll claimed?"

"Indeed. The old king was half-dead, of course, by the time he spoke to anyone, but he was very clear about it. He said the boy had bright red eyes, and he summoned fire to his hands." Áed could practically hear the man's smile. "Now, you know what that sounds like."

Boudicca forced a laugh. "It sounds ridiculous, Father. Seisyll probably caught himself on one of the torches and imagined the rest."

"Oh, perhaps, perhaps." The man stopped talking and made a gruff little grunt. "Say, did you have company?"

Áed froze, and he heard Boudicca do the same. "I'm sorry?"

"Company, yes. You've got leftover food on the counter and plates in the sink."

"Oh." She paused. "It was only Cynwrig and myself."

"All those dishes?"

"Cynwrig doesn't clean up after himself."

Their father chuckled a rasping laugh. "Really? That's new. But Boudicca, are you certain it wasn't a young man?"

"I'm not seeing anyone, Father." And her footsteps tapped back into the kitchen.

"Boudicca, dear," her father cut in, his voice slightly raised to be heard in the kitchen, "May I use your bathroom?"

Áed froze again, horrified. Ronan was still in the bath, no doubt keeping perfectly motionless the way Áed was doing at that moment, and Áed was occupying the other bathroom. There was nowhere to go.

"Oh," Boudicca's voice came, more clearly now as she stepped out of the kitchen. "I'm afraid that they're both malfunctioning. Something's wrong with the pipes."

"That's fine, dear, I only wish to wash my hands."

"None of that plumbing is working," she said, and Áed was impressed by the steadiness of her voice. "But you could use the basin in the kitchen."

"The kitchen?" He scoffed. "My dear, I am a gentleman. I will try the bathroom, and if it's broken, then I'll resort to the kitchen sink."

Áed heard footsteps coming toward the bathrooms, and then Boudicca's lighter ones hurried to stand in the way. "Please, Father, I assure you it's broken. In fact, I'm afraid you could make it worse, so please don't…"

"Nonsense, child, I've never heard of such a thing."

"It's true, Father," Cynwrig's voice cut in smoothly.

Their father was still for a moment, the floor creaking gently while Áed's heartbeat hammered in his ears. "Right," the man's voice came slowly. "Now, is it my imagination, or are you keeping something from me?"

"That's ridiculous," Boudicca said quickly.

"Really," her father said shrewdly. "Fine, then. I'll not

touch the sink. I only want to look in the mirror."

Boudicca sighed exasperatedly. "Why are you doing this? I'm hiding nothing."

There was a quiet tumult of footsteps, and then the heavier ones were directly outside the bathroom door. "Dear," the voice came, almost jovially, "You can't lie to me."

Áed put his hands behind his back and cast his eyes to the floor as the door opened, stepping back toward the far wall. There was a flustered huff from Boudicca and then a deep, gruff chuckle from the older man as footsteps approached. "My, my." Boudicca's father laughed knowingly. "Hiding nothing, Boudie?" Áed kept his eyes down as the man stepped into the room, but he couldn't justify to himself why he was postponing the inevitable. *Two bad hands and eyes like fire.* This man would recognize him, and it was only a matter of time. "Hello, my boy," the man said, addressing Áed. "I apologize for my daughter's rudeness, that she didn't introduce us immediately. My name is Elisedd, Master of the Northeastern Quarter, and Councilor of the King. What are you called?"

"Áed," he responded quietly, ignoring the man's outstretched hand.

"Come, shake my hand. And look me in the eye, for Gods' sake, you aren't a servant." Elisedd turned back to Boudicca. "He's not, is he?"

"No."

"I didn't think so. Doesn't stand like one." He turned back to Áed. "Do you have a reason not to shake my hand, boy?"

Áed, giving up, met Elisedd's eyes. The man was bald with a silver beard, and wore rich clothing. Elisedd gasped, "Your eyes!" The man's own yellow eyes sparked with growing interest. Áed reluctantly brought his hands around in reply to Boudicca's defeated nod, and he thought the old man might faint as Elisedd reached for them, quivering with thrill. "Why... you... you..." He glanced to the ashen Boudicca, his face alight like a beacon. "Is it truly him?"

Boudicca's chin bobbed tersely.

"My Gods!"

"Please, Father, calm yourself," Cynwrig said firmly.

"Calm myself! For how long have you been sheltering him?"

"Since I arrived in Suibhne," Áed answered for himself.

Elisedd's jaw dropped. "Well! Well please, come into the kitchen! The tea is ready, surely, and we must talk..."

"Father," Boudicca interjected, and there was a drop of steel in her voice. "Please do not presume to entertain *my* guest in *my* home. Áed is a friend, and I'll thank you not to begin your maneuvering before he's even recovered from his time in the dungeon."

"Maneuvering? Boudicca, for shame! Áed, *Your Grace*, please don't perceive me poorly on her account. I would offer counsel and nothing else, and *certainly*," he added, casting a look at his daughter, "not before you are willing to be counseled." He stopped short of bowing, but nodded respectfully. "Not to pry, Your Grace—"

"Áed."

"Ah, forgive me. Not to pry, Áed, but I *hear* that you had a rather bloody time in the dungeons. Óengus...?"

"That," Áed said quietly, "is not your business."

"Absolutely correct, Áed, my humblest apologies." This time he did bow, and Áed bit his lip to keep from snorting. "Now, would you please excuse my daughter's forthright rudeness and have a cup of tea?" Without waiting for a response, he strode out of the bathroom.

Áed was stunned. "Boudicca," he murmured, "what is the *matter* with your father?"

"*Step*father," she corrected, shaking her head. "Be careful, Áed." She glanced into the living area furtively, and then stepped into the bathroom to be out of her father's line of sight. "Elisedd is self-motivated. Agree to nothing."

⌇⌇⌇

Áed sat carefully across the table from Elisedd, all too conscious that his back and arms lacked bandages. Perhaps removing them had been a mistake, for he felt vulnerable as Elisedd leaned back in his chair and scrutinized Áed unapologetically. "Tell me, Áed," he said slowly. "You will take the throne, yes?"

"I haven't decided."

Elisedd nodded, keeping his eyes on Áed's face. Áed resisted the urge to look away, and he forced himself to meet the older man's eyes without wavering. "I advocated for you, you know. My fellow councilors didn't want such an unknown quantity on the throne, but I was on your side from the beginning."

Áed didn't answer, only met Elisedd's gaze. The perceptive instinct in Áed's chest swirled warningly, full of distaste. "What did you say your title was?"

The man promptly recited that he was the Master of the Northeastern Quarter and Councilor of the King. "That's a smart question, Your Grace," he added. "As a young man, it's not unreasonable to assume you might be in need of some guidance." He smiled, flashing his teeth in the candlelight. "I have been the Master of the Northeastern Quarter since I was a no older than you, as was my father, and my father's father before him. Seisyll appointed me to his Council, where I served for twenty years. Always, my line has been loyal to the king."

"I'm not the king."

Elisedd waved him off. "You will be. My point stands that I am forever a loyal advisor to you. It would do me a great honor if you would accept my help. And, if I may be bold, I could be greatly beneficial to you as well."

Áed frowned as he regarded Elisedd thoughtfully. The man was pitching hard. "Elisedd," he said slowly. "I take it that your position as Master of the Northeastern Quarter is hereditary?"

"Why, yes, Your Grace. Áed."

"And your position as advisor to the king is subject to change."

The man bristled somewhat. "My family has served the crown for generations. It would be foolish to cast aside my services."

That left a decidedly threatening aftertaste in Áed's mouth, and he knew with certainty that he wanted nothing to do with this man now or in the future. Still, he decided not to make an enemy so soon, and shook his head. "It's just a question."

Elisedd relaxed a little into his chair, apparently chalking the query up to ignorance. "Yes, of course." He leaned back, taking his teacup with him. "Tell me, what was it like in Smudge?"

Áed allowed himself to be diverted. "Ghastly. Though perhaps fixable."

"Oh? And how is that?" Elisedd's tone had just done something subtly unpleasant, had taken on an edge as if he was humoring Áed.

Áed put his palms on the table and pushed himself up, finished with the conversation. He didn't have to bother with this, had no *capacity* to bother with this. "Again, sir, that is not your concern."

Elisedd stood too, and set his cup on the table. "It is my concern, Áed. This kingdom is my concern."

Áed wasn't sure from where the conviction came, but it didn't matter. He leveled the man with a stare and didn't move an inch. "No, Elisedd," he corrected, automatically keeping his voice quiet and forcing Elisedd to exert himself to listen. "It's mine."

Áed left his tea untouched and stalked off down the hallway, leaving Elisedd to recover.

⌇⌇⌇

CHAPTER TWENTY-SIX

WHEN ELISEDD HAD GONE, Cynwrig, Ronan, and Boudicca sat around the radial table. Áed found himself too uneasy to sit, and so he paced back and forth, glad that he could move painlessly enough to do that. He only stopped long enough to lean on the back of his empty chair and glance around the assembled faces. "Would someone please explain what that was?"

Boudicca sighed, tipping her head back as Áed resumed pacing. "You just had the displeasure of meeting Elisedd, Cyn's and my stepfather, who is *thrilled* at your youth and lack of experience and will do his best to use you as a puppet." She raised her eyebrow at him in a way that said *'though I don't think he could.'* She laced her fingers on the table. "That's why he went to such lengths to ensure the Council accepted you as the only lawful heir."

Strange conviction was still humming behind Áed's breastbone. It had felt right, declaring the state of the Gut to be his concern, and that was both exhilarating and guilty. He could feel Ronan's eyes on him as he stalked restlessly back and forth, but there had been a funny feeling of relief that had come when he'd spoken so surely, like he had made the right decision.

Cynwrig had started talking. "Áed, I know the politics are complicated, but I *would* be cautious about rejecting Elisedd."

Áed sighed. "Why?" Based on Elisedd's demeanor, he had a hunch, but he wanted the General's opinion.

"He's a powerful man," Cynwrig explained. "If you don't keep him on your side, he's influential enough to make things difficult for you."

"That's unfortunate." Áed turned his chair around and sat down in it, resting his arms on the back. He looked back and forth between icy and roseate eyes. "What's his story?"

Boudicca propped her wrists on the table. "Our father died when I was seven, and Elisedd married our mother. She passed soon after, and Cyn and I think Elisedd was pleased. Éamon—Elisedd's son—was rising through the ranks, and Mother left an open position full of ties to the southern quarters of the city. Elisedd made Éamon take it."

Cynwrig nodded and finished his sister's thought. "Elisedd likes power, but indirectly. He prefers to act *through* people. He gets others to do what he wants, always. When he wanted the Council to respect Seisyll's orders and accept you as heir, the decision was made."

"There are a few more in the court who are a bit like him, though not as skilled," Boudicca mused, and her brother agreed with a curt bob of his head.

"Elders who like their comfort and are smart enough to get others to keep it for them, and young ones who see it as a way up."

"Leeches," Boudicca added. "Growing fat off the power of the king. Each king selects his own court, which is why Elisedd was trying so hard to convince you that he was worthy."

For the first time in the conversation, Ronan spoke, folding his little hands on the table thoughtfully. "You're all talking like Áed's going to take the throne."

Áed pinched his bottom lip and stared at the pattern of the wood on the table. It made a twisting triplet of spirals that knotted where they merged, like the whole table was ready to spin.

Ronan picked at his thumbnail. "If you *did*—and I don't want you to—could you just get rid of everyone in the court and start over with people you like?"

Cynwrig nodded slowly. "He could, but a move like that makes enemies."

"But if they aren't in the court, what can they do about it?"

"They're still powerful men. More often than not, they have plenty of people living off their money, people whose best interest is their master's best interest." Cynwrig paused to look at the faces around the table, then settled on Áed's. "Even if you retired the advisors, their sons would hold grudges, and their sons' sons. You'd turn family lines against the throne for generations."

It really was time to make a decision. Or rather, since Áed knew deep inside that he'd already made one, it was time to share it. He stopped pacing and leaned on the chair again, turned his attention to where Ronan was looking unhappily at the table. "Ronan, can I talk to you for a moment?" Ronan stood, and Áed nodded to Boudicca. "We'll be right back."

Ronan followed him into the guest room, and the boy didn't take his gaze away from his feet the entire time. When they were in the bedroom, Áed leaned on the doorframe and Ronan sat on the edge of the bed. "I know what you're going to say," Ronan mumbled.

"What's that?"

Ronan looked up, emerald eyes dejected. "You're going to

take the throne. I know you are."

Running his tongue over the tops of teeth, Áed nodded slowly. "Yeah. Yeah, *ceann beag*, I am." He moved to the bed and sank down next to Ronan, who wouldn't meet his eyes. "I wanted to tell you first." Gently, he turned Ronan's chin. "Hey. Look at me."

Unwillingly, Ronan did.

"Tell me what you're thinking."

Ronan frowned. "I thought it was obvious."

"What's obvious is that you don't want me to be king. Tell me more."

There had been a phase, back when Ronan had only four or five, when the boy had stopped talking. Neither Áed or Ninian had been sure why, but when Ronan had started up again a few months later, they'd worked hard on his communication. Even so, and even years later, times still arose when Ronan couldn't seem to say what he wanted. This was one of those times. His mouth pressed into a line, and he sat in frustrated silence.

Áed thought for a moment. Sometimes, open-ended questions like 'tell me what you're thinking' helped to get Ronan's thoughts flowing, but sometimes, they were too hard to parse. "Can you tell me what you think would be different if I was king, and why you wouldn't like it?"

Ronan nodded, and Áed knew he'd asked the right question. "It's not what I wanted when we came. That's what it is. I thought we were going to find somewhere quiet. I like it here with Boudicca, because it *is* quiet, but if you're king, then you'll be busy all the time. It'll be so different."

There, that was it. Ronan had gotten it out, and Áed understood. He drew Ronan close, for a moment forgetting to mind his injuries. The echo of pain, masked by Boudicca's medicine, didn't distract him. "I know what you mean, *ceann beag*. We were supposed to have time to grieve, to rebuild, right? And you think if I'm king, I won't pay you attention."

Tentatively, Ronan nodded, and Áed pressed his forehead to the top of the boy's head. Ronan's thick, damp hair smelled like Boudicca's soap.

"Ronan," Áed said softly. "I would *never* let that happen." He squeezed the boy's shoulders. "We still have time here, as much time as we want. Let's take it. And Ronan?"

Ronan blinked at him.

"You *are* my priority. Not a thing in the world can change that."

The boy relaxed a little under Áed's arm.

"If you have anything else on your mind, *ceann beag*, you can tell me."

Ronan shook his head, and Áed knew that was all.

The weight of worry lifted considerably from his chest, which made him sigh with relief. "Can we go tell Boudicca and Cynwrig, then?"

The boy seemed to appreciate being asked permission, because he sat up a little straighter. "I guess."

Together, they went back to the radial table, where, once again, Áed didn't sit. Ronan stayed close to him, brushing against his legs, and Áed dropped a hand to the boy's shoulder. "Ronan?" he said. "Do you want to tell them?"

Ronan took a look at the General's cold eyes and Boudicca's warm, curious ones and shook his head.

"Alright." Áed felt Ronan lean on him. "Well, Ronan and I have talked." Cynwrig raised a skeptical eyebrow, and Áed leveled a glare at him. "Ronan cannot be excluded from this. *We* have talked, and we've come to a conclusion."

"And what have you concluded?" Boudicca had spoken, and her voice told Áed that she already knew.

"I will accept the throne." Cynwrig slumped ever so slightly, and it was Áed's turn to note the motion with the flick of an eyebrow. "The fact is, I've waited all my life for the chance to do something good. And maybe, to some extent, I have." He brushed Ronan's long bangs out of the boy's little face. "But now, this chance… I can't pass it up."

Cynwrig still looked faintly disappointed, but Boudicca was nodding. "Áed," she said, "It's good that you're sure, but please know that there's still no reason to rush."

"I know," he replied. "I don't want to hurry. I think Ronan and I both need some time to get back on our feet."

Boudicca stood and wrapped her arms softly around both of them. "Take all the time you need."

CHAPTER TWENTY-SEVEN

SIX WEEKS.

In six weeks, everything was in motion.

After six weeks, Ronan's hollow frame had filled out so that his ribs were no longer prominent enough to feel when Áed hugged him. His eyes were bright and his cheeks were rosy. More often than not, his boyish chatter filled the flat; when it didn't, it meant he was most likely studying Boudicca's books with intense curiosity.

After six weeks, Áed no longer needed bandages on his back or arms, but even as the weather warmed, he wore long sleeves. His scars were deep blue, nearly black, and he hid them as best he could. The only place where any of Óengus's work showed was where the tattoo on Áed's back emerged just slightly above the collar of his shirts in an artful snarl of curves, and Áed had fallen into the habit of brushing his knuckles over the marks to explore the spiny peaks of the design. The tattoos fascinated Ronan, but the boy knew better than to say so.

After six weeks, Áed was slowly learning to recognize written words, though he still struggled to hold a quill. Boudicca bought books for him, simple books that were usually petty and frustrating, but that he could understand. Ronan had been curious, so Áed had taught him what he knew, and had found it helpful to teach. Ronan picked it up quickly, and sometimes Áed became his student.

From the books, Áed learned more than just words and the order of letters. Boudicca sat with him often and explained passages about battles, heroes, kings, and disasters. Áed had only truly finished one book, a small volume about a fire that had burned through the city, but the feeling of achievement had been marvelous.

Six weeks was longer than he'd thought he would need, and although Boudicca insisted that it was fine, Áed could see the strain growing in the city. The General's face grew more haggard by the day as the August Guard, without a king, began to fracture. The nights grew more chaotic as the Guard could no longer quash the rabble-rousers who either lusted for the throne themselves, frothed with hatred about the murder of the king, or hungrily awaited the arrival of the heir.

Six weeks.

On the last day of the sixth week, Áed was ready. He could wait no longer, he had learned what he could, and it was time to leave.

⌇⌇⌇

Morning came quickly that day.

Áed dressed simply, adding a jacket that hid the back of his neck, and peeked out the window at the wakening streets. Ronan rallied sluggishly as Áed slipped out of the room.

Boudicca met him in the hall, and Áed groaned.

He had underdressed. Significantly.

Boudicca's hair, done in an ornate tiara of perfect

braids, caught the sunlight, and garnet ornaments rested weightlessly in the waves of her locks. A pattern of amber beads danced over her sleeves and spilled down the front of the dress to her waist, where they hung as if a sparkling stream had frozen mid-tumble.

She looked him over and crossed her arms. "Áed," she said as her eyes surveyed his clothing. "Have you forgotten what we're doing today?"

Áed brushed his fingers over the back of his neck. "I didn't realize *that* was the expectation."

She sighed again and beckoned with a wave of her hand. "People know you're from Smudge, so you're going to need a little extra to assure them you're one of us. Fortunately, I'm prepared. Come on."

When he followed her into her room, he stopped in the doorway. "*A thiarcais*." Hanging from Boudicca's wardrobe were garments, clearly meant for him, and he tried to back out of the door. Boudicca beat him to it.

"Not a chance, Áed."

He groaned. "Isn't it a little much?"

"It's a bit underwhelming, actually, but it's what I could get my hands on. Don't worry, you're tough. You'll live." She smiled mischievously. "Besides, you might have to get used to it." Áed slumped, defeated, and Boudicca sensed her victory. She pointed to the clothes on the wardrobe. "Go into the closet and put those on."

⁂

He didn't like it. Boudicca, scrutinizing him in the middle of the room, looked pleased, but Áed was not happy.

The fabric was heavy and shimmering, and the depth of the colors made him do a double-take every time he looked at his sleeve or down at his chest. He would, without a doubt, attract attention. Boudicca had thought of everything, even including a fashionable flame-blue scarf to cover the back of his neck, and when Áed caught a glimpse of himself in Boudicca's mirror, he looked taller, more confident, and slightly otherworldly.

He *really* didn't like it.

Boudicca nodded approvingly. "Oh, *Áed*," she said, clasping her hands in front of her and beaming proudly. "You look so handsome."

"Stop it," he groused.

Her hands found his shoulders and tried to steer him toward the full-length mirror in the corner, but he resisted and she frowned. "You don't believe me?"

He shook his head, scowling. "I don't like looking at myself."

The smile slid from her lips. "That's…" She shook her head. "Later. The good news is that for the next stage, your eyes will be closed."

His eyebrow flicked up. "There's *more*?"

"Of course."

He shook his head decisively. "Nope. This is fine." He went for the door again, but she blocked his path. Her fingers closed on his wrist and he turned reluctantly. "What?"

"Please?" Her eyes were soft and begging, and she blinked at him pleadingly. "It's important. You need to show that you understand the people."

"What are you going to do?"

She nodded toward a chair by the window. "Sit, please. It's just a bit of paint, nothing absurd."

"Paint?" He resisted the urge to laugh. "Boudicca. Seriously."

"I'm being serious!" she insisted, and he could see she was. "It's what people do for formal occasions. I'm going to accentuate your eyes, it will look very striking."

"I have red eyes," he said as he let Boudicca steer him toward the chair. "I've been told they're pretty striking already."

She just bobbed her chin, satisfied. "When I'm done with you, nobody will be able to look away."

The chilly paint felt smooth as Boudicca applied it to his face, and with his eyes closed, Áed could feel every brush stroke, and his nose tickled at Boudicca's breath as she blew lightly on the paint to dry it.

Boudicca patted his shoulder and chirped a cheery "All done!" In the same movement, she turned his shoulders so that he faced the reflective glass in the corner. "Feel free to compliment me."

It took a few blinks before Áed recognized himself.

All in all, it could have been worse. The paint's color could have been plucked from the last beams of a sunrise, and Boudicca had been right about its effect on his eyes. The warmth of the paint drew heat from them, and his shifting irises flickered as if with flames. A single brushstroke flicked up his forehead as if hinting at a crown. He raised his eyebrows and looked away. "I'll admit it's not what I expected."

Boudicca cracked a smile and opened the door. "You're free to go."

Áed pushed himself up and crossed to the door in three steps, and Boudicca leaned out the door. "Ronan! I have something for you!"

Áed turned back to her with a smirk. "Ronan, too?"

"A little."

He shook his head. "Good luck."

Ronan pattered up to the doorway and skidded to a stop. His gaze darted up and down Áed's person once or twice before moving on to Boudicca, who was lurking behind the door. "What…?"

"Boudicca," Áed answered, and Ronan shot Boudicca a wary look.

"Well!" Ronan flashed Áed a hasty grin and took a step backward. "It looks great. I think I should probably… go get Cynwrig…" He turned, but Boudicca caught him by the collar. Ronan squawked. "Help!"

"Oh, come *on*!" Boudicca said, exasperated. "You'd think I was trying to pull your teeth out!" She hauled Ronan through the door. "I have some clothes for you, that's all!"

The young boy stopped struggling, though his eyes still flitted about as if he suspected a trap. "That's it?"

"Yes! I don't even have paint for you!" She sighed, flustered. "The whole point is that everyone looks good, but nobody distracts from Áed."

Ronan's eyes skated over her brilliant red dress and the gemstones in her hair. "Uh-huh."

"What?" she demanded, and Ronan shrugged.

"I don't think that will work."

Áed snorted, but tried to disguise it with a cough. Fortunately, Boudicca just seemed flattered, and Áed decided to get out of the way.

He looked up as the door to the flat opened, and Cynwrig pushed his way in, looking flustered. The General often looked flustered recently, for which Áed didn't blame him. Both Boudicca and he had been pressing Cynwrig for insights into court life, customs and taboos, which families hated each other, and the ins and outs of the palace. The General had warmed to Áed the more time they'd reluctantly spent together, and though they weren't *friendly*, they'd managed a few conversations without glares or barbed remarks. The progress had been necessary, seeing as Áed didn't intend to replace him as General of the August Guard. They'd have to get used to each other.

The General's eyebrows went up at the sight of Áed, and

Áed gave a halfhearted wave of greeting. "Good morning."

Cynwrig dropped onto the couch, and Áed noted with some jealousy that he wore only simple pants and a neat shirt. The General tugged a cigarette from his pocket and glanced away from Áed to light it. "You look different."

Áed plucked absently at the material of his sleeve and felt the golden embroidery around the cuffs. "Thanks, I guess. Blame your sister."

The momentary silence that fell between them broke presently at the sound of Boudicca's door opening and Ronan stumbling out. Boudicca followed, seeming pleased as Ronan tugged at his collar with an expression of irritation.

Áed grinned at him. "You look great, *ceann beag*." To allow silence to fall would be to invite reluctance into his head, and so he didn't. "Shall we go?"

⌇⌇⌇

CHAPTER TWENTY-EIGHT

THE MOOD STAYED REFLECTIVE, BUT it grew even quieter as they piled into Cynwrig's waiting carriage. Their plan, on which Áed concentrated to avoid letting nerves into his head, was relatively simple. Áed would go straight to the throne room while Cynwrig used his authority to convene the various nobles, advisors, and Quarter-Masters that constituted the Council of the King, and they would meet in the throne room. From that point forward, Áed would be recognized as the Coming King, and the decisions would come from him.

The carriage clattered down the bustling streets, and people cleared out of its path. Despite the August Guard's presence, the number of people hiding under cloaks or hoods had increased, and a furtiveness dominated the people's manner. It showed in the way that women looked over their shoulders and men held themselves up to look stronger, and shadows darted in and out of alleys, bypassing the guards as they spread lies and stolen goods. There were no more children on the streets.

The palace loomed, that white monolith in the heart of

the city, and Áed's gut twisted at the sight. Directly beneath the carriage's wheels, the dungeon coiled like a ball of worms through the ground, and Áed could almost sense its chill under his feet. As the carriage and its occupants wound their way nearer to the palace, Áed found his fingers itching for heat. He curled them as tightly as he could and ignored the urge.

People noticed the carriage. Cynwrig's face was familiar to them, and they glanced at him and then quickly back at their feet. Their obvious wariness only drew them closer, as people are attracted like moths to flame to anything out of the ordinary. By the time the General guided the horse to a stop, a crowd had gathered around the palace gates that was pretending not to be a crowd at all.

The realization of what he was about to do hit Áed squarely and suddenly, as if he had not been bracing himself for it for weeks. The throne of a kingdom and the responsibility it brought were about to land upon his shoulders, the tattooed and scarred shoulders of Áed from the Maze, the shoulders of a recently-illiterate bastard who still couldn't write, the finery-and-gem-clad shoulders of someone who had never worn finery or gems until that morning. He pressed his forehead against the cool window as Boudicca pushed her door open and swished out.

A worried Ronan tapped Áed's shoulder, and Áed gave him a quick smile and a hug before pushing his door open. He didn't want time to change his mind.

He strode over the white cobblestones toward Cynwrig, ignoring the increasingly interested glances from the not-crowd in the corners of his vision. The General looked him up and down, certainly taking in the flush that tinted Áed's cheeks and the muscles twitching in his hands. "Are you alright?"

Áed nodded curtly.

Boudicca put a hand briefly on Áed's shoulder, but let it slip off before anybody's eye could catch on the motion. There was wisdom in that. He shouldn't show weakness by accepting comfort, no matter how much he wanted it.

Áed fell into step in front of Cynwrig, who walked a half-pace behind while Boudicca and Ronan followed. The horse nickered, and Áed decided to believe that it was wishing him good luck. Their footsteps echoed against the walls of the palace as they approached, and then they quieted, those echoes fading into silence. The guard on duty, a young man with daffodil-colored eyes and mousy hair, snapped smartly to attention and focused on Cynwrig. "General!"

Cynwrig nodded. "Quinn." He gestured with his chin toward the door, and the guard, Quinn, moved to open it. As his attention diverged from his general's face, though, his gaze slid over Áed, and the man froze.

His eyes flicked from Cynwrig to Áed, then back to Cynwrig.

Cynwrig raised an eyebrow. "The door, Quinn."

The guard's flabbergasted stare raced over Áed's clothes, the paint, Áed's eyes and hair. "Are… is that… General, is that—"

Cynwrig nodded shortly. "This is your future king. You had best open that door."

Quinn was still spellbound and stuttering. "But I thought… everyone said… Óengus—"

"Yes," Áed replied. His voice, he was impressed to note, held steady even as the rotten stench of the torturer's breath and the gleam of the man's instruments flashed through his memory.

Cynwrig leveled a cold glare at Quinn, who snapped out of it. The guard hurried to pull the door wide. "My apologies, Your Grace, and General Cynwrig, please forgive me." He bowed deeply, and the group swept through.

The palace had become no less revolting in the absence of a monarch. When Boudicca reached out to touch a jewel-encrusted candle sconce with something like awe on her face, Áed could only scowl, though he tried to force his features into the same regal blankness as Cynwrig's.

The General was businesslike. "Right," he directed. "Áed, come with me. Ronan, go with Boudicca. You remember where to go, Boudie?"

She nodded, squeezed Ronan's hand, and together they broke off down a different hallway.

"Perfect." Cynwrig said. "Áed, I'll show you to the throne room and then inform the Council of the King."

Áed followed him until the gilded door to the throne room loomed malevolently before them. The softness of the fallen-gem light from beyond made his heart race as Cynwrig pushed it open, and Áed's palms began to sweat so that it took nearly all of his composure to step over the threshold onto the marble.

The cavernous chamber whispered with shifting replies as the two of them crossed to the spur of the throne. The shadow of Seisyll lurking around the edges of the room did little to ease Áed's jitters.

The General squared his shoulders, collected and confidant. "I'll be back."

⸙

Áed clicked his tongue experimentally, and the sound reverberated once, twice, and a third time as it fractured on the walls and returned. The sound bounced, it was lively, and it sprang across the distance with crisp energy. Quiet expanded into hollow, faraway echoes in the arching space; the entire room sighed as Áed let out a breath. It felt dangerous to speak. Anyone could hear.

The wait didn't last long before a new sound bubbled from the end of the hall. Áed drew himself up in false confidence as the first person entered the room, followed by another, and then another. As murmurs and hushed voices filled the space, Áed could only hope that the men wouldn't set upon him, vengeful and frothing, for the death of their king, because he would be sorely outnumbered in a fight. Then he realized that he'd reverted back to his old way of thinking, where every person was a threat, and so he must have been more anxious than he'd realized. The Councilors he saw had more fat around their middles than murderous intent in their eyes.

A few bold souls strode quickly toward Áed, followed by their warier peers. Finally, a few men ambled in slowly, as if it was no matter to them whether or not they had a king. Áed determined to keep an eye on them.

The Council stopped short about ten feet from where Áed stood near the throne and gaped, unwilling to draw nearer. Áed linked his hands behind his back. "Good afternoon, Councilors."

There were a few uncertain replies.

"I am Áed, son of Seisyll." The words felt wrong, but he spoke them anyway. The truth wouldn't stop being true because he avoided it. "And heir to the throne."

For just one fragile, tenuous moment, the great hall stayed quiet save for the retreating echoes of his voice.

Then it exploded into noise.

Áed held up his hands to quiet the crowd, and all of the councilors' eyes fixated upon their forms. Just like that, the focus of the room snapped to him, and a little shiver ran over his skin. "Thank you." He cleared his throat and did a quick sweep of the crowd for Elisedd, but fortunately, the Master of the Northeastern Quarter seemed to be absent. Councilors retreated before him as Áed stepped off the dais. "It's true that Seisyll is no more, but I *am* his son. It is my right that you welcome me."

His argument was met not by an uproar but a muted buzz of voices, and Áed nearly bit his lip. Entitlement in his words was a necessity. It was a show of power to speak in such a way, and these men respected that.

Still, without their trust, their respect meant little.

"I would like to be open with you," Áed said, spreading his arms. "You may ask me what you will."

At first, the crowd split around him as he walked through it, and councilors avoided being the first to present themselves. Clearly, nobody had prepared. Even the men who looked willing to step forward were cowed by the expressions of their peers, and the throne room remained silent, save for the hush of uncertain whispers. Áed had to maneuver himself before a councilor and engage him in unwilling conversation before anyone would approach, but before long a small cluster of interested councilors were listening in. Áed felt as though he was channeling Ninian; Ninian was rarely more at ease than amidst a crowd, and Áed had learned from his easy mannerisms.

Áed intrigued the Council of the King. They wanted to know about his hands, his eyes, how he had lived in Smudge. They wanted to know how Seisyll had died, and Áed explained that the king's robes had caught fire on one of the torches that lined the hall. Given Seisyll's madness, the old king's story about a man holding fire in his hands was easily dismissed, and Áed accepted the Council's sympathy for being the victim of such a terrible rumor. More delicately, one of the councilors asked about Áed's time in the dungeons and the punishment he'd suffered. Instead of replying, for the words might still quiver in this throat, Áed pulled aside his scarf and let the men crane their necks around one another to see the top of the tattoos.

Councilors gaped and gasped, and some looked faintly sick, but it changed the tenor of the room. Perhaps it humbled them. Perhaps they respected him for surviving.

Eventually, the questions trickled to a stop, and the Council no longer looked at him leerily. "Councilors," Áed addressed them, raising his voice so that the room quieted. It was a powerful feeling. "I'm going to retire for today. We will talk further tomorrow."

Without waiting for the councilors to say anything, because he didn't want his words to be construed as a request, he nodded to the General and walked through the crowd, smiling at the Council's goodbyes.

It was time to find Boudicca and Ronan. He hurried down the hall at a fast walk, Cynwrig wordlessly ahead of him. He didn't want to be caught by any advisors before he had a chance to clear his head, so when they reached the stairs, Áed bounded up two at a time and let Cynwrig speed up to match his pace.

Gilt walls transitioned to white stone as Cynwrig led him through the palace, and beyond that, candlelight gave way to sun and fresh air. They passed into an arching walkway that cut through the gardens in the palace courtyards, and the wind, fresh with the smells of flowers and clean soil, filled Áed's lungs and helped breeze the nerves from his head. A final door greeted them past the courtyards, which opened to a dizzying spiral staircase that they followed up to what was now Áed's quarters.

The General's knuckles had scarcely rapped the door before Boudicca threw it open, and she stepped aside to let them in. "How did it go? Is the Council accepting?" She kept talking, but Áed missed everything else she said.

The room that he had just entered was not a room. He'd expected something like Boudicca's flat, maybe a little smaller. He had not expected arching windows whose glass was as fine as sugar, a floor whose colorful tiles were too artful to step on, or a sweeping staircase that arced weightlessly to a second floor.

"Áed?" Boudicca was saying, and he snapped to his senses as she nudged his arm. "Are you alright?"

"What? Yes, I'm alright." He shook his head in disbelief at a magnificent bookshelf in the corner of the room, stacked with beautiful volumes. Above him, an elegant chandelier held a multitude of white candles. "Where's Ronan?"

She gestured to the staircase. "Upstairs. I doubt he heard you come in."

Áed crossed over to the swooping staircase and took the steps one at a time, still amazed at the luxury around him. "Ronan?"

The boy's head popped out of one of the doors. "Áed?" He stepped into the hallway. "Did it go well?"

"That was my question," Boudicca's voice floated up from downstairs.

"Yes, I think," Áed responded to both of them. "At least, I don't think anyone hates me too passionately. How do you like it here?"

"It's better than I expected," Ronan confessed. "It's quiet."

"Can you show me your room?"

Ronan held the door open in invitation.

"Well, *ceann beag*," Áed said, stepping in. "This is nice." Empty shelves lined the walls, waiting to be filled, and Áed saw that Ronan had arranged his marbles on the nearest one. Beyond the windows, a dizzying drop plummeted into a garden far below, and the entire palace spread out before them, checkered with courtyards, walkways, and white verandas. From this direction, the great wilds were visible where the city dropped off, and the cliff plunged to grasslands ringed by those low, purple-blue mountains in the distance. "You have quite the view."

Áed sat down on the bed and slouched against the wall. After a moment of contemplation, Ronan sat beside him and leaned his head on Áed's shoulder. "You know what I keep thinking, Áed?"

The tone of his voice suggested his thoughts. "What?"

Ronan turned thoughtfully away from the cool breeze tumbling through the window. "I keep wondering what Ninian would say. If he were here."

Áed gave his shoulders a squeeze and didn't let go. "Oh, *ceann beag*. I wonder that all the time." Ronan looked up at him, and Áed leaned back so that the breeze ruffled Ronan's hair away from his face. "But I think he's watching."

Ronan nodded, a little smile on his lips. "I think so too."

CHAPTER TWENTY-NINE

ÁED MINDLESSLY RUBBED HIS thumb on the back of his neck under the soft scarf. Boudicca had gone home, and the General was elsewhere in the palace, probably ordering the Guard about and stubbornly not smiling. Outside, evening was dimming the day into colorless night.

There was one more thing that Áed wanted to do that night, something that had been bothering him in the back of his mind. The only problem was that, despite the duty he felt, the thought of completing the task himself made cold fingers of nausea spread through his stomach, and imagining the smell of the dungeon's air made goosebumps prick up on his arms.

That was fine. Judoc wouldn't want to see him, no matter Áed's intentions.

Áed crossed to the door and leaned into the hall, where two guards flanked the doorway. He addressed the one on the right. "You follow my orders, don't you?"

The guard, a dark-haired woman, nodded. "Yes, Your Grace. Yours and General Cynwrig's."

"I need you to do something for me." Áed explained what he wanted, and the guard bowed shortly.

"I'll fetch him."

"Thank you. Find a room for him, and tell him anything he wants to know."

The guard departed, and Áed retreated back into his chambers. Ronan's off-key humming floated down from upstairs, and Áed dropped onto the couch to wait.

Judoc had been Áed's only comfort during his time in the darkness, and yet Áed had left him feeling betrayed and alone. That wasn't entirely Áed's fault, but it wasn't entirely Judoc's either, and so the debt of gratitude that Áed owed the old man still had to be repaid. Hopefully Áed's guard inspired less terror than Áed would.

The beautiful chambers fell into darkness while Áed waited, and candlelight from Ronan's room made shadows on the walls that shifted like ghosts as the boy moved and the flame flickered. The warm candlelight was at odds with the cool darkness that waited beyond the windows, and Áed realized that from these chambers, despite their lofty height, he could not look toward the Maze. The Red Sea, the tipping buildings, the gray filth on the streets, and the ragged humans that scurried and fought among them were hidden from sight and thought. It would be so easy to ignore everything that happened on the other side of the Gut. It would be so easy to relax in his sumptuous new chambers, dine on fine foods, and walk through the gardens with Ronan, pretending he had forgotten.

But he wouldn't.

The long day had caught up with him enough to make his eyelids sag when a brisk knock at the door stopped him from dozing. Swiping at his eyes, he hurried over to answer it.

The guard he'd sent stood in the doorway, sharp and straight. "It's done, Your Grace."

"Thank you." He leaned back inside and called to Ronan

that he'd be back in a little while, then stepped out and closed the door behind him. "What did you tell him?"

"I told him I was there on your orders, and he asked how that could be. I explained that you were the heir to the throne, Your Grace, and he didn't say any more. He's in the chambers a floor below us, Your Grace." She gave a neat bow. "Will you go to see him now, Your Grace?"

"Yes. And you can call me Áed."

Looking startled, she made to follow him down the stairs. "Oh. Alright. Well, I'll accompany you."

"Thank you," he repeated.

She showed him down the stairs to an unassuming door and took up position beside it. Áed's focus, however, wasn't on her any longer as he raised his hand to knock.

There came no answer from within.

"Judoc?" he called tentatively. "Are you there?"

The old man, if he heard, didn't reply.

The door was unlocked, and Áed nudged it open to find a dark room that smelled of dust. Taking a candle from a bracket outside the door, he stepped inside, and the flame illuminated hulking forms of furniture lurking in uneven shadows. He squinted into the darkness and jumped back when, closer than he expected, a phantom-like form seemed to materialize before him. "Judoc?"

The phantom moved away and drifted into one of the skeletal chairs. "Áed."

"Yes." He took another step in, holding up the candle.

Judoc's pale silhouette made a humming sort of noise. "I didn't expect to see you again."

Áed took a deep, dusty breath and set the candle on a table. He couldn't think of what to say, but he recognized the distrust that still lurked in Judoc's voice.

With a thin hand, Judoc pointed accusingly to the candle. "What are you doing with that, anyway? Don't pretend you need it."

Casting a concerned glance at the guard, Áed hastened to close the door. "Judoc, please. I want to explain."

The wariness in the man's eyes didn't abate. "How much of what you told me in the dungeons was true?"

"All of it. I swear."

Judoc narrowed his eyes. "Now, I believe that you killed the king. But the lost loved one, the child who needs you, the torture… that was real?"

In response, Áed pushed up his sleeve and let the old man's eyes take in the cruel tattoos around his arm. "I never lied. About any of it."

A slightly less acerbic expression crept over Judoc's features. "I know what you are," he said, his voice wary and guttural. "You're one of them. The ones across the veil. I'll be damned if I know how you're here, but you can't deny it."

Áed took a chair and gave Judoc a questioning look, and Judoc nodded grudgingly. Áed sat, the seat creaking softly. "I don't deny it. Not entirely, anyway." Judoc's expression stiffened, and Áed propped his elbows on his knees. "I'm *half*. Half-fae." Áed could feel the old man's disbelief, then shock. "I only found out when I got out of the dungeon," he said. "Honestly, I didn't know what I was doing any more than you did."

Judoc mouthed the word. *Half…*

"Somehow, Seisyll managed to assault my mother. She burned him, but evidently not enough to stop him." Áed gestured to himself uncomfortably. "So here I am."

He could almost see the gears turning in Judoc's head, his distrust thrown by the truth. "When you burned the king…"

"He recognized my mother in me."

Judoc leaned forward. "Does it come easily to you? The

fire, the manipulation?"

"The fire does. I'm not manipulative, but I can read people." He nodded to Judoc. "You're feeling betrayed, not a little afraid, and you've had the last six weeks to resent your memory of me—that's hard to overcome. But it wasn't your very first impression, and the kindness you felt toward me when we first spoke is returning, just bit by bit. Now, you're curious, in a guarded kind of way."

Judoc interlaced his bony fingers on his knees. He didn't seem to believe Áed would hurt him, and that was progress. "That was impressive," he said slowly, and then his clear eyes flicked to look at Áed's hands. "I want you to show me the rest." He pointed to Áed's crooked knuckles. "Your fire. Show me."

Áed was hesitant, but Judoc fixed him with a stare against which he dared not argue. Áed chewed on his lip as he extended his hand and allowed the smallest flame that he could make to dance between his gnarled fingers. It rippled in a draft from the old room, colors shifting from gold to white at its source, and for a moment, it distracted him enough to grow. He quickly pulled the heat from his hand. "I'm better at controlling it now," he said, pushing both hands into his pockets. "But it's still tricky."

"Áed," Judoc said warningly, eyes still fixed on the place the fire had been. "You mustn't let anyone know about that."

"I know."

The old man leaned forward insistently, and his ratty beard brushed at his thighs. "I'm serious. I believe, now, that you didn't mean me harm, but I can't think of many who would give you a moment to explain. Fae on the throne? Áed, you'd be killed. You are not one of a well-loved breed."

Judoc's warning held weight; when he'd told Áed of the dangers of escaping prison, he'd very nearly been right about Áed's reward.

"In fact," he went on, "you must act with caution anyway. Whether or not they believe you killed Seisyll, and whether or not they know your little secret, you are the dead king's bastard son from the slums across the way. Not everybody will be pleased to have you on the throne, especially if they find they can't use you for their own ends. Which, given what you are, I suspect they shall."

"Ah."

Judoc looked at him sideways, his gray-clear irises full of the candlelight. "What? Has something already happened?"

"Maybe. I'm not sure." He recounted his meeting with Boudicca's stepfather, and the old man's face folded with the intensity of his listening.

Judoc frowned, his deeply-lined face uneasy. "Elisedd. I knew him when he was seven years younger. I say, that man." Judoc swayed his head slowly from side to side. "That man could talk his way into, out of, or alongside any situation the mind can create." He rubbed the back of a finger across his chin. "Are you meeting with the Council soon?"

"I plan to. There's a lot to talk about."

"You'd best be careful, Áed," Judoc said again. "My gut says it'll be awhile before you have more friends than enemies."

⌇⌇⌇

CHAPTER THIRTY

SOMEONE WAS KNOCKING on his door.

Áed pushed himself up, brushing sleep from his eyes, and ran his hands through his hair, which stuck up anyway. Boudicca had gone home, so the chambers held only Ronan and himself. He dragged himself out of bed and slipped on the shirt he'd worn the day before, yawning at the soft morning light and the polite round of knocking that came again.

The hall was quiet, though soft voices rose from beyond the door. Remembering Judoc's warning, Áed kept a hand behind the door, ready to defend himself if he had to, but his guards would surely not allow an obvious threat to approach. He opened the door a crack.

Elisedd stood beyond, his piss-yellow eyes examining his nails.

A second person, an unfamiliar young man with nearly-white hair, snapped to attention at the movement of the door, and Elisedd looked up a half-second later, almost lazily. "Elisedd," Áed greeted him warily, and nodded to the man whose name he didn't know.

Elisedd smiled greasily and bowed. "Áed, I'm honored to

see you again. Has the move to the palace been comfortable?" An undertone of distaste ran beneath his words.

Áed only held his tongue, waiting for Elisedd to state his business.

After a couple of uncomfortable seconds, Elisedd cleared his throat. "Allow me to introduce you to my son, Éamon. He is still a novice in the ways of the court, and I hope to educate him."

"Oh?"

Éamon offered an uncomfortable smile, but quickly looked away when his father shifted in front of him. Áed wasn't entirely sure what Éamon's education had to do with him, seeing as Áed wasn't particularly knowledgeable himself, but it occurred to him that that may have been Elisedd's underhanded point.

"Your ascendance to the throne provides a valuable lesson on the nuances of politics," Elisedd explained.

"Really." It still wasn't clear why Elisedd had come, but Áed didn't want to engage in a verbal dance. Not this early in the morning. "Then I'll offer some advice."

Elisedd blinked in surprise. "Why, of course."

Áed turned to Elisedd's son, who, he noticed, had his father's cheekbones but lacked his calculating eyes. "Inviting yourself to the private chambers of the Coming King and waking him early is not the best way to win his favor." He smiled. "It's just advice. But Elisedd should know better." Without waiting for either of them to say anything, he turned back inside.

He'd almost made it to the stairs when he heard footsteps behind him and turned to find Elisedd reaching for his shoulder. Automatically, Áed dodged the councilor's hand and sidestepped, and Elisedd lost his balance and stumbled to steady himself. When the man straightened, his face was flushed. "Áed—"

"What are you doing, Councilor?" Áed demanded.

"I have done nothing but try to serve Your Grace," the councilor managed, but his jaw was tight.

"I didn't ask for that." Dangerous or not, Áed felt instinctually that keeping Elisedd close was even more risky than pushing him away. Keeping him at arm's length might at least diminish the councilor's ability to use him.

"Then you're a fool," Elisedd snapped. Immediately he seemed to realize what he had said, for he pursed his lips and then closed his eyes. He drew a deep breath through his nose. "Your Grace."

Áed looked down his nose at him. For all his robes and power, Elisedd did not intimidate him. "Councilor, calm yourself."

Elisedd's eyes narrowed, confused for just a moment.

Still looking down on him, Áed inclined his head. "There's the door."

Elisedd reddened. For what Áed suspected was the first time in his life, sugared words didn't ooze smoothly off his tongue. "I… you—"

Áed just raised an eyebrow.

"Your Grace, I—" He exhaled sharply and closed his eyes, sparing Áed the sight of their slimy-looking irises. "In truth, I came to offer you my service once again." Stiffly, he bowed. "I hold influence over many members of the court. While they are not all *entirely* dedicated to you, Áed," —Áed noted the unspoken *'but I am'* in Elisedd's speech— "they are dedicated to me. Were that I could sway them to your side, but allegiances are not easily shifted, not allegiances forged over decades. Rather, I offer my influence to you."

Áed's perception didn't fail him. The transparent insult of Elisedd's fellow councilors, the suggestion that Áed could not garner allegiance on his own, the easy request that Áed offer more power to Elisedd by accepting his offer… those were all grotesque attempts to manipulate him. It was difficult to tell whether Elisedd was using those attempts to shield his subtler message, but it didn't matter. Áed recognized the threat.

Elisedd had influence.

There were councilors who had little loyalty to the throne, and a great deal of loyalty to the Master of the Northeastern Quarter.

Be careful, Elisedd was warning. *I can ruin you.*

Áed kept his face mask-like as he offered a thin smile. "Thank you, Elisedd," he said. "That's kind."

He bowed low. "Anything for the Coming King."

"I know that reputations are fragile," Áed continued, and thought he saw a strange expression flicker across Elisedd's brow. "Perhaps it's wise for both of us to tread carefully."

There. A threat and a peace offering, neatly packaged.

He was *good* at this.

Elisedd's face revealed nothing as he walked slowly down the stairs, beckoned to his son, and departed.

⁂

After working slowly through a book in one of his chamber's soft armchairs, Áed opened a window and let the air flood in to wake him properly. It brought the sounds of a waking palace with it. The courtyards buzzed as gardeners tended the flowers, a cook selected herbs and fruits for the kitchen, and a lady sat on a wicker bench to soak in the early sun. While the palace itself was not as vivacious as Áed had imagined, court life flourished beyond its walls; realization dawned on Áed that at that very moment, he felt like a king surveying his domain.

He would meet with the Council again today, but this time, it wouldn't just be pleasantries. When he'd told Judoc there was a lot to talk about, he'd understated the truth. Not only would he have to ascertain the Council members' true loyalties, but the more tangible issue of his coronation needed to be addressed, plans arranged and set in motion, and customs hastily learnt. Even with the cool morning breeze sweeping in from the window, the politics of it made him want to go back to bed.

For the second time that morning, a knock sounded at the door. Thinking perhaps it was Boudicca, he hurried over to answer it before the knocking woke Ronan.

Instead of Boudicca in a flame-colored dress or the General being dutifully polite, a man with about eighteen years stood outside the door. Though he hadn't particularly caught Áed's attention the first time they'd met, he recognized the young man immediately. "Éamon."

Elisedd's son bowed, and his hair, pale as corn silk, obscured periwinkle eyes. "Your Grace."

Áed looked around the narrow hall, but it was empty save for Éamon and Áed's guards. There was a pleasant lack of conniving about Éamon's manner; his father oozed untrustworthiness, but the young man had an earnestness in his expression. "What brings you here again?"

"In truth, Your Grace, I came to apologize." Éamon glanced left and right, as though Elisedd could be listening. "May I please come in?" Áed considered his face, found no malice, and stepped aside. Éamon nodded gratefully and moved inside, and Áed closed the door. Once inside, Éamon relaxed visibly. "Your Grace, I wanted to beg your pardon for my father's actions earlier. He isn't used to people seeing through him." At that, a faint smile touched Éamon's lips, and they parted over perfect teeth. "I admit, it was pleasant to watch."

Áed regarded him with interest. He was certain that Éamon was there of his own purpose. Elisedd hadn't sent him. Besides, Boudicca had spoken highly of her step-brother, and Áed trusted Boudicca. "You aren't much like Elisedd, are you?"

Éamon shook his head. "No, Your Grace. I believe I take after my mother."

"I know the feeling," Áed said under his breath. Then he raised his voice and did his best to make it sound kingly. "I appreciate the apology. Thank you for coming."

Éamon nodded, but didn't move to leave. "Pardon, Your Grace, but there's something else."

Áed leaned against the wall and examined the young man's eyes. "What's that?"

"It's just…" Éamon glanced about again, though they were alone in the antechamber. "A warning, I suppose."

"A warning?" Áed quit leaning on the wall.

Éamon nodded again. "Of sorts. I don't have any evidence except for what I know of my father, but I'll tell you that I've never seen him as angry as he is now." Éamon's fingers found the hem of his shirt and lifted it up, and he turned so that Áed could see the clear mark of a bruising handprint on the toasted-sugar-colored skin of his back. A single strike, furious and controlled. "I'm not even the object of his anger." Éamon let his shirt fall, and more of Áed's reservations evaporated. If Elisedd's son was willing to risk his father's rage to come to Áed, then Áed was less chary of trusting him. "Be careful of him, Your Grace. *You* are the one he wants to hurt." Éamon rubbed the bruise on his back and winced faintly. "And I believe he will try."

"Thank you," Áed said again, but this time, there wasn't much kingly about the words. His gratitude was genuine. He had already pegged Elisedd as one to keep an eye on, but the risk Éamon was taking meant that the danger was serious. "Here," he said. "Boudicca left some herbs with me. I have something that'll clear that bruise."

Éamon brightened a little. "Really?"

Áed nodded. "It works, I can attest to it." He led Éamon to the table and sifted through the basket of food and supplies that Boudicca had brought earlier. "Here." He awkwardly gripped the smooth bottle and offered it to Éamon, who took it. "I'll be careful of Elisedd." He nodded at Éamon's back. "Perhaps you should be, too."

Éamon shrugged. "I don't think he'd do real damage." He rolled his eyes and pocketed the balm. "I'm just his favorite child."

"Rotten bastard." The words were out of Áed's mouth before he could catch them, and he immediately bit his tongue. "Sorry." That hadn't been very regal at all.

But Éamon only laughed. "Gods, I like you better than Seisyll." Then he hastily added, "Your Grace."

Áed waved it off. "Call me Áed. Please."

Éamon's chuckle turned into a grin. "Well, Áed, I like you much better than Seisyll. Quite frankly, I'm hopeful that my father doesn't win this one. I've seen that too many times, and it's taken its toll on me." He put his hands in his pockets as he turned toward the door. "Oh," he said as he made to step out. His broad shoulders turned back toward Áed. "I hardly ever get to see them, so if it's no trouble, could you give my love to Boudicca? And my brother, too?"

"Of course."

"Good luck with the Council today, Áed." Éamon smiled, showing those perfect teeth again. "It was a pleasure to properly meet you."

⌇⌇⌇

CHAPTER THIRTY-ONE

BOUDICCA ARRIVED WITH BREAKFAST shortly after Ronan woke up, and they shared a quiet meal. Boudicca's face lit up when Áed told her about Éamon, and she smiled and sat back. "You know, Cynwrig never liked him much, but Éamon and I always got on well. He's kind." She tilted her head. "And do you know, I doubt he has more than a year or two on you. Perhaps you two would be friends."

They finished breakfast, and Ronan, black hair puffy and tangled, gave Áed a hug and slouched back upstairs to wash up. "Ronan," Áed called up the stairs, and the boy turned at the landing. "I have to go talk to the Council, alright?"

"I'll be staying here," Boudicca added. "We can play marbles if you like."

"Alright." Ronan gave Áed a little wave. "Good luck, Áed."

"Thanks, *ceann beag*. I'll be back before you know it."

He took another bit of bread, and Boudicca trapped him in a pleasant hug before he left. When he closed the door behind him, his guards stood at attention. "Are you going to the Council Chamber, Your Grace?" asked the guard who had fetched Judoc.

"I am."

The guards' presence was welcome as they walked with him through the chilly, vaulted halls. Áed didn't know why he had imagined the palace as a bustling hub of life and politics with couriers rushing to and fro or nobles sweeping through the corridors in their finery, but the reality of the stillness brought an eerie relief.

"Áed, Your Grace!"

Áed startled; he'd been too focused to have noticed Elisedd, but now the man emerged from where he'd leaned easily behind one of the corridor's vaulted ribs. He was wearing dark gray that day, his charcoal robes trimmed with black fur and adorned with silver embroidery, and he looked like a plume of smoke as his clothing shifted with his stride.

Elisedd broke into a conspiratorial smile. "Áed, I'm so pleased to have found you. You're the very man I need to see right now."

Áed raised an eyebrow. Elisedd was in high spirits, very clearly recovered from the embarrassment of that morning, and Áed did not like that at all. "Is that so?"

"Indeed, indeed. Although, I regret to say that I wish to speak to you of a rather delicate topic, so perhaps we may find privacy a moment?"

Though Elisedd's face remained composed, Áed could feel the man's glee beneath the tempered smile. "What topic?"

Elisedd pressed his lips together, forehead wrinkling in affected concern. "I'm afraid it pertains to you, Your Grace. Come, walk with me, there's a private place this way."

"I'm busy at the moment, Councilor." Áed said the words experimentally, and their effect told him what he needed to know.

Elisedd's smile twitched up at the corner. "Oh, Áed," he

said, his voice almost singsong in his giddiness. "I think you have time for me."

This couldn't be good.

Áed reluctantly followed Elisedd down a branch of the hallway, where the Master of the Northeastern Quarter unlocked a door with a key from his pocket. "Right this way, Your Grace." Beyond the door was a small room, adorned with nothing but a table. Shelves lined the wall, heavy with papers and leather-bound ledgers. "This room houses the Council records," Elisedd said, closing the door behind them as Áed's guards stationed themselves outside the entrance. "It's as private as any place."

"Why have you brought me here?" Áed crossed his arms, but Elisedd didn't note his impatience. The man took his time, finding the table and leaning against the edge, and then he simply sighed and fixed Áed with a stare.

"Áed," he said, his smile growing once again. This time, it was patronizing. "You impress me, you know." He ran a hand along the edge of the table, then brushed the dust off on his robe. It left a pale streak against the dark garment. "I'm sure if you tried to guess why I've brought you here, a young man of your intuition could find the truth."

Áed didn't like the way Elisedd had said 'intuition.' Something about that word in particular made Áed narrow his eyes at the silver-bearded man who leaned so casually on the table. "Perhaps you overestimate my intuition," he said slowly, choosing to acknowledge nothing. All he felt was Elisedd's excitement, and instinctive uneasiness in his own gut that warned him to tread carefully.

But Elisedd only sighed, still smirking. "Somehow, I think not." Áed regarded him warily as the man pushed away from the table, but Elisedd only ambled to the side of the room. "Somehow, I think that you're reading my every intention, easy as breathing."

In ainm dé. But Elisedd didn't know. There was no way he could know.

No expression crossed Áed's face. "Strange flattery, Elisedd. What do you hope to achieve with it?"

Elisedd sighed. "Your Grace, why do you assume that I flatter you?" He absently ran a hand across the records on the shelf beside him. "I've been doing some research—such dull work befits men of my humble status—and I thought it my duty to inform you of my findings."

The councilor, unable to remain still, made his way back to the table. Áed hadn't moved, and he watched Elisedd carefully. "Really."

The Quarter-Master folded his hands in front of him. "Your Grace, I've been examining some interesting stories." He wetted his lips. "I started with the story of our murdered King."

Áed's breath caught at 'murdered.'

Elisedd continued, observant eyes on Áed's face. "I was there, you know, as the poor man died, and I heard his side of the events. He said that you pushed him, and with your touch came fire." He adjusted his robes easily. "So I went to the throne room, and I stood in the place where he'd fallen, and I found that the nearest wall-torch was some fifty paces away."

"He ran," Áed said. "He was panicking."

"Perhaps," Elisedd said thoughtfully. "Or perhaps not." The councilor was opposite the table from Áed, and he slowly began to move around the edge. "I decided to follow a hunch. Since this morning, I've been reading some interesting things—care to guess?"

"Not particularly." If Áed left now, even if he made an excuse to leave, he knew it would affirm Elisedd's theory.

"I'm certain that it's already crossed your mind," Elisedd replied. "You see, I started reading about our neighbors across the veil. The *fae*." He shrugged, but the smile on his face ruined his nonchalance. "Fascinating, truly. Did you know, for example, that all of the fae share the same eyes?" His smile turned into a grin, spreading across his face. "It's said they're as red as blood. Or, perhaps more astutely, fire. Their eyes are all red as burning, deadly fire."

Áed managed what he hoped was a bored sigh. "This is ridiculous, Elisedd."

"Ah, please, Your Grace, I haven't finished." The councilor cleared his throat. "I found, too, that there's a certain… *perception* with which the fae are gifted. They know a man's intent at the sight of his face, or perhaps a word of his voice—the legends disagree on that point, but they concur that the emotions of a human being reveal themselves to the fae as naturally as if they were read from a book.

"And finally, the fire." Elisedd spread his hands. "The legends say that, incredible as it is, the fae can call fire to their bodies. They can walk in it, can control it with a thought." He shook his head. "*Amazing*, isn't it?"

"You sound like a child," Áed retorted. Boudicca's and Judoc's warnings were clamoring in his head like alarm bells, and his mind was moving quickly. "This is your research? You're grasping at straws, my friend, and you're humiliating yourself."

Elisedd was quiet for a breath. Then: "Have I touched a nerve?"

Áed rolled his red, red eyes. "You've brought me here to accuse me of what? Of being one of the fae? *Listen* to yourself."

"I have been," Elisedd replied softly. "And I've found myself very rational." He took another step in Áed's direction. "The late king was a human. And yet it seems that you, Áed, are not. Tell me, what does that make you?"

"I don't have to waste my time with this." Áed turned to

the door, heart hammering.

Elisedd's voice stopped him cold. "I wouldn't," the councilor said quietly, and the simple words were full of deep, deep threat. The texture of them rolled over Áed, powerful and horrible, and he shuddered at the sensation of their intent. "Áed," Elisedd said amicably, "I have no issue with your claim to the throne. I advocated it, and I stand by that. But the rest of the court, the rest of the *city*..." He clucked his tongue and shook his head in mock regret. "I'm afraid that they wouldn't be so openminded." As if his point needed elaboration, the councilor drew a finger delicately across his throat. "I'm quite sure that the August Guard would be more than a match, even against fae fire."

One foot before the other, Áed turned back to face the Master of the Northeastern Quarter. "You can prove nothing."

But Elisedd only echoed Áed's instinct: "I don't *need* to."

Áed nodded slowly. "Alright." He ran his tongue across his bottom lip, taking a slow breath. "So this is to be a game of threats, then." Before Elisedd could respond, Áed had crossed the room to stand directly in front of him. Áed was taller by only an inch or so, but the man cringed gratifyingly at the power in Áed's eyes. "I am better at this than you are," Áed murmured. "I *can* read your intent." He rested a hand on the councilor's shoulder, right at the base of his neck, and felt Elisedd's pulse. A thought from Áed, and that pulse would boil away. Áed spoke quietly. "I know exactly how afraid you are to have me so near you, and I can tell you that your fear is well-placed. I can tell you, too, that I am capable of swaying every man in that Council chamber until they would roast you on a spit at my command, and I can tell you that you don't stand a *chance*." He moved a hair closer, until Elisedd was pressed against the table. "And if that doesn't pacify me, I'll just burn your head off your shoulders."

He took a step back and lifted his hand, letting Elisedd swallow and take a few deep breaths.

"Don't you dare," Áed said, "threaten me."

Without waiting for the man to answer, Áed turned and marched out of the room.

⌇⌇⌇

Alone with his guards in the hallway, Áed allowed himself a few deep, stabilizing breaths.

Elisedd knew.

Áed wasn't naive, and he understood the Quarter-Master's intent. Elisedd wanted to hold that secret over Áed's head, threatening to let it slip if Áed didn't act as his puppet. But with Áed's threat in return, what was to stop Elisedd from deciding that Áed was too dangerous to be worth the effort?

He needed to collect himself. He would address the Council briefly, putting this in the back of his mind for a moment; so long as Áed was in the council-chamber, he didn't think Elisedd would attempt anything. But Áed knew that Elisedd had just established himself as the most dangerous threat in the city, and when the opportunity arose, Áed would have to take action.

With another long breath, he nodded to his guards and set off for the Council of the King.

The buzz of voices echoed down the hallway from the Council chamber, so Áed needed no direction once he and his guards drew close. The guards wordlessly took up positions on either side of the great wooden doors; Áed stopped, observed how the point of the arch met the very center of a seam in the masonry above, and straightened his shoulders.

Steeling himself, he placed one hand on each side of the double doors and pressed them open.

The moment he did, a ripple of silence fanned out across the room.

It was tempting to freeze in the doorway, pinned in place by the stares, but he propelled himself to the front of the room as if he belonged there. "Good morning, Councilors. I trust you are all well?"

A middle-aged councilor whose eyebrows begged reminiscence of spiny sea-urchins upon his forehead stepped forward. He bowed deeply, to the point where his cloak spilled onto the floor. "Your Grace. Shall we commence with the business of the Council?"

Áed nodded with as much authority as he could. "Absolutely."

The councilor nodded and moistened his lips. "I am Lord Muir, Your Grace. As you surely know, the August Guard has overseen the kingdom since the departure of King Seisyll."

Áed nodded. "I'm aware."

"This must change. Your Grace, Suibhne is in a strange position."

Áed inclined his chin toward the man, listening, forcing himself to concentrate on what was happening around him rather than what had just happened in the dusty record room.

"The Council may debate among ourselves all we want, yet there is little we can act upon without a king." A swell of murmured assent rose and fell. "The people need a leader. The August Guard serves admirably, but its power is limited. Duty is upon us to *govern.* Fortunately, fate has shown us the way." Lord Muir spread his arms wide, gathering the entire chamber of councilors into his speech, though a few councilors did not attempt to hide their disdain. "It falls on the members of this Council to crown the next king, and the law allows no dispute as to who that must be."

Áed let the words brush over him, and he permitted no emotion to cross his face.

"Our only enemy, Your Grace, is time."

"Explain."

The man's shoulders rose and fell in a heavy shrug that seemed to bear the weight of the room. He handled the attention of the Council far more easily than Áed did, though perhaps Áed could achieve such calm through practice. "Suibhne cannot carry on this way, Your Grace, and many of us fear that we've waited too long already." A hint of supplication crept into his voice. "Our circumstance is very unusual, indeed. We never contemplated such an heir from Seisyll, nor a king from Smudge. Never has the throne changed occupants in such an *unexpected* manner. Even so, you must be crowned."

"When?" Áed said, taking a step toward Lord Muir and ignoring the reverberation of a few dissatisfied grumbles. He wasn't intimidated, no. No, his palms weren't sweating.

There was a collective hush in the hall as every man waited for the councilor to respond. "Well, Your Grace, if it would suit you…" Muir looked to the assembly as if reaffirming the support of his peers. A couple nodding heads encouraged him, and he turned back to Áed with an apologetic smile. "Tomorrow."

Áed blinked. "Tomorrow?"

The councilor nodded. "Your Grace, the Council of the King is nothing without a king to counsel. If we also consider the civil order that is currently dissolving—there are, Your Grace, many people who wish for your place, and many who would stop them, and many who would serve their own devices—haste is very necessary." He shrugged. "It's not completely unusual. The Queen Fiona, who ruled before Seisyll, was coronated the same day as her father's funeral."

Áed forced a thoughtful nod. This was not what he had expected; he'd been ready for a few weeks of acclimating to court life and getting to know his advisors. He had thought, perhaps foolishly, that he had more time.

Lord Muir bowed once again and spread his arms regretfully. "We will send someone tomorrow to help you to prepare."

"Thank you," Áed said stiffly.

Lord Muir who, for his honesty, Áed was beginning to like, readjusted his slipping cloak. "We can discuss the details of the ceremony whenever Your Grace is ready."

Áed did not need time to think that over. He wanted information quickly so he had time to sort through it. "Now seems as good a time as any."

"Then by all means, Your Grace," the councilor replied, giving up on his crooked cloak much the same way he must have given up on his eyebrows. "Let us go to someplace quiet where we can talk." With a flick of his wrist, he summoned a man from among the councilors, and together they attended Áed to a table at the edge of the room with a number of chairs whose worn cushions attested to a long life of use. "Forgive the furniture, Your Grace," the councilor apologized. "It is intended for men of humbler status."

"Although his Grace is unlikely to complain, I would expect," the second advisor mused.

Lord Muir spoke sharply to his companion. "Mind your place, Lord Ross."

Ross's beady eyes slid smoothly back to Áed. "I meant no harm, Your Grace."

Lord Muir cleared his throat with a sound like a wet mop and rubbed his hands together. "Your Grace, this is Lord Ross, head of the silversmiths' guild. As I introduced myself before, I am Lord Muir, Master of the Southwestern

Quarter. We will attempt to be of service in any way that we can." As he spoke, his eyebrows crept downward with earnestness. "Our state of affairs is unusual. I pray that you do not take easy offense."

"Not at all." The Councilors were still standing, and Áed sat without invitation. The other two men followed suit with a faint air of surprise. Áed waited until they were both seated before he drew a deep breath. It tasted of wax, paper, and ink. "I would like to get to the matter at hand, if you don't mind."

"Are you impatient, Your Grace?"

The question came from Ross, though Muir shot him another glare. It was hard for Áed to resist the urge to shrug nonchalantly. He didn't need to supply an answer. Instead, he turned to Muir and rested his wrists on the table, cutting Ross out of the conversation. "Lord Muir, I presume that the Council has prepared a plan?"

Muir nodded. "Yes, Your Grace. With your assent, the ceremony will begin tomorrow evening. Around midday, we will send servants to prepare you." Muir drew a deep breath and settled more comfortably into the chair. "If you require any accommodations, we will surely adapt."

For just a moment, Áed almost rubbed his eyes with his thumbs, or pinched his lower lip in thought, or pushed his hair back the way he did when he was overwhelmed. Anxiety incited the impulse, and arresting it forced him to confront his nerves. He drew a deep breath and allowed himself a moment of solitude behind closed eyes. Of course he was anxious. Why wouldn't he be? "And who will be present at the coronation?"

"The entire court, Your Grace," Muir replied promptly. He spread his hands. "And, of course, the August Guard."

A quick laugh trailed under Áed's breath before he could stop it, and Muir offered an amenable smile. Áed let out a sharp sigh to get a handle on his nerves. "How will the ceremony proceed?"

Muir, though seated, endeavored to bow, and the result was that his forehead nearly smacked the table. He didn't notice, because he'd clearly been waiting for the time to answer that very question. "If it pleases Your Grace, Lord Ross and I will accompany you to the throne room and explain all in detail."

⌇⌇⌇

CHAPTER THIRTY-TWO

ELISEDD WAS WAITING FOR HIM in the hallway, hands folded behind his back, when Áed finally stepped out of the throne room with Lords Muir and Ross. Éamon stood behind his father with his head down. Muir and Ross bowed their goodbyes, and Elisedd flicked up a calculating eyebrow and fell into step next to Áed. "Your Grace, if I may have a moment of your time?"

Áed glanced to Elisedd's hands, which were twitching. Everything about the councilor was on high alert, and Áed was no different in that regard. "What is it?"

The man forced a bow, and a vein popped in his forehead despite the calm of his expression. "I spoke very inappropriately this morning," he said carefully. "I would like to make it up to you."

Something was afoot, that was certain. Áed didn't know what action the Councilor had planned, but he was wise enough to be wary of it. Áed glanced to Éamon, but Elisedd's son had looked away.

"Your Grace, it would set me at ease if I could show you my remorse. Please, won't you give me just a moment?"

This time, when Áed looked back to Éamon, the young

man didn't turn quickly enough. A second was long enough for Áed to see the caution in his face and the gigantic, fresh bruise over his right eye. Áed stopped walking and faced Elisedd, but turned his body to include Éamon. "Is everything alright, Councilor?" He shot Éamon a concerned look with the words, but Éamon wouldn't meet his eyes. He looked a little dazed.

"Hm?" Elisedd followed Áed's eyes to his son's injury, and Áed could tell Elisedd was pleased that Áed had noticed. "Oh, Éamon? He fell, Your Grace."

The lie tasted bitter, Áed could sense it in the air. He looked again to Éamon.

Éamon flicked a nervous glance to Elisedd, which affirmed Áed's suspicion. "Yes, Your Grace," he said quietly. "I fell."

Elisedd raised that eyebrow again, sliding his gaze from his son to Áed. "Your Grace, it's very kind of you to care. I don't think he'll make the same mistake again, but perhaps it would be best if he rested for a while. I wouldn't want him to fall again. Please, won't you accompany the two of us back to my suite?"

Áed gritted his teeth as Elisedd's words hit their mark, and he recognized the situation: Elisedd had shifted tactics. No longer did it matter if Áed perceived Elisedd's intent—in fact, the councilor was counting on Áed to understand the threat. Elisedd could not fool or blackmail Áed into doing what he asked, but he could still leave Áed very little choice. "Fine," Áed said softly, and he felt the undercurrent of heat beneath his voice. He would not leave Éamon to suffer for him. "My guards will follow."

A decaying kind of smile crept over Elisedd's face, and he set off down the hallway at a brisk walk. Áed lagged behind for a moment where Éamon hadn't moved. Now Elisedd's son looked at him straight, if a little vacantly, and Áed saw that his black eye was truly impressive even though it had not yet fully bloomed. A gash, dark with blood, cut through his eyebrow and cheekbone, and Éamon's blue-violet eyes weren't quite focused.

"What did he do?" Áed asked quietly.

Éamon's fingertips found the cut on his cheek and came away blotted with half-dried blood. "Used a candlestick."

"Did he find out what you did? This morning?" Áed didn't bother to ask if Éamon was alright—he knew the answer to that.

Éamon broke his stare at the blood on his fingers, blinking slowly. "Maybe. I don't know." Farther up the hall, Elisedd stopped, turned, waited. Éamon squinted at his father's form and started forward. "Áed, you shouldn't talk to me. Please. I'm sorry."

Áed bit his lip and nodded, and he beckoned to his guards before following Éamon and Elisedd. Elisedd waited for his son to catch up to him before putting an arm around Éamon's shoulders and drawing his head sharply toward the young man's ear. Éamon stiffened, and Elisedd pushed him away again.

Elisedd's chambers, as Áed was unsurprised to discover, were cold. The opulent carpet and the framed portraits that hung, all-seeing, over the doorway didn't bring any sense of home to the place; no evidence of habitation appeared amongst the upholstered chairs and the wall hangings. The man gestured vaguely to his son. "Éamon, fetch some wine." Éamon cringed, and Elisedd glared at him with danger in his eyes. "Do as I say."

Áed watched Éamon's retreating back, shoulders unbowed but tense.

The Master of the Northeastern Quarter bowed deeply to Áed, though his face rebelled enough for Áed to see how that chafed. There was something dancing in his eyes. "Your Grace, forgive my humble lodgings. I'm unused to entertaining those of your status. Oh, please, do sit."

Áed sat slowly, and Elisedd, a polite moment later, did the same. Áed was still in the process of discerning Elisedd's ultimate motive, but every pore in his body screamed at him that danger was rolling from the man like sweat. Could it be that the Quarter-Master had come with another threat? Or could it be that he planned to demand something from Áed, given his new influence? Áed's guards had stopped at the door, as always. Áed knew he could call them in quickly if the need arose, but he prayed it wouldn't.

Éamon returned with wine, and Áed noticed that his hands were shaking. A bead of sweat rolled down Éamon's temple, and the young man winced when the droplet ran along the plane of his face and melted into the cut on his cheek. Elisedd appraised his son coolly and accepted the glass from his son's right hand while Áed took the one on the left. Without offering his son a seat, Elisedd raised his cup. "Your Grace, to your health and prosperity." And he took a drink.

Éamon, left still standing, caught Áed's eye while his father's glare was hidden in the cup and mouthed the word: "*No.*" Then his gaze dropped to the ground as his father lowered the glass.

Áed wasn't foolish enough to drink anything that Elisedd offered him anyway, but now Elisedd was watching him expectantly. Curious, Áed held the wine under his nose and took a breath.

Well. That was familiar. Beneath the fruitiness of the elderberry, bitterness traced its tendrils.

Áed set the glass on the table and frowned at Elisedd thoughtfully. "You were going to do it yourself?"

Elisedd's eyes darted from the cup to Áed's face and frantically back again. "Your Grace?"

Folding his hands behind his head, Áed nodded to the

cup.

Elisedd's visage had grown faintly ruddy, which made his yellow eyes look like two infected welts. "I'm sorry, Your Grace. Is the wine not to your liking? My son will bring something else."

"Enough, Elisedd," Áed cut him off sharply. He pointed to the wine. "You thought that after *seventeen years* in Smudge I wouldn't recognize that?" Elisedd's face grew blotchy now, and his fist clenched and unclenched at his side. "I'm surprised at you."

Elisedd's mouth opened wide, snapped shut. No words came out.

"Then again," Áed went on, "not a bad choice of poison. Wouldn't work for oh, a day or so. Plenty of time to set someone up." Something dawned on Áed, and he let himself smile. "You've done this before, haven't you? When someone becomes more trouble than they're worth to you?" Yes, that was the truth. Áed could feel Elisedd's reaction, and he knew it was so. "It is your kind of murder, I think. Subtle, hard to trace, and you needn't get your hands dirty a bit."

"I didn't know," Elisedd said with a sickly smile. "The boy!" He raised a quivering, incriminating finger to his son, whose mouth fell open. "It was the boy, Your Grace, I swear it." He was gaining steam now. "He's not right in the head, Your Grace, I didn't realize the danger he posed—"

"Oh, shut your mouth." Áed turned to Éamon. "Can I trust you to tell me the truth?"

Éamon put a hand on the back of Áed's chair for balance, and the sharpness in his eyes was directed at Elisedd. "My father told me that if I didn't do as he said, he would kill my sister. I'm so sorry, Áed." He licked his lips. "I poisoned the wine. I tried to warn you."

Elisedd blanched, all ruddiness draining from his face.

"Éamon," he said softly. "You'd best be careful."

But Éamon shook his head. His eyes had grown more lucid with fear—of his father, or of Áed's retribution it was impossible to say. "I won't."

"Boy, if you're wise, you'll quiet yourself now." Elisedd's face was furious. "Your Grace, don't listen to him. He doesn't know of what he speaks."

"He would do it," Éamon posited desperately. "He would really kill Boudicca."

"Éamon," Elisedd snapped. "You have no proof."

"You were careful about that, yes. But not careful enough." Éamon pulled a little jar from his pocket, wrapped in a scrap of paper, and offered it to Áed. "This is what he gave me to use."

Elisedd's face went perfectly blank as Áed accepted the jar and loosed the paper from around it. It was a little slip of parchment, scratched in an unfamiliar hand and signed in a loose, curling scrawl.

"A receipt of purchase," Éamon said, and Áed looked more closely at the dark powder in the jar that he recognized as the bitterness in his drink. "Signed in my father's own hand."

Áed carefully read the receipt and found Éamon's words to be true. He set the jar and paper down and sighed. "Well," he said softly. "I'm afraid it's over, Elisedd."

Elisedd replied by staring.

Áed raised his voice. "Guards!" Immediately, the door flew open, and Áed's guards stood at attention. "Take this man away."

"Wait!" Elisedd protested as the guards took hold of his arms. "Where?"

"The dungeon for now. Not too deep, not yet." He didn't think he could condemn anyone—except perhaps Óengus—to the horror of those deep, lightless cells, no matter what they'd done.

The guards nodded perfunctorily and half-led, half-dragged a protesting Elisedd, whose silver words shattered uselessly on the ground.

Éamon covered his mouth with his hands and sank back down into the chair. There was a trembling in his shoulders. "I can't believe…" He looked up, and his lavender-blue eyes, one ringed by that horrible bruise, found Áed's face, wordless.

"I'm sorry."

But Éamon only closed his eyes. "No. That was too long in coming." He looked up at Áed, and the haze fell back over his expression. "Gods, Áed, I am so sorry. So sorry."

"Éamon, why didn't you tell me? If he threatened Boudicca, we could have had Cynwrig protecting her, even protecting you."

"I couldn't." Éamon grimaced. "I'm so sorry. Elisedd has people everywhere, and it would take a *word* from him to have Boudie dead in an hour. No time. No time at all." He cupped a palm to his eye. "My Gods. My head."

"Here, let me see." Áed nudged Éamon's hand out of the way. "You said he used a candlestick?"

"The one on the mantle."

Áed eyed the heavy bronze and gave a low whistle. "Was he trying to kill you?"

"Not sure." Éamon replaced his palm over the injury. "Usually he doesn't hit places that show." His uncovered eye blinked. "My head's all foggy."

Áed wasn't surprised. "Alright. Let me get rid of this wine, and we'll figure out what to do." He carried the glass to the room where Éamon had prepared it, and then he poured it down the drain.

When he returned, he gave Éamon his hand and helped him up. Elisedd's son swayed for a moment before he steadied. "Áed, do you believe how sorry I am?

Áed nodded. "I do." Éamon had risked a lot by warning Áed, and Áed was still grateful.

Éamon sagged with relief. "What will you do with my father?" His voice wavered just slightly. "The punishment is death, I know that."

Áed didn't plan on keeping to that. No more blood on his hands. "I'm not going to execute him. Perhaps I'll banish him to No-Man's-Land."

A little more relief relaxed through Éamon's shoulders. "Maybe I shouldn't be glad of that…"

"He's your father."

Éamon nodded, and Áed gestured toward the door.

"Come on. Boudicca's in my chambers, and you two should talk. The General, too, if you can find him around."

Éamon nodded and followed him out.

⁂

The mid-afternoon sunlight streamed through open windows. Boudicca sat, knees tucked up, on the couch next to Ronan, and her face brightened as Áed came in with Éamon behind him. Then her mouth fell into a perfect 'O,' and she was up from the couch in a moment. Her stepbrother slumped into her arms, and she hugged him, hands worried on his back, before she pushed him away to see his face. His eye had begun to swell closed. "Éamon," she gasped. "What happened?"

"Where's Cynwrig?"

"I don't know. Why? Éamon, what's happened to you, are you alright?"

"We need to talk. Cynwrig too."

Boudicca shot Áed a worried, questioning look. "Would you tell me what's happened?"

Éamon replied. "Elisedd tried to poison Áed."

Boudicca's mouth dropped open. "*What?*"

"I'll explain," Éamon mumbled. "I'll do better when I can think straight."

"Gods… alright. Alright. Áed, are *you* alright?"

Áed nodded assuringly. "I'm fine." His eyes fell on Éamon, who had leaned heavily on the wall. "Elisedd assaulted him with a candlestick. Do you think it'd be a good idea to bring him to your flat for a little while?"

"I was about to suggest that." Her hands gently touched her stepbrother's injury, and Éamon winced. "Where is Elisedd now?"

"I ordered him to the dungeons for now."

She blinked and shook her head. "I can't believe it. Well, I *can*, but… Gods. I'm so glad you're safe." She gave a little gasp. "Oh! What did the Council say?"

"The coronation is tomorrow night, which is sooner than I expected, but it'll be fine, I think."

She put a hand to her forehead. "Goodness." She shook her head again, as if to clear it, and moved to take Éamon's arm. Éamon didn't argue. "Áed, I'll come back tomorrow, but I have to tend to Éamon. You'll be alright for tonight?"

"Of course. Boudicca, thank you so much for everything." He gave a little wave to Éamon, who managed a pained smile. "Heal quickly, Éamon. Thank you for warning me."

"I'm sorry. Again." He returned the half-wave. "I'll see you at the coronation. Be damned if I miss it." Then, obeying Boudicca's concerned murmurs, he let her steer him from the room.

CHAPTER THIRTY-THREE

"ARE YOU NERVOUS?"

Ronan had been up for hours and was bouncing from one foot to the other in Áed's room. Áed nodded slowly. "Yes, a little."

"*I'd* be nervous. Why aren't you more nervous?"

"Don't worry, it'll catch up with me." His nerves *were* doing their best to squirm through the fray of his thoughts. Nerves about the coronation, about humiliating himself, about what he would do afterward. He'd been planning since he first decided he'd take the throne: First, he would send supply carts to the Maze, under guard to prevent the gangs getting hold of them or people killing each other for a basket of apples or a bushel of wheat. It wouldn't be a popular decision, and nor would the one in which he sent troops to break up the gangs, healers to tend to the damaged, and governors to prevent anarchy.

He let out a breath. He'd be busy.

Áed jumped a little when a knock sounded at the door, and he moved to open it. A page no older than Ronan stood outside, and the boy took off his cap and bowed low when Áed came to the door. "Your Grace," the page said, straightening again. "I have a message from General Cynwrig. He says that if you meet him in the dungeon's antechamber, he has something for you to attend to."

Áed frowned. "The dungeon's antechamber?"

"It isn't an unpleasant place, Your Grace," the page assured him. "Just a room with a door to the dungeon. I'll show you the way, if you please."

"Ronan," Áed said over his shoulder, wondering what this could be about. "I'll be right back."

He followed the page down the stairs and through the palace halls with which he was gradually becoming familiar.

"Did the General say his purpose?"

"No, Your Grace," the page replied promptly. "But he had a man with him who seemed rather frightening."

"What did this man look like?"

"Frightening, Your Grace."

Áed sighed. After the previous day, he thought he was probably ready for anything, but that didn't mean that he was excited for whatever scene awaited him.

A door like any other door greeted them, and the page held it open for Áed. "Your Grace," he said politely, bowing again. "General Cynwrig awaits inside."

"Thank you," Áed replied, and the page took his leave with another half-bow.

The antechamber was dimmer than the hallway, making Áed blink for a second, but when his eyes focused, he saw Cynwrig standing before him. "Your Grace," the General said in his customary, professional tone. Something was different, however, something that didn't show in the man's voice but that Áed felt nonetheless; it was almost… friendly.

"General," Áed replied curiously. "What is it?"

"Something that I thought you might like to see." He beckoned Áed to follow, and started walking down the long room. The floor sloped gently downward and the walls were bare stone, which Áed didn't like, but the air was warm enough and didn't carry the dungeon's oppressive dampness. At the end of the room, a forbidding door was barred tight, and Áed guessed with a shudder what lay behind it.

"Why does the dungeon need an antechamber," Áed asked, "if it has openings elsewhere?"

"This serves as the guards' lounge," Cynwrig explained. "But I've cleared everyone out for the moment." He stopped walking and turned to his right, and Áed followed his gaze.

There, manacled to a cleat in the wall, sat a greasy-haired man with eyes of flat darkness.

A frigid shiver ran from Áed's head to his toes, and he took an involuntary step back as the torturer's eyes flicked over him, grim and gummy about the edges. "Cynwrig," Áed managed, swallowing hard and glancing back toward the entrance, toward the hall and safety. "What the *hell*."

Cynwrig folded his hands behind his back. "Your Grace, when you arrived half-dead at my sister's flat, I recognized the work of this man." He nodded toward Óengus. "I recognized, too, that he had never been given an order to harm you."

Óengus's black hair lay lank on either side of his face, and his nose shone with oil. He looked smaller than Áed's memory had attested, but he still gave Áed a curling smile. Áed looked away, heart stuttering a little. He had never wanted to see this man again. Never. "I thought… I thought it was a punishment for what happened to Seisyll."

The General shook his head. "Your punishment would have been a simple death had Cadeyrn not taken mercy on you. And, seeing as Cadeyrn *is* the merciful sort, he never gave this man permission to lay a finger on you." Cynwrig fished a cigarette out of his pocket and, placing it between his lips, lit it. He exhaled the smoke into the torturer's face. "So I took it upon myself to bring justice." He shrugged, holding his cigarette carelessly between two fingers. "I didn't approve of you, Áed, but this was too much to ignore. Far too much."

"General," Áed said slowly. His heart was beating hard just from being in the same *room* as Óengus, but he was beginning to make sense of Cynwrig's intentions. "I might actually be starting to like you a little bit."

Cynwrig took another puff of his cigarette, the smoke making the room hazy. "I'm flattered. My point for bringing you here is that my men finally caught this rat trying to leave the palace—evidently he's been hiding in the dungeons—and arrested him. He's yours to deal with as you choose."

The torturer, Áed noticed, was terrified. His beady little eyes darted around the room, and every time they landed on Áed, the man turned a shade paler, until he was the color of a corpse. He looked ready to piss himself.

Good.

Gathering his courage, Áed took half a step closer to the man who had so thoroughly ruined him. "General," Áed said thoughtfully. "What would ordinarily be the punishment for his crime?"

Cynwrig smiled, just a little bit. "He'd be tattooed as a criminal and left to beg on the streets."

"Hmm," Áed said, braving another step. Óengus's stink stopped Áed from coming any closer, and Áed wrinkled his nose. "I think that would be a sorry punishment for the streets."

"What would you have me do, Your Grace?" Cynwrig raised an eyebrow.

"Please," the torturer croaked, but Áed ignored him. "Please, Your Grace, have mercy on your misguided subject."

"You're looking for mercy in the wrong place," Áed replied flatly. He turned to Cynwrig. "Tattoo him as a criminal," Áed directed. "And bury him deep in some gods-forsaken cell." He put his back to Óengus, facing Cynwrig alone. "Then forget about him."

With a brief nod, Cynwrig extinguished his cigarette and placed his hands professionally behind his back once more. "Your Grace," he said. "Consider it done."

The torture-master moaned pitifully as the two began to walk away, but his complaint fell on impassive ears.

"His fate seems rather vengeful," Cynwrig observed to Áed as they crossed the long room again, heading back toward the hall.

Áed considered it. The General wasn't wrong. "Do you begrudge me that?"

Cynwrig shook his head. "Not at all, Your Grace. Not at all."

⁂

The General bid Áed good luck and left to prepare the August Guard for the coronation ceremony, and back in his chambers, Áed flopped onto the sofa and let out a long breath. Ronan climbed up next to Áed and leaned on him, and Áed dropped an arm over the boy's shoulders. "You ready, *ceann beag*?"

"Are *you*?" Ronan adjusted himself so he could see Áed's face. "You look stressed."

Áed chuckled. "A little, mate. I didn't like the person I just had to go see."

"Cynwrig?"

"No," Áed said. "Someone else." He sighed. "Can you believe it, Ronan? Tonight—"

"You'll be *King*," Ronan finished for him. "Are you

excited?"

Áed deflected. "Are you excited to be a prince?"

At that, a slow smile unfurled over Ronan's face. Clearly, he hadn't thought of that, though in the six weeks before their move to the palace, Áed and Cynwrig had discussed it. Ronan would be the ward of the King, a king with no children; he would be heir to the throne. Prince of the White City and all the Gut. "I'll be a prince?"

Áed smiled. "You sure will."

A knock at the door presently announced a visitor, and Áed got up from his seat to find two people that he had not seen before. One was a portly woman with a cheerful expression and hair done up into a dimpled bun on the top of her head, and the other was a girl of perhaps Áed's age with a quiet face and hard, observing eyes.

The two of them, dressed in servants' garb, stepped into the room at Áed's invitation and curtsied in unison. "Your Grace," the woman said modestly. "We've come to make you ready."

"Of course. Thank you." He offered a smile that, he realized, probably held a hint of nervousness. "What are your names?"

The girl looked surprised that he asked, and the woman responded. "I am Aifric, and this is Aileas."

Aifric and Aileas. He wondered how many times he would call them by the wrong names until he remembered which was which. They had no supplies with them, and he frowned. "Are we to go someplace else?"

"Yes, Your Grace," Aifric replied with another curtsy. "We will escort you, if you will follow."

Áed gave Ronan a hug, murmured a "See you soon," and then they were off.

⁂

They arrived at a room, and Aifric bustled inside. "See that door there?" she said, pointing, and Áed nodded. "That opens to the throne room. When we're finished, you'll walk right out there." Aileas ambled over, and Aifric nudged Áed in her direction. "Get him dressed," she directed, "while I prepare everything else."

Aileas nodded to Áed and turned away, and Áed followed.

Aileas led him behind a folding screen, a space shared with an enormous wardrobe and a chair, and she opened the doors of the wardrobe and began rifling through the clothes. It all looked immensely rich. Without even looking over her shoulder to speak to him, she ordered: "Undress."

"What?"

Aileas pulled her head out of the wardrobe and fixed him with a strange look. "Undress. Take your clothes off."

"With you here?"

She sighed in exasperation. "How am I supposed to dress you if you're already wearing something? Leave your underclothes on, I don't care, but we don't have time for modesty. Have you ever done this before?"

"No."

"Then do what I say."

"Your rudeness is refreshing," Áed grumbled, and Aileas turned back to the wardrobe as he pulled his shirt over his head.

"You're no older than me," her voice came, muffled by fabric. "Coming King or not."

"Are you always like this?"

She pulled herself out of the wardrobe again, looking critically at a piece of clothing in her hands. "You're to be king because Seisyll was completely mad. Now, *I* think he had it coming, dying like that, but *you* were just lucky. I don't see how you deserve my deference—" Her words stopped abruptly as she looked up at him. Her hand flew to her mouth.

Áed dropped into the chair to pull off his shoes as her eyes flitted over his exposed upper body. "Luck's a funny word for it."

"I'd heard," she said quietly. "But I didn't..."

Áed dropped his shoes next to the chair and stood. Aileas's gaze followed the motion. "Didn't believe it?"

She shook her head. "They were just rumors."

He shrugged. "I wish they weren't true."

She straightened her shoulders and seemed to reclaim her confidence. "Perhaps I've overstepped my bounds."

"How about we do this properly?" He held out his hand. "I'm Áed. Nice meeting you."

Aileas gingerly shook his hand, and she didn't even try to disguise her stare at its crumpled shape. "Aileas."

"No assumptions, yes? We've just met, after all."

"Do you actually want me to call you Áed?"

"Yes, please. I *like* my name."

She nodded, and the way she looked at him had changed. He was almost sure he noticed a hint of respect in her eyes.

That gave him a bit more hope for his future as King.

⁂

Áed had never even *touched* material so fine, not even when Boudicca had prepared him for the move to the palace. Aileas refused to let him look in the mirror yet—in fact, she covered it with a cloth—but when he looked down he thought he was practically shining. The colors were muted, but they captured the light with impossibly fine threads, held it, and threw it back in a way that shifted when he moved.

Now Aifric took over and steered him into a chair. Contemplatively pinching her lip between forefinger and thumb, she leaned back to scrutinize his face. She turned to a side table that was covered with colored bottles, and after musing over them for a minute or two, she selected a couple of them and returned.

"What's that?" Áed asked, with a sinking feeling that he already knew.

"Paint."

He groaned internally. "Dare I protest?"

"No." Aifric swirled the first bottle a few times and held her hand out to Aileas, who supplied her with a brush. "Stay still, Your Grace."

Ultimately, he didn't mind it too much. It wasn't gaudy, it wasn't bright, and the result was that it complemented his face rather than distracting from it. This was a remarkable feat, seeing that paint covered his visage almost entirely.

Aifric's handiwork dusted his cheekbones with amber and hid his eyebrows beneath a layer of gold that peaked downward between them. She'd dragged three paint-drenched fingers down his lips and over his chin, gold-silver-gold, and used the same blunt technique to color the space under his eyebrows. Below his lower eyelashes, gold streaks followed his cheekbones and made his eyes appear to glow.

Áed blinked and felt the light resistance of the paint on his eyelids, felt it shimmering. "I feel so strange."

Aileas leaned against the wall. "I hope you're ready, Your Grace. It won't be long now."

⁂

An hour later, Aifric fastened a cloak over Áed's shoulders, and though her face was focused, her eyes shone. With a few gentle pushes, she adjusted his posture, and then stood back appreciatively. "Shoulders back, chin high. Oh, perfect." Áed closed his eyes as Aifric steered him to the door. Suddenly, he couldn't even muster a breath. "Come, Your Grace, it's time."

He nodded, and she opened the door.

The hall was packed with people, strangers in different clothes and perfumes and jewelry, and above the sensory clamor drifted the smoky scent of incense and the clarion, glass-like tones of singing. The spectators were silent.

The crowd stared, and Áed did not stare back. In fact, he could scarcely see them. His vision had narrowed, and the only subject clearly in his sight was the throne and, beside it, a man and a child. The child held a pillow. The pillow held the crown. Though crimson fabric lay between the soles of Áed's shoes and the marble floor, his footsteps seemed to echo throughout the vaulted space, and the fading daylight glowed through the stained glass, which cast its shower of gemstones.

He stopped before the throne, and, remembering what he was to do, dropped slowly to his knees. The dark cloak puddled on the ground behind him, and the singing faded.

In the full hall, sound was suspended.

The man who stepped toward him was old and silver-bearded, and behind his weathered brows, moss-brown eyes pierced Áed's like spears. Áed took a deep breath as the man approached, and he bowed his head.

The man turned to the child beside him and took up the crown. "Áed, son of Seisyll, King to Come," the man said in a voice as soft as well-worn leather, and Áed looked up. The crown was just as he remembered it, a simple band with details like battlements, but it no longer glittered with white jewels. Instead, the brackets secured gems that shifted with the light, that flashed red and black and a stunning golden-yellow as the man held up the crown and the room held its breath. "Do you swear to lead with honor and with integrity?"

Áed licked his lips. "I do."

The man cleared his throat quietly. "Áed, native of Smudge," he intoned. "Do you promise to lead with courage and loyalty to your kingdom?"

"I do."

With a faint nod, the man spoke again. "Then, Your Grace, I bestow this crown into your keeping."

His wrinkled hands lowered the crown onto Áed's head, and Áed felt its cold weight on his brow.

"Rise, Áed, Monarch over Suibhne, Emperor of the Darklands of Smudge, High King of the Gut." As Áed rose, the man stepped back. "Long live the king!"

The room took up the cry, and Áed stepped up onto the dais. The hall was ringing, or perhaps it was just his ears as his heart thundered, and he turned to face the shouting masses. There, in the corner, were Boudicca and Ronan, and Éamon behind the two, and though Áed knew it to be wishful imagination, he thought he felt Ninian's familiar presence in the hall with them. Ronan wiped at his eyes with the backs of his hands, and Boudicca wore a look of the fiercest pride; it gave Áed the courage he needed to smile.

This was what he was meant to do. He felt it, then, with a sureness that resonated in his bones, in harmony with the roar of the room. The White City would be cleansed, the Maze reborn. He would do what was right. He and Ronan would have their better life, and all would be well.

And so, to the cries of the vast, color-struck chamber, he sank into the throne.

ACKNOWLEDGEMENTS

The Hidden King would not exist if not for the work and support of some truly remarkable individuals. The people here—many of whom I now think of as my teammates—gave me a greater gift than I had ever asked for: they lifted me up to create something lasting. For that, I am grateful in ways that words cannot express… but I am an author, and I will try.

It seems only right to begin with Erin Radcliff, my mother, who was with me from start to finish. Ever the wind in my sails, she encouraged me not to let *The Hidden King* sink beneath the waves of daily life, and it was she who pressed me to stay the course through the occasional foggy night. Beyond that, she volunteered to do the mountains of research that went into the publication process, and I greatly appreciate that her technical prowess outstrips my own by leagues. She stepped into the role of designer, publicist, tireless organizer, and true friend.

Next are my constant supports, my sounding-boards and providers of honest feedback: Tim Radcliff, for never letting me talk myself down, and for his deep spring of inspiration. Michelle Haller, for her always-open ear. Vida

Cruz, Lisa Fanelli, Maggie Schroeder, Lynne Kern, Woody Ward, Grace Phillips, Leah Gleason, and Mark Reed for beta reading and providing reactions: their honest input made *The Hidden King* a better book. Thanks to Mimi Black, Alyssa Williams, Jackie Crnkovich, and Alyssa Murphy of the Elmhurst Public Library, for the extraordinary depth of their consideration, the bluntness of their feedback, and their encouragement that I was on the right track. Additionally, my thanks to Catherine Herina McGovern and Máiréad Ní Chatháin Uí Chonchúir for their help with the Irish expressions that I used as the language of the Maze.

The rest of my team consists of my wonderful editors and designers. Kelsy Thompson, developmental editor extraordinaire, helped me sculpt *The Hidden King* by her clever insights and ever-patient willingness to answer a tide of questions; her suggestions nudged me to place emphasis on everything important, and she discerned these importances with an artist's touch. Thanks to Beth Dorward, copy editor and proofreader, for the repair of many a minuscule inconsistency. Affirming her extraordinary nature, she even offered insights beyond the scope of copy editing, which proved just as clever as her command of the minutiae. Last, though very far from least, the brilliantly-talented Micaela Alcaino designed a stunning cover with adaptability and vision, and I'm impressed by her patience with my ever-changing mind.

To all those who provided a word of encouragement or a passing suggestion: I extend my gratitude to you as well. Those little motivations kept me going through this long, hard, oh-so-worth-it process.

ABOUT THE AUTHOR

E.G. Radcliff is an incurable writer, lifelong imaginer of worlds, and author of the *The Coming of Áed* series of books. An insatiable reader and researcher with a penchant for all things Celtic and a love of the mysterious and magical, she brings a knowing touch to her Young Adult fiction.

She enjoys adventure, reading on the train, and dreams about flying.

She is based in Chicago, Illinois.

CONNECT WITH E.G. RADCLIFF

www.egradcliff.com
info@egradcliff.com

@egradcliff

Join the mailing list from **www.egradcliff.com** for news about upcoming books in the series, book giveaways, blog updates, and limited edition book swag!

Thank you for reading this book!

If you enjoyed this book, you can be an author-reader matchmaker by leaving an honest review on your preferred book-buying platform.

Post a picture of the book on Instagram, Facebook or Twitter and tag **@egradcliff**!

MORE BOOKS IN *THE COMING OF ÁED* SERIES

The Last Prince (August 2020)

Book 3 (coming in 2021)

CPSIA information can be obtained
at www.ICGtesting.com
Printed in the USA
LVHW050111060620
657508LV00001B/135

9 781733 673327